Price of Freedom

By L.M. Somerton

By Ethan Stone

What's his Passion?
Vegas Hustle

Anthologies
Racing Hearts: Just my Luck

By Molly Ann Wishlade

Anthologies
Racing Hearts: Horses and Harleys

Racing Hearts Anthology

THE LONELY ONES
BAILEY BRADFORD

RACING FOR HOME
MORTICIA KNIGHT

THE SECRET OF DELVILLE WOOD
HELENA MAEVE

KEEPING THE LUCK IN
L.M. SOMERTON

JUST MY LUCK
ETHAN STONE

HORSES AND HARLEYS
MOLLY ANN WISHLADE

Racing Hearts
ISBN # 978-1-78430-967-1
The Lonely Ones ©Copyright Bailey Bradford 2015
Racing for Home ©Copyright Morticia Knight 2015
The Secret of Delville Wood ©Copyright Helena Maeve 2015
Keeping the Luck In ©Copyright L.M. Somerton 2015
Just my Luck ©Copyright Ethan Stone 2015
Horses and Harleys ©Copyright Molly Ann Wishlade 2015
Cover Art by Posh Gosh ©Copyright December 2015
Interior text design by Claire Siemaszkiewicz
Pride Publishing

Published in 2015 by Pride Publishing, Newland House, The Point, Weaver Road, Lincoln, LN6 3QN, United Kingdom.

THE LONELY ONES

Bailey Bradford

Dedication

With love.

Chapter One

Marshall Evans parked his rental in the driveway of the dilapidated residence. The whole place — land, house, barns, stalls, equipment — looked much worse than he remembered. Selling it might be more of a problem than he'd expected.

The slight throbbing that had started up behind his eyes after his flight had landed became a more intense pain. Marshall sighed and tried to remember where he'd put his migraine meds. *Not in the carry-on, damn it.* He'd have to get out in the hellish heat and retrieve his suitcase from the trunk.

Closing his eyes, he tried to take a few deep, cleansing breaths, counting silently as he did so.

The *whap* to the driver's side window almost gave him a heart attack, and Marshall screeched at an embarrassingly high-pitched level. His head pounded as he whipped it around to glare at the man bent over and glaring back at him. Even through his own anger, Marshall could see how attractive the stranger was, and it made him even more pissed off for some reason.

"What the *fuck* is your problem, man?" Marshall growled, reaching for the window switch. He only thought how foolish it might be to lower the window after the fact. By then, the glass was halfway down and he could think of no way to salvage his pride—if that were possible, considering his squeak of alarm— should he raise the window up again.

"You're trespassing," the stranger drawled, his dark brown eyes glittering with irritation or some other unfriendly emotion. His thin lips were pressed together so tightly the skin around them was almost white against the rest of his darkly tanned face.

"I'm not trespassing, *you* are," Marshall snapped back at him. "So—"

"I live here."

Marshall shut off the car. "Oh really." It wasn't a question. He made it sound as snotty as possible. "Funny that wasn't mentioned when Mr. Rogan called me." Allen Evans' attorney hadn't mentioned anyone else living on the property.

The man blanched and after narrowing his eyes until they were almost closed, he looked away toward the house. "Yeah, well. Rogan is a son of a bitch, and your grandpa wasn't much better."

Marshall opened his mouth to argue, but promptly closed it. There was, after all, a reason he'd never been back to visit his grandpa after that last time. Then it occurred to him that he was at a serious disadvantage, because the stranger knew who he was, at least in a general way.

"Who are you, and why are you here?" he asked. "And can you back away so I can open the door?" He hated having to ask that last question, and had even fleetingly considered just opened the door and hitting the annoying fool with it.

"I'm Rex Martinez, and I've been working here for almost five years," Rex replied, taking off his stained straw hat before running his fingers through his sandy blond hair. "Been living in the garage apartment since there ain't a bunkhouse here all that time too. You might have known that had you ever bothered to talk to your grandpa."

"Yeah, well, that's not your business," Marshall said. "You practically called him a son of a bitch. Like you have any room to judge me."

"At least I knew him well enough to know what he was," Rex informed him while surprising Marshall by opening the door for him. "For all you know, he could have been a great man in his later years."

"He wasn't. People don't change," Marshall stated flatly, unbuckling his seatbelt. He got out and slammed the door shut. "I can get my own doors, thank you very much."

Rex rolled his eyes and put his hat back on. "Prissy. Figures."

"Asshole," Marshall retorted. He was angry and out of sorts, in no mood to put up with shit from anyone. "And you're fired." *Let him deal with* that!

Rex laughed at him—literally bent over and held his stomach, he was laughing so hard.

Marshall failed to see the humor in anything just then. He crossed his arms over his chest and glowered until Rex straightened up and swiped at his eyes.

"Hot damn, you're funny," Rex finally said.

Apparently, firing Rex wasn't going to have the sobering, 'Aha! I got you!' effect on him that Marshall had hoped it would.

Rex looked right at him, and Marshall almost gaped. Sure, the man was handsome as sin in a rugged, inbred cowboy sort of way, but since when had cowboys been

Marshall's thing? *Why do I want him? You know why, idiot. He's like the love child Paul Newman and Robert Redford would have made together, if they'd been able to...* Marshall's train of thought derailed as Rex's slow grin ratcheted up his attractiveness to a whole new level of hot.

"You think you can take care of the horses, go right ahead and have at it. I'll still be packing my bags when you're ready to come ask me to stay." And with that, Rex winked at him then walked away.

It took Marshall a full minute of gawking at Rex's very fine backside to get his brain into functioning gear. By then, Rex was almost out of sight. Marshall gave himself a shake, and Rex's parting words registered — "Horses?" *The lawyer didn't say anything about there still being horses here! Or an angry cowboy! Jesus, what other surprises are waiting for me?* "Fuck!" Marshall squeezed his eyes shut and tried not to panic. He didn't know jack about regular horses, much less racehorses like the ones his grandfather had bred and trained. He was so screwed.

Chapter Two

"Of all the annoying, flashy, city-dwellin' snobs…"
Rex searched for some more suitably insulting terms
for Marshall Evans. He'd known *exactly* who that little
punk was when he'd pulled into the drive, despite
acting otherwise. The lawyer had told Rex to expect
him, just as he'd told Rex, "Tough shit, cowboy. Allen
Evans didn't leave you anything except a month's pay,
and that's with the stipulation that you work the whole
month without missing any days. I can tell you, now
that he's gone, he never had you in his will despite
what he might have said. He was never leaving his
ranch to a *ho*-mo-*sex*-shual." Of course the lawyer had
drawn the word out, and said it like being called a
homosexual was an insult when Rex didn't see it in any
such way.

He also hadn't been aware that Allen had known he
was gay. That'd been something Rex hadn't shared
with the old bastard because he'd been such a hateful
cuss at times. "Most of the time," he muttered, digging
out a duffel bag from his small closet. Rex took his hat
off then leaned against the wall and closed his eyes.

"How'd everything go to shit?" He'd spent five years working for a man who'd been bitter and mean more often than not, but he hadn't been able to leave. Five years training racehorses, Allen's, and others that were boarded at the ranch for just that purpose. Rex had also worked hard on improving the breeding stock. He'd done everything he could to make the ranch more profitable and successful. "And for what?"

Rex shook his head. It didn't matter. He'd been honorable, and he guessed that he could think of a couple of good things about Allen, such as, he'd always paid Rex on time. And when he'd been sober he hadn't been that bad of an employer, even if he hadn't been a very good person. It was when he'd been drunk that he'd been truly awful.

There at the end, he'd been drunk more often than not. The way Rex figured, the heart attack was an easier death than liver disease, which surely would have claimed Allen eventually. That, or he'd have wrecked driving drunk like he used to do the times that Rex wasn't quick enough or around to stop him.

Rex thumped his head against the wall. Loyalty was overrated, as far as he could tell. That was his lesson for spending five years helping out an abandoned old man. Yeah, he'd gotten paid for it, but he could have left and worked elsewhere. "Probably." As long as wherever he'd have applied hadn't checked references or backgrounds.

With his luck, Marshall Evans would either fire him for real, or he'd start snooping into Rex's past, find out about his arrest, *then* fire him. After all, Marshall had been clear on his belief that people didn't change. It wouldn't hurt to keep most of his stuff packed.

Rex highly doubted Marshall knew jack shit about horses, specifically the Thoroughbred racehorses there, or running the small ranch he'd inherited. All the horse training had been Rex's responsibility in the last couple of years, with Allen doing little more than barking out orders and drinking his booze. That was part of the reason the place looked so run down. Rex didn't have time to make it pretty when he was working with the horses every day, and Allen had said he couldn't afford to hire anyone else.

Rex tried not to give way to panic over his certainty that he'd soon be out of a job. He had a little money saved—very little, since he'd had to buy his own truck when the ranch one had finally bitten it for good. He'd also purchased four horses over the past year and had planned on using them to start his own breeding program. He wouldn't have done so had Allen not told him he'd inherit the ranch.

When had that changed? Rex tried to pinpoint when Allen had found out he was gay, when the old man's nastiness had increased, but it was impossible to tell. *Maybe he knew all along. Maybe he never planned on leaving me anything. Maybe he just said that to keep me here, working for him because he knew damn well no one else would put up with his drunken shit.* It was a lot of maybes, yet Rex suspected there was truth in all of them. It was quite possible that Allen had done a background check on him after all—or he'd had his shithead of a lawyer snoop around.

Whatever had happened, Rex was screwed. He didn't even have his own trailer to move his horses, and he didn't have anywhere to go. "Fuckin' Allen," he muttered, a little heartsick at having been naïve enough to trust the man. He should have known better.

Rex pushed away from the wall and walked to his battered dresser. Most of the furniture in the apartment belonged to him, including the crappy appliances.

Allen hadn't done more than give him a mattress and a coffee pot when he'd first started at the ranch. It'd taken months of scouring roadside trash pickup piles and the local flea market to furnish the apartment. The belongings weren't worth much, but they were Rex's, and he didn't want to leave them behind. He'd have to rent a trailer for the horses, and load everything else into the back of his truck, even if he had to stack it up ridiculously high. He'd just have to avoid going under low overpasses and such.

Rex tossed the bag onto the bed. He opened the top drawer of his dresser and pushed the socks and underwear aside. He took out the small jewelry box he kept hidden there and was about to open it when someone—and he'd bet he knew who—banged on the door. Rex set the jewelry box back in the drawer and closed it.

"Marshall must not be too bright," he mused, figuring Marshall had finally realized that he couldn't run the ranch on his own. "Took him long enough." Rex tried not to be too smug when he opened the door and grinned at Marshall.

Marshall didn't appear to be repentant at all. In fact, he pushed his way into the apartment, poking Rex in the chest as he started ranting. "You think you're so smart, don't you? There aren't any horses here. I looked in the barn. You're full of shit, trying to pull a fast one over on me. I knew Rogan hadn't mentioned horses in our phone call!"

"Did you already drive over and check the pasture out past the mesquite trees? Not sure your little rental car would survive the trip, though it ain't very far. Just, you know, bumpy. So did you head out there?" Rex asked, catching hold of Marshall's finger since the man still had it pressed to Rex's chest. "You know, the one I put the horses out in most of the time, unless I'm working with one of them?"

Marshall sputtered and his face turned an alarming shade of red. He snapped his mouth shut, his teeth clacking together.

"Good thing your tongue wasn't in the way or you'd have bit it plumb off," Rex observed.

Marshall ground his teeth, his jaw twitching. He jerked his finger free.

Rex noticed that Marshal had fisted his hands at his sides. "Really? You're gonna deck me?"

Marshall snorted, reminding Rex very much of a high-strung Thoroughbred he'd been trying to train. That horse, Orion, was his own, and his favorite. Now that he was looking for similarities, Marshall had almost the same, rich brown coat — *hair! Hair, damn it! —* as Orion.

"I don't believe in practicing violence," Marshall said. "I get that it might be *your* way of dealing with issues, but it's not mine."

"That's enough," Rex bit out, fed up with all the attitude coming his way. "You don't know jack shit about me, so don't go acting like you do. For someone who isn't into violence as a way of handling *issues*, you sure are borderline violent, barging in here and jabbing me in the chest, all full of piss and vinegar when the only person between us that's done anything rude and obnoxious is you." He immediately wished he hadn't said all of that, just on the off chance that he would have been able to talk his way back into his job.

Marshall had narrowed his eyes to tiny slits, and his face had gone all red again.

Rex waited for an insult, or more angry words, but Marshall suddenly drooped like a human willow tree, shoulders rounding, head hanging, defeat clear in the curved lines of his body.

"Jesus, I *am* being an utter jerk," Marshall whispered. "Fuck. Fuck, I'm sorry, man. I don't usually act like this." He pinched the bridge of his nose, then pressed his fingertips to his temples. "The lawyer was a smug asshole on the phone, and I had the feeling he was pulling one over on me but I didn't see how. I never wanted this place. Maybe when I go talk to him tomorrow in person, he'll have some suggestions on how to sell the ranch."

"You haven't met with him in person yet?" Rex didn't know why that surprised him.

"No, he called and told me Allen had passed away, that he'd been cremated immediately as he'd requested, with no funeral service or anything." Marshall shrugged. "I didn't *know* him, but I knew enough about him. Allen."

"Your grandpa," Rex added, pushing, curious about that bit of information. "You never visited or called him the whole time I worked here."

"Yeah, well." Marshall sucked his bottom lip in between his teeth, then let it pop back out. "There was a reason for that."

Rex would just bet there was. He didn't plan on giving Marshall an easy way out of the conversation, however. "What reason?" He'd just poke right into the man's business.

Marshall blinked, looking surprised at Rex's intrusive question. "That's kind of personal."

"Not seeing a lonely old man or even giving two shits about him is personal? Hell, I put up with him for years," Rex scoffed. "So your way sounds pretty damn impersonal to me." *Is impersonal a word? Shit. Shit! Is it?* He panicked inwardly at the idea of sounding ignorant.

Marshall drew himself up, shoulders going back and nose almost tipped into the air. "It's not any of your business."

Rex didn't have a way to break down that shield of snootiness. All of the sudden, he felt as stupid as he'd feared Marshall would think him to be. "Whatever. I'm not a realtor, so you'll have to deal with selling this place. I'm just a dumb redneck who takes care of the horses. You can let yourself out."

He turned and walked into his bathroom, shutting the door softly when he really wanted to slam it. Whatever else Marshall had to say could wait to be heard. Until he got a better grip on his temper, Rex didn't trust himself not to take a swing at Marshall if he talked down to him one more time.

It'd been a long time since anyone had pissed Rex off as much. Even Allen, with his obnoxious bigotry and drunken fits, hadn't fired up Rex's temper so quickly. Then again, he'd expected the crap Allen had thrown at him. Marshall was an unknown force, one Rex felt an almost magnetic pull toward.

He wasn't sure he cared to have such a strong reaction to Marshall, whether it was a negative one or a positive one. Especially not when he was all too aware of how attractive Marshall was. He had thick brown hair that gleamed in the sunlight, and eyes so green they reminded Rex of his mother's emerald ring, the stone bright and warm and rich. There wasn't a wrinkle or flaw on the man's face, with his straight, pert nose and nicely defined lips.

Pretty, Marshall was not. Handsome, in that classical, could be a male model way — that was him to a T.

Rex had no need for a man like that in his life. That was what he told himself as he began to strip for a cold shower. His half-hard dick didn't mean he was a liar.

Right. Somehow he couldn't make himself believe that line of shit. Marshall turned him on, and that was a complication Rex really didn't want.

Chapter Three

Instead of hanging around and waiting for Rex to come out of the bathroom, Marshall left, not even bothering to enter Allen Evans' house. There wouldn't be anything of sentimental value in there for him. When he and his mother had left years and years ago, she'd taken all the photographs and mementos that had held any meaning for her, having had the foresight, or enough knowledge of her dad's violent behavior, to have packed them up beforehand. And when she'd died, Marshall had inherited them.

Marshall closed his eyes against the pain of her loss. It'd been almost three years since she'd been murdered, and it still hurt almost as much as it had at first. Sometimes he still had nightmares about that, about finding out she'd been killed.

The nightmare was always factual, an exact memory of what had happened that day in September. He'd opened up his door to find a somber police officer standing on the other side of it, and Marshall's insides had turned to ice—jagged, freezing pieces that made him ache and his eyes sting before the officer ever spoke.

Then the crushing blow, to learn that he'd lost her, the one ally he'd always had, the one person in the world who loved him, gone because some criminal had wanted her Escalade. Maybe he'd have some kind of closure if her murderer was ever found, but that wasn't looking likely.

Marshall forced his mind back to the present, and the meeting he was about to have with Ed Rogan, Attorney At Law, as his sign proclaimed. After taking a steadying breath, Marshall was ready to meet with Allen's lawyer. He got out of the car and immediately began to sweat.

The New Mexico heat was enough to almost make Marshall get back in his rental car and drive home. For one split second, he considered it—just saying *fuck it* and letting Rex deal with the ranch however he wanted to. As tempting as the idea was, Marshall wouldn't do it. He tried to be responsible, and for whatever reason, Allen Evans had left the ranch to him.

No, Marshall knew the reason. There was no one else left with the family name. There were some distant second or third cousins he vaguely remembered meeting when he'd been a kid, but they'd had a different last name, and by all accounts from Marshall's mom, Allen Evans didn't consider them to be family.

Marshall didn't feel guilty for not having had anything to do with his grandfather. It wasn't like the mean bastard had ever tried to reach out to him, either. Honestly, Marshall was surprised Allen had even known where he was. Then again, it was entirely possible the lawyer had hunted him down.

Aware that he was stalling, but not sure why, Marshall chided himself and forced his feet to move.

The law office was a lot cooler than it was outside, and Marshall came close to whimpering with relief at the blast of cold air when he entered.

There was no one at the reception desk, and no one else in the waiting area. "Hello?" he called out, feeling rather foolish.

"Just a sec," someone hollered back in a tone that didn't sound very friendly.

"Sorry to freakin' inconvenience you," Marshall muttered as he wandered over to look at a framed photograph by the desk. It was one of those cowboy-in-shadow pictures, with a cowboy sitting astride a horse, forming one black silhouette against a sunset.

"You must be Marshall Evans."

Marshall turned to look at the man who'd spoken. Tall, close to six and a half feet, and probably in his late sixties or early seventies, with a shifty-eyed expression that made Marshall immediately not trust him. "Mr. Rogan?"

A curt nod was all he got in response before Mr. Rogan gestured to the hall. "Come on back, then, and let's get this done."

Rogan didn't seem all that professional to Marshall, but what did he know? He hadn't dealt with a lot of lawyers in a professional capacity. Even his mother hadn't had a will or an attorney.

He followed Mr. Rogan into a small, dark-paneled office that reeked of cigarette smoke. Logan sat with a huff and opened a file on his desk. "Allen was a friend of mine," he began, his bushy white eyebrows pulling together until they almost touched as he frowned. "I counseled him against including you in his will, seeing as you never once bothered to contact him."

"*That* is none of your business," Marshall snapped, anger burning up the length of his spine. "Do your job without the judgmental commentary, or I can just have my lawyer call you." His heart pounded and his palms felt clammy. He hated confrontations, yet he was having his second one in less than twenty-four hours. Plus, he didn't have a lawyer. Rogan's attitude was getting on his frayed nerves, though, and Marshall wasn't going to put up with it.

Rogan huffed. "I can tell you could have used your grandpa's influence. He'd have taught you some manners."

Marshall fisted his hands then willed himself to stay calm. He wouldn't discuss Allen Evans beyond what he had to in order to get the will dealt with. "The will, Mr. Rogan. Stick with that."

"You get it all," Rogan said, each word clipped and conveying the lawyer's anger. "With the stipulation that you can't sell it to that queer."

Shock jolted through Marshall. "What?" Had he heard wrong? He hadn't been confronted with such blatant hatred before. Having been raised up in Los Angeles, he'd of course heard plenty of stories about people confronted by homophobes, but he'd been lucky, and sheltered to an extent, until he'd left home. Even then, he'd never had anyone hassle him for being gay. He wasn't quite sure how to react in the face of such bigotry, and the shock of it stunted any rebuttal he might have made.

Rogan seemed unaware of Marshall's inner turmoil. "Yes, that's the only stipulation in here. Rex Martinez wanted to buy the place, and Allen might have let him, might have even given it to him in the will if Martinez hadn't turned out to be a fag and a—" He closed his mouth and smirked, his expression smug as could be.

Marshall's first reaction was a surge of exultation that Rex was gay, which was stupid, because he wasn't interested in Rex. Then the words Rogan had used burned into him like a brand, making him feel as if he were suddenly marked with a scarlet G. *Should I tell him? God, how he can be so...so fucking hateful? But what if he wants me to say I'm gay? What if there's something in the will that — But I don't want anything from Allen. I don't want his money or land. If I don't take it, what happens to Rex? And what was Rogan going to say about him?* Marshall told himself not to ask. Whatever Rogan had been about to say, the fucker was getting a big kick out of holding it back, and he clearly wanted Marshall to wonder and enquire.

Coupled with an odd feeling that it was best to keep his mouth shut on the topic of his sexuality, for the time being at least, he also wasn't giving Rogan the satisfaction of showing any curiosity. "Okay, so I can sell it to anyone else, then?"

Rogan's smirk vanished and he went back to frowning. "Of *course* a California boy like you wouldn't know anything about running a ranch, even a small one like Allen's. Really, it's more of a boarding and training facility—oh, never mind. Wouldn't want to bore or confuse you."

Despite how obvious it was that Rogan was trying to get to him, Marshall couldn't figure out *why* the man was being such a jerk.

Until Rogan came out with, "I am prepared to make you an offer on the place, though it's not worth much."

Marshall stood up. "I'll keep that in mind if I can't find another buyer. And you know what? I'll have my lawyer call you." Just as soon as he found a lawyer. "Have a good day."

Rogan stood as well. "Mr. Evans! We aren't done here. There are accounts to go over—"

"Then stick with business and stop being a jerk," Marshall retorted, fed up with Rogan's shitty attitude. "Act like a professional. Do that, and we can get this done."

"I want the ranch."

"Well, that was pretty damned blunt," Marshall said. "Let's get one thing straight. I'm not the naïve fool you seem to think I am. You aren't bullying me into anything. I'll have a realtor I trust come out and look the place over, then decide on the price. *You* don't get to set that."

Rogan's eyes were narrowed, making them even beadier in appearance. "I'm friends with every realtor in this county. Most of them in this state."

Marshall doubted that last part, yet he guessed he could be wrong. "So? I never said I'd use someone local. Now, what do I need to sign?"

Rogan pressed his lips together, and for a moment, Marshall thought the lawyer would refuse to do his job. Then, grudgingly, Rogan began to speak again, anger still tinging his voice as he explained what Marshall had inherited.

* * * *

It was a very uncomfortable hour spent in that office, and Marshall was as glad as he could be to get out of there. Even the hellish heat was welcome after dealing with Rogan. The lawyer had kept it professional for the most part, once Marshall had made it clear he wouldn't put up with anything less.

But the one thing Marshall had learned was that Allen really had intended to sell the ranch to Rex up until a few months before Allen had died. Somehow, Allen had discovered, supposedly, that Rex was gay.

Marshall kept telling himself that there was no proof in regards to Rex's sexuality. He hadn't asked Rogan why Allen was certain Rex was gay, just as he hadn't asked him about whatever else Rogan was keeping back. Marshall knew there was more, and he suspected it had to do with Rex.

If that was the case, he'd probably never know what Rogan was gloating over. Rex sure wasn't going to tell Marshall, not after the fit he'd thrown yesterday. Marshall groaned and felt his face grow warm not with the heat of the sun, but with a blush brought on by shame. He wasn't given to tantrums. Yesterday he'd been very out of sorts, scared and angry and wigged out.

"Still not an excuse," he muttered as he got in his car. If his mom had seen him acting like that, she'd have ripped him a new one, and deservedly so. Marshall could understand why Rex had been angry, too, if he'd been led to believe he'd get the ranch, then it'd been yanked away from him.

And Marshall really *couldn't* sell it to him. Well, he'd have a lawyer look the will over and see if there was a way around that. First he had to find a lawyer, though, then hire her or him if possible. "God, what a mess." A faint throb, a reminder of yesterday's migraine, echoed between his temples. "What a fucking mess."

Chapter Four

Rex saw Marshall first, before Marshall spotted him. Rex was coming around the barn, having just given Orion a thorough brushing before turning him out in the corral for a little while. Marshall looked thoughtful, a frown on his handsome face as he sauntered past the house. Rex wished he could see Marshall's eyes, but Marshall was wearing large, black aviator sunglasses. They lent him a dangerous, bad-boy air that he hadn't had yesterday.

Marshall was lean and average height, Rex would guess, maybe five-ten or so. The tight black jeans he wore emphasized the taut muscles in his thighs, and Rex really wanted to get a look at his ass. Though the front view *was* mighty fine. He liked the way Marshall dressed, with a long-sleeved button up left open enough to show a hint of dark chest hair peeking out of the white V-neck T-shirt underneath.

The fact was, Marshall turned him on, physically, at least. His personality left something to be desired, from what Rex had seen.

And maybe Rex shouldn't have been so judgmental about Marshall not having anything to do with Allen. He knew for a fact that Allen was mean and prone to violent outbursts when drunk, which at the end, had been damn near constantly. There was a good chance Marshall and his mom, Allen's daughter, had stayed away for a justifiable reason.

Rex needed to stop taking his anger out on Marshall regarding being screwed over on getting the ranch. Yeah, Allen had said Rex would get it when he died, but there was only Rex's word on that. No one would believe him.

About the time that Rex was going to clear his throat to draw Marshall's attention, Marshall looked his way, raising one hand up to push those sunglasses down his nose. Rex got his shot of those green eyes he'd been hankering to see again, and the sight of them sent a bolt of heat right to his dick.

Marshall slowed down, never taking his gaze from Rex's. Rex found himself unaccountably nervous when he had no cause to be. He overcompensated by puffing his chest out and trying to scowl, but somehow he ended up gulping and fidgeting with his belt buckle.

He had a flashback to tenth grade, when he'd had a crush on Billy Owens, the quarterback of the football team, and it had just been him and Billy in the boy's restroom at school. Rex had learned then that his gaydar was finely tuned, but for a few seconds, he'd thought Billy was glaring at him in anger, not lust.

He'd caught on quick back then, and he was catching on quick now, too. Marshall was checking him out, that hot green gaze dipping down to Rex's groin and lingering before raising back up to meet Rex's eyes.

Rex was still nervous. Not every gay man he'd met had been comfortable with themselves and their sexuality, that was for certain. He licked his dry lips and saw Marshall's Adam's apple bob as he gulped. *This guy's not my friend. He wants to put me out of a job and home. Hell, I thought he was going to punch me yesterday!* But as much as he tried to reason with his traitorous dick, that part of him kept growing firmer with every heartbeat.

In an act of desperation, Rex whipped off his hat and lowered it over his groin as he tried, nonchalantly, to run the fingers of his other hand through his hair. He even rubbed the back of his neck and moved his head from side to side like he had a crick he was trying to work out of it, all the while hoping he'd managed to hide his erection from Marshall.

Marshall stopped in front of him, perhaps a little too close, on the verge of invading Rex's personal space. "Did Allen tell you this place was yours? Or did he say he'd sell it to you?"

Rex blinked, startled by the question. He hadn't thought that fucker Rogan would tell Marshall about that. "Doesn't matter."

Marshall scowled and took his sunglasses off before clipping them to the lowest part of the V-necked collar. "Just tell me what he said."

"He said lots of shit, and none of it matters," Rex replied. "He talked about you every now and then, but in a vague way. I'm not sure he even knew where you lived."

"I don't know, either," Marshall said. "My mom didn't change her name or anything. She and I were both Evans, even after he beat her so bad he almost killed her. That was when I was about four, when she came back here hoping he'd changed, hoping he'd help us like he'd swore he would because he was sober. Lying fucker." Marshal spat out the last two words, his high cheekbones going ruddy. "He broke her nose, cracked her ribs, broke two of her fingers, and it wasn't the first time he'd hurt her. She told me stories, later on, said her mom had supposedly run off but she always wondered if her dad had killed her. Mom had to have been desperate in order for her to have come back here, and he knew it, and he used it against her. *That's* the kind of sleazy fucker you worked for."

Rex felt ill. He'd known Allen wasn't a good person, but he hadn't had any way of knowing he'd been an abusive father and husband. Allen had never mentioned any of that.

Marshall leaned in, penetrating Rex's space. "I was just a little kid, and he backhanded me, knocked me across the room. I remember running into the living room because Mom was screaming at him to stop, and he hit me. I was bleeding, both my lips busted. Mom hit him with the lamp, and we left. She drove like that, all busted up, until we hit LA. Never cared to see him again. Didn't tell him when Mom died. He didn't fucking deserve her, or me. Did he deserve you?"

Rex tore his gaze away from Marshall. He'd thought the man was furious yesterday, and he had been, but this, today, this was a cold, deeply entrenched rage that Marshall was completely entitled to hold on to. Not that hating a dead man was going to do him any good.

"I knew he was a mean drunk, and not much better when he was sober, but I didn't know— He took a swing at me once. Fell and landed on his ass, and I left him there." Rex shook his head. "I figured it was a fluke since he never did anything like that again. Sometimes he'd throw something, but it never came close to hitting me. Just put it down to him throwing a tantrum." And now Rex got it, why Marshall wouldn't want to keep the place. Rex hated that his own dreams were being demolished, but he couldn't blame Marshall for that.

"Yeah, well, maybe he preferred to beat women and children who weren't strong enough to fight him," Marshall said. Then he sighed, and the anger seemed to flow right out of him, leaving his mouth softer-looking and almost too tempting to resist.

Rex wanted to kiss him, to pull Marshall right up close, chest to chest, groin to groin, and kiss him until they were both moaning and hard, aching for more.

Marshall inhaled sharply, and he took a half-step closer to Rex.

Rex couldn't look away from Marshall's lips, both of which now had a wet sheen to them, since Marshall had just licked them. As tempted as he was to kiss the man, Rex forced himself to hold still rather than reach for Marshall.

But Marshall seemed to have none of Rex's reticence. "I'm going to kiss you. If you don't want me to, now would be a good time to walk away," Marshall warned, and Rex could feel Marshall's body heat, his breath across Rex's neck and chin.

Rex's fingers twitched as he fought against moving toward Marshall, then it wasn't a concern anymore because Marshall was gripping his hips and pulling Rex close. When their bodies touched from chests to thighs, Rex let out a low moan he couldn't hold back. He slid his arms around Marshall and leaned in, pressing his lips to Marshall's.

Marshall moaned as well, pushing the sound into Rex's mouth. Rex tightened his hold on Marshall as they parried and nipped, each trying to take control of the kiss. Then pleasure began to well up in Rex, and he forgot about dominance, forgot about trying to put on a show of strength, and he simply let his body take over, kissing, rubbing, touching Marshall.

No longer a contest of wills or a declaration of strength, the kiss became something else, with Marshall giving up on taking it over. It became a sharing, a mutual give and take as the sun beat down on them and a light breeze cooled their heated skin.

Marshall buried his hands in Rex's hair. Rex had dropped the hat and was happily holding Marshall at the nape and hip. They moved almost as one, Rex walking backwards, Marshall right there with him, until they were in the barn, and Rex's back was to a wall.

It was pure need that made him tremble as Marshall rubbed up against him, sliding one leg between Rex's thighs. Rex's head spun as lust blanketed him. He moved his hands down to cup Marshall's butt, kneading the firm mounds as Marshall began to rut, working himself on Rex's thigh.

As good as what they were doing together felt, Rex couldn't shut his brain off all the way. He wanted Marshall, very much, but it wasn't even a full day ago that Marshall had been shouting at him, and certainly hadn't seemed to like Rex at all.

Thinking about yesterday was the equivalent of someone dumping a bucket of ice water on Rex. He shivered and turned his head aside, breaking the kiss as he moved his hands between him and Marshall so he could ease Marshall away. Rex did so gently, not wanting to hurt him.

Marshall tightened his hold on Rex, then let him go, stepping back and gasping as he stared at Rex. "What—" Marshall shook his head and wiped his mouth with the back of one hand. "Shit. Shit! I just— You were there and listening and I— You're so damned sexy, Rex, but

I shouldn't have assumed anything. I just jumped you like you wouldn't mind if I did it. I'm sorry."

Rex didn't particularly like knowing Marshall was sorry for what they'd just done. It kind of stung his pride. Even so, he told himself to be reasonable. He had been the one to push Marshall away, after all, and Marshall deserved an explanation for that. "I'm not sorry," he said, though, because he wasn't.

Marshall snapped his gaze up and stared at Rex. "You're not?"

"No." Rex hitched one shoulder up in a lazy shrug. "Not at all. Just didn't understand how you went from wanting to punch me yesterday to *wanting* me today. Kind of confusing."

Marshall grunted. "Yeah, I guess. Even though I was pissed off yesterday, I noticed how attractive you are. Woulda had to have been dead to miss it. That still didn't give me the right to maul you."

"I could have stopped you any time if I didn't want it, or if I didn't want you," Rex pointed out. "I wasn't fighting you off, not even when I pushed you away. I didn't want you making a mistake you'd regret since I figured you hated me."

Marshall tilted his head to one side, giving Rex the impression he was perplexed. "But I don't hate you. So," Marshall drawled. "Then you stopped me because you thought I'd regret having sex with you."

"Sex? We were making out," Rex protested feebly, because he knew where they'd been headed. Sex had been happening, with all the humping and groping. It still made him blush for some reason to hear Marshall say it.

"Yes, *sex*," Marshall said, suddenly closer to Rex once again. "Sex. You blushed. It's a very appealing look on you, those red cheeks and shy smile. You can't be a virgin."

Rex barely managed to shake his head. "N-not a virgin, no. It's been a long time. Years. I stayed on the ranch except for when I needed to pick up supplies or Allen wanted me to drive him somewhere. Doesn't matter, though, because I thought you hated me."

Marshall backed off again as he sighed. "Yeah, I can see where you'd get that idea. I was a shit yesterday, and usually, I'm not so obnoxious." He gestured around the barn. "Being here made me remember it all. I was little when Allen last beat Mom, so sometimes the memories aren't so clear. Yesterday I kept fighting them, and I was hot and pissy on top of that. Didn't know you were here, or the horses. Not that any of those things are an excuse for my behavior. Rogan hadn't told me shit, then today he tells me things he should have mentioned sooner." He cast a speculative look Rex's way.

Rex didn't wait for him to finish. "He told you I'm gay, and what else?" He tensed, waiting to hear Marshall call him a criminal.

Chapter Five

Groping and kissing Rex hadn't been a part of Marshall's game plan when he'd arrived back at the ranch. Yet he couldn't regret having done so, and Rex had been an eager participant.

It took Marshall a moment or two to get his head together so that he could ignore the rampaging need inside him. While he gathered his wits, he noticed how nervous Rex seemed, and that he was trying desperately to hide it. Marshall was torn between prying and cutting Rex some slack. He settled for the latter, since he'd been such an ass yesterday.

"What else did he tell me? He went over the accounts and property values and, oh yeah, he wants this place," Marshall said. "He didn't beat around the bush about that."

Rex nodded and put his hat back on. "Figured as much. Allen didn't trust him. I don't think Allen trusted anybody. He was okay with me most of the time unless he was drunk, then he could be as hateful as Satan himself. He used this place against me, and I was stupid enough to let him."

Marshall wished he felt something other than anger toward Allen, but he didn't. "I told you some of the story about when Mom and I came here years ago. All Mom wanted was some help, a place to recover after she'd lost her job. It wasn't like she could turn to my father for help. She told me she never even knew his name. I wouldn't judge her on that, but Allen sure did. It started out with him being nice, then he began to make snarky little comments. I don't remember them, just Mom's reactions to them. Mom told me about it once, when I was about fifteen or so and I asked. Eventually, Allen did what he did, and we were gone. I don't get why he left this place to me. It's a sure bet he didn't know I was gay, if that's what kept him from selling out or giving it to you. Where will you go when I sell it?"

Rex grimaced and glanced out toward the house. "I don't know." He looked even more dour as he swiped a hand over his mouth.

Marshall had the impression that Rex was very much alone in the world, and rather than there being a romantic feel to the image a lone cowboy, Marshall's heart ached for the man. He wasn't sure how to get past his behavior from yesterday, but figured owning up to it was a start, and maybe, if they both wanted to, they could be friends.

Or more. Jesus, kissing Rex just about burned me up inside. Marshall cleared his throat, and held out his hand to Rex when Rex turned back to him. "Hi, I'm Marshall Evans. I was hoping we could have a do-over since yesterday I had a flaming case of assholeitis."

Rex appeared startled, then he gave Marshall a shy grin and shook his hand. "Rex Martinez, and I was having a case of it, too. But I wonder…" He lowered his hand to his side.

"What do you wonder?" Marshall asked.

Rex sucked in his bottom lip then released it, leaving it darker pink and glistening. Marshall wanted to suck on it, too, but he refrained.

"Rex?" he prodded, tucking his thumbs into the front pockets of his jeans to keep himself from reaching for Rex.

"Er, I...I was just... You said something yesterday." Rex tipped his chin up, like he was bracing himself for a hit.

It made Marshall wonder about Rex's past, and why he was defensive at times. "I said lots of shit yesterday. Can you be specific?"

Rex snorted softly, and the grim expression he wore lightened just a bit. "Yeah, I can do that. It was about how people don't change."

Marshall wanted to smack himself upside the head. He'd screwed himself over with that statement. "Well, I didn't mean that, exactly. I'm not always a raging asshole like I was yesterday. In fact, I can't recall being so obnoxious before, except, you know, when I was a snotty teenager who thought he knew everything. Or the time I decked Matt Crowley because he beat me in the spelling bee, but to be fair, I was six and he laughed at me for misspelling banana — entirely too many 'n's in that word. I was referring to people like Allen, and it doesn't sound like from what you've told me that he *did* change."

Rex toed the dirt, digging at it as he grunted.

Marshall wondered what was going through Rex's mind.

After almost a minute of silence between them, Rex grunted again and nodded, which Marshall took to mean he'd come to some kind of internal decision.

Then Rex looked at him, and Marshall thought there was a hint of fear in Rex's dark eyes. He wanted to tell Rex it would be okay, but the fact was, Marshall didn't know if it would or not, or even what *it* was.

Finally, Rex spoke, his gaze darting away from Marshall. "See, I came here five years ago, after...after I got arrested for assault. I was lucky I didn't get jail time, but I still have a record. I'm not violent. I'm *not* like Allen. I learned from my mistake. It's why I don't drink, not even a beer every now and then."

"Why are you telling me this?" Marshall asked, trying to decide how he felt about Rex's confession.

"Because you kissed me," Rex replied. "And it seems dishonest even if you hadn't, with your history with Allen, and you believing people don't change. Sometimes they do."

Marshall wished he could take those words back, in a way. "Did you have a habit of drinking and fighting?"

"No." Rex shifted his weight, cocking one hip and leaning against the wall. "I mean, I had a few beers with friends on the weekends. I hadn't ever had a problem before, which is why I didn't end up serving time. I...I seriously hurt the guy I hit, Marshall, and if I'd been sober, I wouldn't have let him get to me enough that I'd have resorted to violence. That wasn't the case, though. I was drunk, and pissed off because the guy I'd been dating was cheating on me. I'd gotten laid off, and none of that matters. Those are just excuses. I chose to get mad when I was taunted, and I chose how to react."

"You think you're like Allen?"

Rex shook his head. "I don't, any more than I think I'm a violent person. I fucked up. I was twenty-one, old enough to know better. He threw the first punch, but he was so intoxicated he could barely stand. I should have walked away. Now I know, alcohol really does impair my judgment. I don't ever want to hurt someone again. Seeing Allen, working with him all these years, was another way of making sure I didn't drink. Didn't want to even have a sip of wine after seeing him sloppy-drunk and piss-mean."

Marshall scratched at his nape. "I've done shit I'm not proud of, either. It's a good thing juvenile records are sealed, because I was arrested once for shoplifting along with another boy, a kind of friend-foe of mine back then. It was a miracle I hadn't got busted before. Seeing my mom cry, I realized not taking a dare didn't make me a wuss. I kind of had a chip on my shoulder about anyone thinking I was weak. Stupid, but the point is, I wouldn't steal anything now. So I revise my statement from yesterday. People *can* change. Some do, some don't." Then he stepped back and chuckled awkwardly. "Well, this conversation has gotten deeper than I'd have thought it would. How'd we get from snarking to kissing to confessions?"

Rex shrugged. "I don't know, man. You're a force to be reckoned with, though."

"Is that a good thing?" Marshall wondered.

"Yeah, it is," Rex assured him. Then Rex asked, "When are you putting this place on the market?"

"I don't know. I have to find a lawyer, and a realtor who isn't buddies with Rogan. Guess I need to go through the house."

"I can do that with you, if you want." Rex gestured to the house. "The going through it. The rest, I don't know about."

"I'd appreciate your help." Marshall told himself to stop being a chicken and just ask for what he wanted. "And I'd like to have dinner with you, maybe kiss some more, if you'd like that, too. I'm not going to toss you off the ranch if you say no."

Rex took a deep breath, then blew it out as he closed his eyes. When he opened them again, he drilled Marshall with an intense gaze. "What if I want more than a kiss?"

"We're two grown men, capable of enjoying one another's company for tonight, and"—Marshall winked at him—"longer, if you want. I'll be here a few days, at least."

"A few days," Rex repeated. "You have to get back to a job?"

"I can work anywhere," Marshall told him. "I'm a software developer, work for myself. I've made some good"—*lucrative*, though he didn't say that—"programs in the past few years."

"Oh. So you're real smart," Rex said. "That...that turns me on, actually."

"I think I like turning you on." Marshall looked Rex up and down. Then he decided, *Fuck it.* "I like kissing you, too." He took a step toward Rex.

Rex met him halfway, closing the distance between them as Rex cupped Marshall's cheek. His other hand went right to Marshall's butt, and Marshall moaned as he parted his lips, welcoming Rex's kiss.

Rex's body was all hard muscles. Marshall pressed against it, feeling the bulge of Rex's cock and the rippling of his abs. Marshall got two handfuls of cowboy buns and didn't want to wait until dinner to feel skin on skin.

But a little voice in his head told him to back off, rushing would be foolish. There was no reason to rush through the attraction they shared. It'd been a long, long time since he'd wanted someone as much as he wanted Rex. Marshall had learned to savor and anticipate.

Chapter Six

Rex was going to lose his ever-lovin' mind! He and Marshall had spent an hour last night making out, kissing and rubbing against each other, but neither had taken it any further. Rex had been surprised and disappointed when Marshall had called it a night, not that Rex had said as much.

Instead, Rex had hurried back to his place and tried to figure out if he'd done something wrong. He'd concluded that Marshall's assertion that he didn't want to rush anything had to have been sincere.

Then Rex had jacked off twice, each time imagining Marshall's touch instead. It was strange, maybe, but he really liked Marshall. They'd gotten off on the wrong foot, each of them prickly for their own reasons. Rex thought they could be friends, and that was exciting, seeing as how Rex hadn't had anyone but Allen in his life regularly for the past five years.

Rex was beginning to see that he'd been serving penance, a self-imposed one. The guilt over hurting someone like he'd done had weighed heavily on him. But, it might be time to let that go, he reasoned, or at least loosen the grip he let it have on him. He wouldn't go out and get drunk again, wouldn't be goaded into throwing a punch. If it came down to it, he'd let someone hit him and not fight back. Rex never wanted to feel bones break beneath his fist again.

And since he knew that now, he could stop punishing himself. Rex finished up with Leona, a mare he'd been training for a client. He gave her a carrot since she'd performed so well for him. "Good girl. You'll be leaving soon, the way you're going." He'd miss her. Rex always wound up attached to every horse he trained, but he was realistic enough to know they weren't his to keep. Except for the ones he'd actually bought.

He spotted Marshall outside on the back porch, stacking boxes of Allen's things that were to be donated to charity.

"I can help you, if you want," he called over to Marshall.

Marshall stretched, placing his hands on his lower back. "I think I'm about done for the day. I'd love some company after I shower, though."

Anticipation rushed through Rex. "Half an hour?" He could use a good cleaning himself.

"Or half that." Marshall smiled. "I've been thinking all day about kissing you again."

"Just kissing?" Rex asked, because he'd hinted he wanted more yesterday, and it hadn't happened.

Marshall sauntered down the porch steps, his bright gaze on Rex. "You know, you looked really good with your lips red and wet, swollen from kisses."

Rex's breath hitched and he warmed up in a way that had nothing to do with the temperature. "Y-yeah?"

Marshall kept approaching him, reminding Rex of a big cat stalking prey. "Yeah. I didn't want to stop. The things I want us to do to each other...mm-mm."

Rex's throat was dry and his hands trembled as he reached for Marshall. "Why'd we stop last night?"

"Because I wanted more than a quick fuck," Marshall explained. "And I would have come in about two seconds if you'd have put your hand on my bare dick. Or your mouth on it. Oh, God, those lips—"

Rex moaned as Marshall kissed him, a fierce clash of teeth and tongues, hunger for Marshall driving Rex to grab and hold and squeeze.

Marshall spun them around, then they were stumbling, walking, kissing while they made their way up the steps and, eventually, into the house.

"I smell like horses and sweat," Rex protested when Marshall nudged him toward the second bedroom.

"You smell like man and hard work, and I fucking love it," Marshall said. "All the times I wasted money on cologne when this"—he pressed his nose just under Rex's ear and inhaled—"aw, man, that's fucking perfect."

Rex wasn't going to argue. His dick was so hard he could barely walk. He stopped trying, instead slipping his hands under Marshall's T-shirt and pushing it up. "Off," he got out as Marshall kissed and nipped at his neck. "Oh Jesus, I didn't know that could feel so good," he murmured, goosebumps racing over his skin. No one had ever taken the time to savor him like Marshall was doing, had done the night before.

Rex understood then why Marshall had waited. It made everything new and brighter today, added a sense of urgency and heat to their attraction.

"Yeah," Marshall whispered before sucking on Rex's earlobe. "Hasn't anyone appreciated you, Rex?"

Instead of answering that out loud, Rex pulled Marshall's shirt off. All the golden, smooth skin available to him—he wanted to kiss it, leave little love marks on it, learn the taste of every inch of it. He started with his hands, caressing Marshall's back, feeling every knob of his spine and every ripple of his lean muscles.

At the same time, Marshall was driving him crazy with kisses and bites, nothing harsh, just with enough sting to make his insides quiver as his need ratcheted higher. Rex couldn't remember ever wanting someone like he wanted Marshall. It wasn't just going without another man's touch for five years. Rex could have waited longer—he'd never been one for fast hookups. It was Marshall himself, with his snark and apologies, Rex wanted.

He was going to get all of Marshall tonight. It wouldn't take but another day or two for Marshall and him to clear out everything from Allen's house, then Marshall would leave and forget all about Rex.

Well, Rex wasn't going to make the forgetting easy. He growled a little as he spun them around, right before taking Marshall down onto the bed with him.

"Oh, I like this aggressiveness," Marshall said, stretching out under Rex. "Kiss me again?"

Like Marshall needed to ask. Rex pressed his lips to Marshall's just as Marshall parted his legs, letting Rex slide right in between them so that their dicks were *right there*, hot and hard, but separated by too many layers of clothes. Rex kissed Marshall thoroughly, tongues dueling, dancing, as he savored each taste and sound Marshall gave him.

Every cell in Rex's body ached with the need to bury his cock as deep inside Marshall as he possibly could. He had a flash of a vision—Marshall's lips stretched around his shaft—and Rex nearly whimpered with the desire to have that happen.

Then Marshall tore his mouth away, twisting and panting as he pushed at Rex's shoulders. "Condoms and lube, under the pillow."

Rex sat up, straddling Marshall's thighs. "You planned ahead?"

"Fuck yeah I did," Marshall said. "Another reason to stop where we did last night. Didn't have supplies. I want you to fuck me after we suck each other."

Rex grinned. "I do like the way you think." He unfastened the button of Marshall's jeans. "A lot." Then he slowly eased the zipper down, his heart racing with every inch of exposed skin.

"Careful," Marshall said.

Rex slipped his other hand down Marshall's pants and found nothing but smooth skin, a rigid dick, and short, crisp hair. "Commando. That your regular thing?"

"No, this is just for you," Marshall replied, sounding breathless. "Aw, fuck, I'm *still* not gonna last long!"

"We have time for more than one round," Rex said. It wasn't like he'd last long this time, either. "But for now—" He freed Marshall's dick, spreading the jeans wide open. "Goddamn. I—" Words weren't going to cut it. Rex bent and took the fat tip into his mouth. He moaned, eyes closing as he lost himself in the scent and taste of Marshall.

"Fuck! Rex, fuck, suck me, suck me please," Marshall begged, pushing at Rex's shoulder.

Rex shoved at Marshall's jeans, and Marshall got the hint, lifting his butt up so the pants could be moved out of the way. Then Rex went to town on Marshall's dick, taking more in while he jacked the shaft, using his other hand to roll and palm Marshall's balls.

Rex had never been able to deep throat, and he sure couldn't take much after years of not having anything nearly as tasty in his mouth. He worked the head with his lips, then his tongue, delving into the leaking slit and tasting the slightly salty pre-cum there.

Marshall began to move, thrusting while holding onto Rex, one hand on his head, not demanding, just there as Rex bobbed up and down, reveling in the experience. Everything about what he was doing, what *they* were doing together, felt right and perfect, and hot enough to have Rex's dick throbbing. He needed to be touched, to slide his shaft into Marshall's hot, wet mouth almost as much as he needed to keep sucking Marshall off.

Rex lapped at the head again, then teased the bundle of nerves on the underside.

"Fuck!" Marshall yelped. "Let me— Ah, fuck, let me suck you, Rex. Please!"

Rex hated to stop what he was doing, but he'd have hated missing out on a blow job even more. "'Kay." He gave Marshall's dick a kiss, then he got up and quickly stripped off his own clothes.

While he stripped, he watched Marshall, all those lean muscles moving as he sat up and got the condoms and lube out.

"You good with fucking me?" Marshall asked. "I can top if you'd rather."

"Later," Rex said. "Next time." He really hoped there would be a next time.

"Yeah." Marshall lay back and opened the lube. He squirted some on his fingers. "Since you're not naked yet..." He raised up one leg and reached down between his cheeks.

"Fuck," Rex dragged out, unable to move while Marshall pushed two fingers right up his ass. Rex stumbled over his own feet as he tried to hurry up and finish with his clothes. His boots were a bitch to get off, but once he had them tossed aside, he only took another second or two to remove his socks and jeans. His briefs were in the mess of clothes too, then he was pushing at Marshall's legs, encouraging him to raise them up.

But Marshall rolled his head from side to side. "Suck me again."

"Can I…" Rex traced the top of Marshall's hole.

"Yes, fuck yeah," Marshall rasped.

Rex took the lube and wetted his fingers, then he slid one in alongside Marshall's.

The sound Marshall made, a guttural, primitive claim of pleasure, almost undid Rex. He eased onto the bed, that one digit still inside Marshall as Rex stretched out beside him, his head by Marshall's groin.

"Over me," Marshall demanded.

Rex got it. He placed his knees above Rex's shoulders, then maneuvered them lower. Slowly, he eased his cock into Marshall's mouth, reveling in the hot, slick glide of tongue and the perfect suction around his shaft. It was every bit as incredible as Rex had thought it'd be.

"Marshall," he whispered, shaking all over, trying not to fuck Marshall's face like a desperate man.

Then Marshall traced Rex's crack from top to his asshole, and Rex moaned, giving himself over to his body's demands. He stopped thinking and let the pleasure wash over him as Marshall tugged on his hips, encouraging him to thrust deeper, faster.

At the same time, he fingered Marshall's hole while sucking on his cock and jacking the shaft.

A volcanic burst of ecstasy shattered Rex. He had no warning, his climax bursting from every nerve ending in his body, pleasure thick and rich as it filled him then spilled out, pumping jets of cum into Marshall's throat.

Marshall jerked and his dick swelled. His asshole clenched so tight Rex had to stop fingering him, had to hold still while Marshall cried out, his seed shooting into Rex's mouth. Rex tried to swallow every drop, but his head was muzzy and dense with his own release. Eventually, the sexual fog cleared and he eased his finger from Marshall's hole.

Marshall's cock wasn't fully hard anymore, nor was it soft. Rex wasn't yet ready for round two. He maneuvered around to lie beside Marshall, pulling the man into his arms just as soon as he could.

For a little while, they rested, neither speaking. Rex wouldn't admit it out loud, but he was fairly sure that no other man was ever going to be able to compete with the way Marshall had just blown his mind.

And for some reason, Rex wasn't even afraid to admit that to himself.

Chapter Seven

The smell of bacon woke Marshall, and as far as he was concerned, that was the second best thing to wake up to. First would have been a certain sexy cowboy, but said cowboy wasn't in the bed.

Marshall sat up and glanced at his watch. He'd dozed off for an hour or so, he'd guess. His belly rumbled and he got up, idly scratching his chest. Little flashes of him and Rex together, the things they'd done, reverberated through Marshall's memory. His hole was still lubed, but he added a little more, then he took a condom with him and went to find his cowboy.

This thing he felt for Rex, it was new and nowhere near over. Marshall wanted more than sex from Rex — but he *definitely* wanted the sex, too, preferably very soon.

He found Rex in the kitchen, plating bacon at the stove.

"Damn, that looks good."

Rex gasped a little and spun around. "Jeez, I didn't hear you. Hey, you're..." Rex swallowed, his gaze going to the condom Marshall held up. "Round two?" he whispered.

"Unless you want the bacon first." Marshall grinned as Rex set the plate down.

Rex did, however, grab a few pieces of bacon before he walked over to Marshall. "Fuel," Rex proclaimed, handing them to Marshall. "You're gonna need it."

"Am I?" Marshall purred and hoped he didn't sound like a dumbass.

Rex narrowed his eyes and his nostrils flared. That wasn't an amused look he was giving Marshall, but one that made it clear Rex was about ready to bend him over and fuck him stupid.

"I'm all for being fucked stupid," he muttered, heart thumping wildly.

Rex gave him that shy smile that Marshall was coming to crave seeing.

"Fuel first," Rex told him. Rex took the condom after Marshall had the bacon.

Rex walked back to the stove, his ass in his white briefs a gorgeous sight to behold.

"Cowboy buns," Marshall mused. He ate a piece of bacon while Rex chuckled.

Rex had a couple of slices, then he wiped his hands on the dish towel and picked up the condom he'd set on the counter. Rex pushed his briefs off. "Now," he drawled.

Just one word, but it set Marshall's dick into overdrive. It was hard in seconds, and he watched, shivering, as Rex opened the package then slid the condom on.

Rex had a beautiful dick, thick and long without being too much of either. Marshall couldn't look away from it as he asked, "How do you want me?"

"Any way I can have you," Rex said, and it seemed to Marshall there was more meaning to the words than he could fathom.

Marshall couldn't dwell on it—his pulse was racing and he was dizzy with lust. He turned and bent over the table. "How about like this—to start." He spread his feet further apart and arched his lower back.

"Fuck," Rex drawled.

Marshall looked over his shoulder and grinned. Rex was staring open-mouthed at him, or at his ass, to be precise. Possibly at his balls dangling between his legs, too. "Like what you see, cowboy?"

Rex made a strangled sound, then he moved quickly, stepping right up behind Marshall. "Are you ready?" Rex asked, his voice gruff. He pushed a finger into Marshall's hole before he could answer.

Marshall moaned and let his eyes close. He rested his head on his forearms and thrust back as Rex fingered him, but he was too eager for Rex's dick to take that for long. "Rex, fuck me already!"

Rex pushed his finger in harder, then curled it and hit that sweet spot inside Marshall.

"Ungh!" Marshall reached down to fist his own dick. "I'm gonna come without you—"

"No you aren't," Rex muttered. He stopped fingering Marshall and something much thicker was pressed to his pucker.

Marshall almost whined with eagerness as Rex slowly moved, his fat cockhead stretching Marshall's ring perfectly.

Once the crown was in, Rex hissed and pulled back, only to fill Marshall's ass with a steady thrust.

Marshall couldn't hold back the moan, or the pleas once Rex began to fuck him, taking long, deep strokes, every other one or so resulting in a perfect nudge to Marshall's gland.

Marshall jacked his own cock as he pushed up on his other hand so he could slam his hips back to get more of Rex's hot shaft in him faster.

Rex gripped Marshall's hips and fucked him hard, but after a few minutes, he pulled out.

"Why?" Marshall asked, ready to beg.

But Rex helped him to stand, then led him over to the couch. "Get up here."

Marshall knelt on the couch, his belly and dick against the faded cushions. He propped one knee on the arm of the couch.

"Perfect," Rex said. He got behind Marshall and thrust in with one swift move.

"Fuck me!" Marshall encouraged.

"Trying," Rex grunted out. He began to pound into Marshall, using a grip on Marshall's hip and shoulder to pull him back into every deep penetration.

Marshall was in a sensual heaven, panting, moaning, grinding back to get more of Rex.

And Rex gave him everything, fucking Marshall, kissing and nipping at his neck and shoulders.

"Grab your dick," Rex demanded. "Gotta come, oh fuck me, I have to…need…more—" His hips battered Marshall's ass as he moved even faster, driving in deeper and deeper until Marshall would have sworn Rex would never be able to leave.

Marshall fisted his own dick, and he ground his teeth as he tried to hold back. He was so close, pleasure pinging off his nerves, bouncing around from one to another like a pinball ricocheting, wild and unpredictable but so, *so* incredibly erotic.

His orgasm slammed into him, and Marshall threw his head back, shouting as pleasure engulfed him.

Spunk spilled over his hand, and Rex loosed a raw sound as he thrust in twice more then stilled, his fingers curling where he held Marshall. Rex grunted as he shot, and after several seconds, he shuddered and gasped.

"Holy shit," Rex got out. "Fuck. I can't—" He eased his cock out of Marshall's ass.

Marshall hissed a little. "You can't what?"

"Talk, think." Rex laughed wildly. "God. Damn. Marshall, you melted me." He plopped onto the couch and groaned.

Marshall would have felt pretty smug about that, but he was kind of certain his bones had turned to gelatin. He flopped down on the other end of the couch and tangled his legs with Rex's. "Same, you know. Never felt anything like what I've felt with you."

Rex was silent for what felt like a long time, but finally, he spoke. "I wonder if...if we have the beginnings of something special between us."

He sounded timid, and Marshall got that. What they could have, what *he* thought they could have, could be...*everything*. Only time would tell if he was right, though, and if he sold the ranch— "You could run this place. I don't have to sell it."

Rex sat up. "I wasn't angling for that."

Marshall nodded. "Yeah, I know. We were just going to fuck, but you feel it, too, right?"

Rex bobbed his head in agreement. "Sure, but I don't want you to think that means you have to keep this place if you don't want it. I'll find something else."

But this had been Rex's home for five years, and Marshall wasn't so eager to take it from him. "No, I think...I think we can give this a try—you and me, and if it doesn't work out, I won't sell this place out from under you. I don't need the money. But, if it *does* work out, I'd want some changes around here. Meanwhile, while we're trying to see if we can have a relationship—"

"We can," Rex said firmly. "If it's what we want."

Marshall liked Rex's enthusiasm. "Well, I don't want to rush us, so I'll go home and we'll take our time, get to know each other."

Rex's smile could have lit up the whole house. It certainly lit up Marshall's heart.

"I'd like that. I'd like that a lot," Rex said. "So what changes would you want?"

Marshall already had a list going in his mind, but they'd discuss it later. "To start with, a kiss."

Rex touched his cheek. "I'd be happy to kiss you, but I think *we* started the second you glared at me in the driveway."

Marshall laughed and pulled Rex down on top of him. "Well, if all it takes is a dirty look to snag you, I can do that, but I'd rather give you smiles."

A whole lifetime of them, if things went as he hoped.

As Marshall got the kiss he wanted, he believed in the future he could imagine sharing with Rex, and in Rex, and himself.

Epilogue

Rex watched Orion run across the field. The horse was gorgeous, his dark mane flying as he ran.

"Think he'll ever let me ride him?" Marshall asked.

Rex nodded. "Sure. He just wants you to work harder for it. A carrot every few days won't cut it with him."

"Well, you know I'm not an experienced rider, and he seems like a whole lot of horse," Marshall said. "I like Lulu. She's safe, and she loves me."

"She sure does," Rex agreed, flicking his gaze to the roan mare he'd given to Marshall for his birthday almost a year ago. "She keeps Orion in check, too."

"Yeah, that she does, cowboy." Marshall slipped his hand into Rex's. "The cleaning crew and the movers are gone. It's finished."

Rex turned to Marshall. "Finally." God, his heart couldn't possibly be any fuller of love, and yet, every day, he fell more in love with Marshall. Two years, almost three now, and they were happier than ever.

"Yeah, finally. Took a while, but we have our dream home now." Marshall tugged. "Come on. You're done for the day, right?"

"Yeah." Rex kissed Marshall, unable to resist that brilliant smile and the joy shining in Marshall's eyes. "Done working, but I have other plans."

Marshall laughed and tugged harder on his hand. "Well then, come on and let's go home! I do love your plans. And, I love you."

Rex took one more kiss. "I love you, too. Take me home and have your way with me."

"Oh, I plan on it."

Rex planned on it, too. He planned on doing a lot of things with Marshall, and he was grateful every day that he and Marshall had taken the chance and the time to build a relationship. He still felt a thrill every time he saw the wedding band, either his or Marshall's.

Rex had a home, and it wasn't a place. It was Marshall, and it always would be.

RACING FOR
HOME

Morticia Knight

Dedication

For my wonderful editor, Sue. ♡

Chapter One

I wish I'd never come here all those years ago.

Charlie lounged in the hay of one of the empty stalls at Piedmont Farms, idly chewing on a bit of straw. As one of the grooms at the top race horse farm in Long Island, New York — perhaps all of the east coast — he'd been designated to prepare the larger stall for Golden Dreams. The champion mare was nearing her time to foal and Charlie had kept himself busy with his chore. The only thing that ever prevented his thoughts from drifting into melancholy waters was taking care of his beloved horses.

Not my horses.

He let out a self-pitying groan then mentally chastised himself. No good ever came of wishing for what could never be. He had to be tough, be a strong man, survive. That's what his papa had told him before he'd sent him off to the farm to live for good when he'd turned fourteen. His ma had been felled by a local influenza outbreak in 1904, which had left his father to care for him and his siblings. The job Charlie had taken at the farm to help ease the family's burden had inspired his father to speak with Albert Piedmont about taking him on full-time. A growing boy about to become a man was much more expensive to feed than his two younger sisters. Once they'd left the area a couple years later, he'd never heard from them again.

Eight years.

For eight years he'd lived at Albert Piedmont's beautiful horse farm, and for five of those years, he'd been in love with Albert's even more beautiful son, Edward. He ran through all the significant milestones from his life in his mind. Losing his mother. Being forced to leave home. The first time he'd locked eyes with Edward and known they were meant to be. Their first kiss. When he'd lost his virginity in the very stall where Charlie currently lay, and they'd declared their everlasting love to each other. The day Edward had left Piedmont to go live with his new bride, Alice Normandy, on her family's estate across the island.

He pushed himself up from the hay, angry that he'd let his musings stray so far. He slapped at the bits and pieces of straw clinging to his woolen trousers, then smacked his newsboy cap back on his head, giving it one final pat before stomping out of the enclosure. The early spring chill hadn't yet given away to the warmth of the impending summer, and he had horses to worry about. Not traitorous ex-lovers.

* * * *

"The rest of my belongings have been crated, Alice. My valet will arrange their delivery. I'll be out of your hair entirely, my dear, within the week."

Edward pulled on his gloves, anxious to leave the Normandy estate with the intent of never setting foot in it again. His soon-to-be ex-wife rose from the settee of her bed chamber then slowly approached him. He couldn't discern the emotion behind her expression, but then, that had always been the case. His own emotions were jumbled, irritation mixed with a deep sadness that gnawed at him. The source of his sorrow wasn't what those around him would assume it was.

She stood before him, close enough to touch. They both knew that there would be no reason to do such a thing — they'd barely had any physical contact at all during their three-year marriage. Although, in Alice's case, she'd not suffered from any loss of affection. There had been plenty of handsome young men willing to keep her pleased. She'd invited him to seek companionship of his own, but she was unaware of his preferences. He hadn't dared take the chance.

Wasn't interested, regardless.

The true source of his despair would be taunting him soon enough by his proximity. Once he returned home to Piedmont Farms, Charlie would be tantalizingly within reach and an agonizing reminder of what he'd lost. He'd broken the sweet boy's heart and he knew Charlie would never forgive him — likely detested him, even.

Perhaps I should go abroad.

The silence between him and Alice had grown more uncomfortable, and as had been typical throughout their sham of a marriage, she stared at him, daring him to say something untoward so she could throw a fit of rage. It was one of her favorite games. Their union had been nothing more than a power play between two very wealthy families who came from a long line of other incredibly rich families. Once they'd been wed and he'd discovered that she was even more unhappy than he was about their forced matrimony, things had only deteriorated from there.

"Alice. It's quite late. Is there anything else you require before I leave?"

"No. I think you realize there's never been anything that I've *required* from you at all."

She'd no doubt thought that she could instigate one last screaming match by flaunting her lack of interest in him physically, as she'd been wont to do on many occasions. He didn't have the stomach for it.

"Excellent. Then I'll be on my way."

He'd already turned to leave when her words stopped him short.

"Back to your horse groom?"

He clutched his derby in his fingers, schooling his expression before facing her again. "My horse groom? What in heaven's name are you going on about?"

The corners of her mouth turned up in what he was sure she thought was a smile. "Don't be obtuse, Edward. I've always suspected your predilection, so I stayed aware to confirm my suspicions. It was dreadfully curious to me that you never dallied with any of the available women of our set, the way I did with the men."

"Perhaps I've been more discreet. It's never been my intention to destroy your honor."

"Ha! How amusing. No, the ladies of our circle revel in intrigues and gossip. I would've known. So I began to watch you around others, see if I could ascertain what the issue was. I'd about concluded that you weren't a man at all, couldn't perform with anyone, until our last gathering at your father's estate." Her face twisted slightly, a flush of anger apparent before she returned to her former mien. "I saw the look of longing on his face, the way you caught his eye before flushing and abruptly turning away. How disgusting."

"You've always had a vivid imagination, Alice. It's one of your shining attributes. Now that you've said your piece, I'll be off. I'd like to get home before dawn. I did you the favor of leaving in the middle of the night to save you from any undue embarrassment in front of the staff, so you could show me some consideration now by letting me be on my way."

She stamped her foot. "You're ten years older than him! He must've been a boy when you first took him, he's been at your father's farm since he was fourteen." She sneered at him. "My God, you're vile."

"I didn't *take* anyone." He'd spat it out before he could stop himself. "Especially not a boy. I'm interested in *men*." He slammed his hat on his head. "And the only thing that's vile is the fact that you'll raise your skirts for any willing cock while I've only ever taken the pleasure of one. That's because he possesses the only thing that you'll never understand. The ability to love."

He ignored the shattering of a glass near his head as he exited her room. The shrill insults she hurled at his retreating figure meant nothing to him either. As he trotted down the steps of what was no longer his home, he was filled with a new resolve. Charlie might hate him, but he still loved Charlie. If the fates were willing to intervene, he would do everything he could to win his lover's heart back.

Chapter Two

"Come on, pretty girl, it's okay. I'm here now, and Doctor Graham will be along in a few hours to check on you. You're going to do a wonderful job."

Charlie was on his knees, gently stroking Golden Dream's head, patting the tuft of coarse reddish brown hair that lay between her ears. Her breathing was steady, a light sweat covering the coat of her neck and flank. She kicked her legs restlessly, struggling to get up. Charlie moved out of the way to allow her the space she needed to likely reposition the foal in the birth canal. She'd repeat the process of moving then resting until she was ready to expel her newborn.

He backed out of the enclosure, shutting the door then engaging the latch.

"How much longer does she have?"

Charlie jumped, clutching the wooden edges of the stall door, his heartrate accelerating along with his breathing.

Why in the name of hellfire is Edward in here?

His ex-lover hadn't set foot in the stables since he'd left him behind to forge a new life with his bride three years before. After that awful day, he'd only ever seen him in passing during infrequent visits to his father's estate.

"She, uh…" He cleared his throat, the sensation that it was tightening preventing him from speaking up, making him sound weak. "I estimate three to five hours. She's done this before." He refused to turn around, fiddling with the metal latch instead.

"Old Carruthers is letting you attend a foaling mare? You've learned quite a bit since I last…"

Edward cleared his throat too, confusing Charlie. Why should Edward be nervous? He'd always been so self-possessed, regal even. He hung his head. He'd been a fool to ever think that a man of Edward's station would truly pledge his love to someone who was essentially an uneducated orphan with no social status.

"What I mean is, that you're obviously very knowledgeable of the care of the horses. I always knew you had a gift with them."

He let out a small laugh that held no mirth. "Yes. I've become rather enamored of them. They're loyal creatures when treated well."

He started at Edward's hand on his shoulder, shrugging it off then finally facing him. His heart slammed in his chest. It was the closest they'd been to each other in three years, the first time they'd touched since their final kiss. He'd sobbed like a baby after Edward had left his bed located in his sparse quarters at the back of the small stable.

"I have to take care of Shadow. Please excuse me."

His words had come out anxious, breathless. He couldn't be around Edward any longer, he'd simply come apart. In his desperation to get away, his foot became caught in the pitchfork he'd leaned against the wall earlier after he'd filled Golden Dream's stall with hay. As he stumbled, losing his footing, he was enfolded in Edward's strong arms. He struggled against Edward, terrified to reawaken the fire that had always burned much too bright between them.

"Charlie. Stop. I'll let you go, but I don't want you to fall and hurt yourself."

Edward released him as he stilled, and he took a large step back.

"What do you want? Why are you here?"

He cringed. He hadn't wanted to give voice to his questions, had only wanted to get away from the torment of being so close to the man he loved.

"Alice and I are divorcing. She's found a man whom she wishes to marry and I've come home to stay."

Divorcing?

It made no sense. Edward and Alice's union had seemed forged in stone, judging by the way his employer and Alice's father had so adamantly insisted upon it. He shook his head, not sure what to say. In addition, Charlie had always wondered just how true Edward's declarations had been that he had no feelings for Alice or any other woman. Charlie assumed that all he'd ever really been was a young man's folly.

"You must be devastated. I'm sorry to hear it."

He *was* sorry. As angry as he was at Edward, the thought of him experiencing the same pain that he'd suffered during the years of Edward's absence filled him with sorrow.

"Charlie. You know I was never in love with her, that we only married under pressure from our families."

He let out another frustrated laugh. "Yes. So you said. And I was supposed to accept your word the same way I did when you swore we'd be together forever."

His words had hit their mark. Edward's brow furrowed, his eyes glistening. He nodded jerkily.

"You're right. I'm ashamed that I didn't stand up to him, that I fell for what turned out to be his lies about my mother's desire for me to marry Alice."

Charlie felt a stab of remorse at his harsh words. Albert Piedmont had no issue using falsehoods to manipulate those around him. Charlie had witnessed it enough times when he'd been present during any of Mr. Piedmont's business transactions. He swallowed, searching for the right words.

"So you're telling me that he pretended it was your mother who wished you to marry Alice, that it was never true? What a *snake*." Charlie bit his lip. He didn't have the same relationship that he'd once shared with Edward. He needed to temper his words if he wanted to remain employed. "Forgive me. I spoke out of turn."

Edward gazed at him with the same pained expression he'd had almost the entire time they'd talked. "Don't. I don't want you to edit what you say to me. And it *was* a despicable thing he did by telling me how much it would break my mother's heart if I didn't marry Alice. I swear that was the only reason. I *never* lied to you, Charlie. Alice and I were never in love. It wasn't until mother was dying that she told me…"

Edward choked on his words and Charlie had to catch himself before he gathered Edward in his arms to comfort him. Edward swiped a finger under his eye before continuing.

"If only I'd known that she'd understood all along, that it was really my father who wanted to marry me off before I caused the family an embarrassing scandal. By the time she insisted that I follow my heart, it was too late."

Charlie remembered the day Edward had come to be with his mother before she died. She'd had what they thought was a mild illness, but she'd gradually become weaker until her heart had given out. By the time the doctor had realized how grave her condition was, it had barely left Edward the chance to be by her side.

"Edward...I..."

He wrung his hands, his heart broken over all that might have been, all the pain they'd both endured since they'd been apart from the other. He glanced up to see Edward staring at him intently.

"But it's not too late anymore, Charlie. I'm back. Alice and I are no longer together."

Hope bloomed in his chest right before it was stamped back out. He snorted derisively. "I see. I'm to be your mistress then, is that it? The dirty secret of the Piedmont horse farm, your plaything until you're forced to marry once again to keep your reputation and inheritance intact? Fuck off, Edward. I'm not some swooning female, bending over at the mere hint that you might favor me with a good rutting."

"Charlie, love..."

Edward reached for him, and he jumped back. "I have work to do. I don't need you anymore, but my...the horses do. I'm sure you can find entertainments elsewhere. If it's a warm hole you're looking for, I've heard that the O'Tierney Inn is always a good source." He grunted. "Sorry. Can't speak from experience. I've never let anyone *touch* me since you."

"Neither have I."

He snapped his jaw shut, his final retort lost in the shock of what Edward had just declared. He blinked a few times, mulling over the implications of Edward's claim. As he stood there, confused, sorting through his emotions, Edward advanced on him. When he was yanked into Edward's strong embrace, his lips branded by Edward's hot kiss, he didn't fight. He melted.

Chapter Three

Edward plunged into Charlie's mouth over and over, desperate for his taste, his sweetness. Even though he was still lean and shorter than Edward, Charlie had developed a compact layer of muscle on his frame and was at least an inch taller since they'd last been together.

So much time lost.

He clutched his fingers in the dark waves of Charlie's hair, held him flush to his body with his other hand. Edward nipped and tugged at Charlie's lips in between licking inside his mouth until he was forced to stop and catch his breath. Charlie wouldn't meet his eyes, but he hadn't let go, his fists still curled in the fabric of Edward's suit jacket. Their hard lengths were pressed together, the throb in Charlie's as pronounced as Edward's own.

"I love you, Charlie, don't ever doubt that."

"Don't. It hurts too much. I can't…"

Edward tightened his arms, peppered Charlie's face with kisses, desperate to soothe his lover.

"I'll find a way for us to be together, I swear. But our options are limited while we both remain here at the farm. That's the reality of this world. Men will never be allowed to openly love one another without fear of the consequences. We have to accept our circumstances, search for the best solution we can." He angled back, making sure Charlie held his gaze as he continued. "But I won't ever abandon you again, my love. I hope you can find it in your heart to believe my oaths once more."

Charlie seemed to catch a sob before he spoke. "Edward. God, how I want to believe. I've exhausted myself these last three years trying to banish the specter of you from my thoughts. I don't know if I can allow myself to give into you. Not like this, not so fast. If I embrace hope now then lose you again... I don't think I could survive it."

"Shh, love. *I'm* the one who wouldn't survive." Edward caressed Charlie's back then cupped his face. "I'll dedicate the rest of my days to making it up to you. To begin with, I won't allow us to be parted again, I swear. But I need time. If I had unlimited access to my trust, I could combine that with what I'll have left over after the divorce. We'd be set. I've saved quite a bit from my business dealings over the years, but it's not enough for us to start over somewhere else yet."

Charlie arched his eyebrows, his eyes widening in surprise. "What are you saying? That you'd actually take me away with you, that you would risk us being together?"

Edward stroked Charlie's hair off his forehead, marveling that he was in his arms, that he was blessed enough to be staring into his stormy gray eyes again. "Yes. Together. We'd still have to hide the true nature of our relationship no matter where we went, but I would be yours the same as you would be mine. No separation."

Charlie's expression remained stunned as he seemed to search Edward's face for answers. Edward was filled with dread that he'd be turned away, that the same anguish he'd unintentionally caused Charlie would be thrust upon him. After a few more moments, Charlie slowly nodded.

"Yes. I want that too."

Edward crushed his lips to Charlie again, still lost in the thrill of having his lover in his arms after so many years apart. This time, he let Charlie have control. He licked inside Edward's mouth, exploring everywhere. Edward gave into his lust, answering back as they battled with their tongues to delve deeper into the other.

They clung to each other as the kiss heated, both of them touching, caressing then seeking skin. Edward shoved first one then the other of Charlie's suspenders down then yanked his cotton work shirt free. His blasted tank was in the way and Edward struggled with the buttons. They finally had to break from their kiss to turn their attention to disrobing.

"Just your shirt, then loosen your trousers." Edward glanced around. "When...?"

"Soon. When dawn breaks. Don't you remember from before?"

Edward fumbled with his own shirt. "Of course. But it's been so long. You're a groom now instead of a stable hand, everything's so different—"

Edward gasped as Charlie encircled his cock with his warm, calloused hand. He was leaking freely, desperate to come. He wanted it to last forever, go slow in celebration of their first time back together, but they couldn't take the chance. The sun was breaking the horizon, and the dark that had felt like a shield around them was ebbing away.

He pulled Charlie to him then shoved his hand down the front of Charlie's pants, tugging him in quick, harsh strokes, his lover's own preliminary emissions slickening the way. Charlie increased the pace of his own strokes as they breathed frantically, Edward working to control his moans. Scared that he would cry out at his completion, he took Charlie's mouth in a bruising kiss right as he released, his seed erupting over Charlie's hand. Almost simultaneously, heat coated his own and he softened his tugs, gently coaxing the remainder of Charlie's spend from him.

They held each other close, their hands stilling on each other's softening member as their frantic breaths slowed. Edward reluctantly let go of Charlie, his lover doing the same. As thrilled as he was that they were near again, that Charlie had given him a second chance, it was agony to have to leave him so soon. There wouldn't be caresses in the afterglow of their spent lust, Charlie wouldn't lie in his arms. They'd never spent a whole night together—it had been too risky—but they'd had moments of closeness after their stolen times. He longed for the day when they could be with each other the way Edward knew they were meant to be.

Charlie kept his eyes averted as he gazed around the stable. "I left some clean rags in the one of the empty stalls. I'll get one for you."

"Charlie. Look at me."

The way he glanced up at Edward with a pained expression, as if he'd done something wrong, tore at Edward's insides.

"Yes?" Charlie's voice was so small, Edward frowned.

"What is it? You act as though I'm going to beat you or tell you to get out. Fetch us the cloths then come back to my arms. Quickly, before I have to leave."

Charlie's eyes glimmered and he scurried to do as Edward had asked. Once he'd returned and they'd both cleaned themselves, Edward pulled Charlie to him. He wrapped his hand around Charlie's nape, holding him there as he pushed past the seam of his lips, hoping to convey with the kiss that his emotions were true, that Charlie needn't fear that Edward would run away from him.

Charlie panted as the kiss was broken, clutching at the lapels of Edward's jacket. "I love you, Edward. God help me, I really do."

Edward placed a finger under Charlie's chin, tipping his head back to stare into his lovely eyes again. "No more than I love you. I'll spend the rest of forever proving how much you're cherished by me so that you'll never doubt again. I don't know if I can ever forgive myself for abandoning you the way I did."

Charlie gripped the fabric of Edward's coat tighter. "Don't. We can't go back. All I care about is that all my tomorrows will be with you in my life."

"They will, Charlie love. Give me some time to take care of things so that we can build our future the way it should have been originally."

He captured Charlie's mouth in another deep kiss, not sure if he could bear to let him go. He had the irrational fear that if he did, Charlie would disappear. That their entire interlude would prove to be a dream.

They both started as two voices outside of the stable drifted to their ears. Charlie gasped, letting him go at once. Edward was keenly aware of Charlie's well-placed anxiety — it had loomed over them the entire time they'd been together previously. If they were to be caught, the price Charlie would pay would be much dearer than Edward.

"I know, my love," Edward whispered. "I'll be back soon. Meet me here at midnight."

Charlie shook his head as the voices grew in volume, the clattering of pails adding to the sounds. "No. Golden Dreams will've dropped her foal by then and Carruthers or your father might be checking on her."

Edward pulled Charlie into the stall from where he'd retrieved the rags. "I must see you. It's too cruel after all these years."

Charlie nodded, a frown still marring his features. "I know. Go to the smaller stable. Hardly anyone goes in there, even during the day. Carruthers put me in charge of it and everyone's accustomed to me spending long hours in there because of Shadow."

"Shadow?"

"Yes. He's a yearling that your father decided wasn't worth his money to train, so he's been banished to the lesser stable."

Edward smiled. Charlie loved lost causes, his heart was so soft. It only made Edward adore him that much more.

"But he's worth everything to you."

Charlie flushed as the door to the front of the stable creaked open along with a muttered curse.

"Go! I'll see you tonight."

Edward grabbed Charlie's face then kissed him hard on the lips. "I love you."

Charlie whispered back, "I love you too."

Edward peered around the corner, grateful to see that whoever had opened the gated door to the stable was busy mucking out one of the front stalls. He carefully made his way out the back, near where Carruthers had set up a small office for himself. Edward was relieved to discover that the small door wasn't latched from the outside.

He paused to give Charlie one final look, only to see his poor love staring back, an expression of longing on his face so profound, it threatened to unravel him. He blew a kiss to him then stepped outside into the mist clinging to the ground, the precursor to a new day. It was time to face his father.

Chapter Four

"When did you get in?"

"Good morning to you as well, Father." Edward let out a casual chuckle as he entered the breakfast room, hoping to convey to his father that all was right with the world. The man could sniff out discord from miles away, and Edward was still reeling from his lack of sleep and the unexpected encounter with Charlie. He could barely contain his emotions. Displaying anything resembling happiness on the heels of leaving Alice would have his father interrogating him to no end, and likely keeping a close watch on him too. That would be disastrous.

He took a seat to the right of his father then plucked a linen napkin from the cherry wood table before laying it across his lap. The solid silver coffee server, which had been in the Piedmont family for generations, was brought to the table. He nodded to the maid, noting that she was unknown to him. He creased his brow before he could stop himself. Since his mother's passing, the Piedmont household had seemed to employ an unusual amount of young, attractive maids.

As he poured himself a cup of coffee, he glanced over at his father who leaned forward, one elbow on the table as he held up his spectacles to examine the *Daily Racing Form*, which he grasped with the other hand. Edward hadn't lived at home for three years, but as he watched his father squint, frown and alternately purse his lips that were crowned with a bristly gray mustache, it could have been the very morning he'd left the estate. As was typical, he was so absorbed in the paper, he hadn't bothered to continue his conversation with Edward.

Edward did as he'd always done. He carried on as if his father gave a good goddamn. "I arrived at dawn. Rawley had the staff bring my trunks to my rooms. He'll be seeing to the rest of my belongings left at the Normandy estate later on this week when Alice leaves town."

He took a measured sip of the hot brew, hoping that the Kentucky Derby — only a little over a month away — had his father too distracted. Albert peered up at him, his look of disapproval apparent as his squinting changed into a scowl.

"I still don't understand the women these days. A fine, upstanding lady leaving her husband to go off gallivanting with another man!" He grunted. "It's indecent, is what it is." He slammed his paper down on the table, dropping his spectacles on top. "And you. What kind of a man allows his wife to disgrace him in such a way?"

"Father—"

Albert smashed his fist down. "I don't want to hear it! I don't care what you told me. All this modern nonsense about seeking happiness with another person, true love — it's preposterous! That sort of hogwash is fine for the uneducated, lesser masses. What else do they have? Let them entertain themselves with sonnets and flowers. Marriage in the upper classes is about building strong alliances, increasing wealth, power." He huffed, crossing his arms over his chest. "Why couldn't she have her end of the house and you have yours? Carry on that way, if you catch my drift?" He narrowed his eyes at Edward who'd decided it was pointless to argue with someone who had no heart. "Is it because she's barren? Is that it? I know the Piedmont seed is strong, so it can't be you."

"Father. Really. It's done and over with. Can we move on from here? Tell me about Lord Blue. He's running in the Derby, correct?"

The scarlet that had risen in his father's face softened a bit at the mention of his prized stallion. "Of course. He's the one, Eddie. Wait until you see George give him his workout on the track. The purse is high, but so will the stud fees be once he's outrun every other horse this season!"

His father had a gleam in his eyes as he spoke, and Edward was certain that the attention on his impending divorce had been successfully derailed. They chattered some more about developments on the farm, his father hinting once again that he wished to have Edward take over Piedmont one day. William, his younger brother, was settled with his family in Boston. He was a lawyer with his own legal firm, which alternately made his father proud and irritated. William had a Harvard education and a successful, respectable trade. But he wasn't working with horses, which in his father's opinion, meant he wasn't *completely* successful.

Edward's thoughts drifted to Charlie, his heart swelling. He held back a smile, but was reminded by his father's rant about William and his brother's distaste for equine pursuits, just how much Charlie loved working in the stables. Wherever they ended up, whatever fate awaited them, there would have to be horses.

Anything. Anything his heart desires.

Chapter Five

"He's back, Shadow. At least I think he is. I might've hit my head on something and am seeing visions."

The coal-black horse snuffled, nodding its great head three times as if agreeing with Charlie. He chuckled as he finished brushing Shadow's soft, shining coat. He took extra good care of Shadow, pampering him more than the other horses. It wasn't only that Shadow was his favorite, but that Charlie felt bad that Albert Piedmont had never given the horse a fair chance to prove himself. The snooty trainer that Piedmont employed was full of himself, and loved to declare to anyone within earshot that he could tell almost from the moment a horse was born whether it was worth its weight in oats.

"He's an idiot, Shadow."

"Is that what you're saying to your dear horse about me? I don't stand a chance then."

Charlie whirled around, his excitement at the sound of Edward's voice speeding up his heart.

"It's true. You're really here."

It was a stupid thing to say, but it had flown from his mouth before he'd had the chance to give it a thought. Edward advanced toward him, his face radiating a happiness that Charlie had missed almost as much as he had the man. He stopped right as he reached Shadow. Edward held out his hand for the brush. Charlie gave a small, snorting chuckle.

"What?"

He handed the item over. Edward took the solid wood grooming accessory and gently brushed over Shadow's side down to his flank.

"I want to see if your horse likes me." Edward winked at him. "If he does, then maybe you'll believe that I'm true to my word. Horses know when a person isn't worth their salt." Edward swept the brush along Shadow's coat in a sweeping arc. "That's what my father always told me."

Charlie shrugged. "Well, he can't be wrong about *everything*."

Edward let out a hearty laugh, arousing Charlie. There was a lustiness to Edward's nature that made Charlie have to stop and catch his breath at times. There had never been another person he'd encountered who was as full of life as Edward. Charlie's chest tightened. The few times he'd seen Edward after he'd left the estate, that vivacity had been absent. The fraudulent life he'd led had robbed Edward of his spirit. Charlie flushed, lowering his head. He hoped that he was the reason Edward was so lively again.

Edward moved nearer, until they were almost touching. Heat built between them and Charlie wasn't sure if it was from how close they were or from the flush building inside him.

Perhaps both?

Edward reached down to caress his cheek, Charlie leaning into the touch. "Your sleeping quarters are still here?"

Charlie nodded, whispering, "Yes."

"Here." Edward lowered his hand then handed Charlie the brush with his other. "When will the others be back?"

Charlie accepted the brush, shaking his head as he did. "I'm it. There's Carruthers, the Head Groom as always, then there are five stable boys. They don't live here on the farm and Carruthers' place is in the main stable."

Edward's expression was one of confusion, his brow furrowed. "I don't understand. There have always been at least a half dozen grooms under Carruthers. What's going on, Charlie?"

He'd wondered the exact same thing. The years since Edward's mother had died, changes had been made that didn't bode well for Piedmont Farms. He gazed up at Edward, sorry that the mysterious issues plaguing the farm had chased away Edward's happiness.

"I don't know the why of it, but your father seems to be dealing with some financial hardships. Staff and horses have gradually been reduced since your mother's passing." Charlie indicated to the rest of the stable with a gesture of his hand. "There are only four horses left in this stable, yet as you know, it used to be full with upwards of twelve at any given time. The main stable is half empty as well. Only the stud horses, Golden Dreams, Lord Blue and one other possible racing contender are left."

"My God." Edward turned away, a hand to his forehead as he circled around the stall, eventually leaning against the open gate, his face a study in anguish. "No wonder."

Charlie swallowed hard. He feared what Edward might have to say. "Do you know something, Edward?"

"I'm not sure, I..." He shook his head, more as if he was perplexed than answering Charlie's query. "He about had a fit when I told him I was divorcing Alice. I knew he'd be upset, knew the Normandy estate was his main concern, yet..." Edward furrowed his brow. "I can't explain it, except that he sounded desperate in a way I've never heard before. He tried several times to convince me to stay with her. It has to be the loss of the Normandy fortune that upset him so." He snorted derisively. "Yet he has no problem affording comely maids for the main house."

Charlie didn't know much about business dealings — not much at all. He couldn't even begin to imagine the amount of money it must take to run an operation the size of Piedmont Farms. Then there was the grand home. It had to be an enormous pressure.

Edward turned back to Charlie. "I've been investing in the farm with some of the Normandy money. Her father expected it to be mine and Alice's one day, but now that we're divorcing..." Edward ran a hand through his wavy hair. "James Normandy will want a return on his investment."

"Oh."

Charlie wished he wasn't so stupid about such things. He could do tack, grooming, exercising, stall upkeep and every other manner of duties as horse groom at Piedmont. But he had no idea how to run an estate or manage money. What possible good could he be as a partner to Edward someday?

Edward advanced on him, gathering his hands up in his own. "My Charlie love. I'll have to find a way to pay Mr. Normandy back right away. I can't take the chance that father might lose the farm and leave me without my share of the income from it." Edward squeezed his fingers. "It could delay when I can leave with you for good, but I promise, I'll find a way to make it happen. Please believe in me."

Charlie nodded his head jerkily, swallowing down the tears building in his eyes, fighting back the voice in his head mocking him. It told him that it had all been a hopeless fantasy, that he'd never be with Edward for good.

"I do believe in you. But pardon me for saying so, I just don't believe in your father."

Edward tugged Charlie to him, wrapping his arms around his waist possessively. "I don't believe in him either, Charlie. I haven't for a while." He ran one hand up Charlie's back. "I love you. He can't take that from me, from us. All that matters to me from this moment forward is finding a way to pay James Normandy back then financing our way out of here."

Charlie chewed at his lips, not sure if he should say anything more. Edward knew about such things, Charlie didn't. But at the same time, he'd seen how it worked over the years. He understood how the horses made Mr. Piedmont money.

"What if you had your very own horse? One who was just as good as Lord Blue, could win races and make lots of money?" Charlie lifted his gaze. "One whose stud fees would pay the bills for a long time, maybe even allow you to buy more good horses?"

Edward arched his eyebrows with a smirk. "Is Shadow this magical horse?"

Charlie's face heated and he lowered his head. He knew he wasn't smart about business, but he didn't like Edward mocking him.

"Now, now. Look at me, Charlie." Edward placed a finger under his chin, encouraging his head back up.

"Tell me about Shadow. What makes you think he has what it takes?"

I'll sound like a lunatic. He shrugged. "It's in his eyes. The way he dances during his hot walk, like he could go on forever and ever. Like he'd never get tired." Charlie knew he was blushing furiously. He'd never dared to give his opinion about a horse to anyone before. Not when he'd been told by Carruthers to shut up so many times over the years. "He wants to, Edward. He wants to show the other horses that he's better than them. I see the way he reacts when they're around."

The corners of Edward's mouth were curled slightly. Charlie couldn't discern whether it was in amusement at Charlie's assessment or if he was taking him seriously.

"My father leaves town this week with Lord Blue for a match race down in Philly. He'll be gone for at least two weeks. Show me what Shadow can do while he's gone."

Charlie blinked a few times. "But the trainer won't be here. He'll be with Lord Blue. And anyway, he'd never touch Shadow. Your father forbade it."

"Shadow doesn't need that tired old trainer. What he needs is you. You show me what Shadow can do."

Charlie sputtered, overwhelmed by Edward's crazy proposition. "But I'm just a horse groom, nothing more."

Edward jostled him. "Stop that. You're much more. You're everything to me and I can already tell that you're everything to Shadow too."

Before Charlie could respond, Edward had slanted his mouth over his, demanding entrance with his tongue. He allowed his body to go limp in Edward's assured embrace. Nothing was as thrilling as Edward's touch, his mouth, his manhood as it drove deep into him.

Edward used his hands to roam Charlie's body freely, squeezing his flesh with his powerful grip. He wanted Edward to take him. They'd only ever coupled a few times during their initial romance. The fear of being caught had been one issue—the other had been Edward's reticence to take Charlie's virginity at first. He'd been afraid that Charlie's feelings were a puppy love, that he was too young for him. Once they'd been together as lovers for over a year, Edward had breached him. It remained in Charlie's mind as one of the most important things that had ever happened to him.

Their shared caresses increased in urgency and Charlie wasn't sure either of them would last until Edward was inside him. Charlie broke their connection, panting breathlessly. Edward's chest heaved as he seemingly struggled to speak.

"I won't penetrate you if you don't want it. Any way I can be with you is wonderful."

"But I do." A flush of heat crept up his neck. "I want you to love me that way. Please."

"Oh, Charlie."

Edward had whispered it before taking him in another bruising kiss. This time when their connection broke, it was Edward's doing. He twined their fingers together as he led Charlie to his quarters in the stable. Edward's return no longer seemed like a fantasy, his promises a false hope. Together they'd find a way to finance their departure and together would be how they'd spend their lives.

Chapter Six

Edward lay back on Charlie's small bed, one arm behind him supporting his head. He watched as his sweet man finished cleaning the sweat, dirt and smell of horse off his lean, sculpted body using the jug and wash basin. It was located on a little wooden table that also held a lantern in the corner of the confining space. Charlie really had matured from the boy he'd appeared to be when they'd first been together. It made him even more appealing to Edward.

"Turn and face me."

Charlie's figure highlighted by the glow of the lantern was spectacular. Edward's shaft leaked freely, the build up from their earlier kiss tightening his jewels. He was anxious to be inside Charlie, to feel the tight heat of his body as it swallowed his cock. Edward raked his gaze over Charlie's frame, his lover's erection angled toward his belly, as ready for release as Edward's was.

"Come to me." Edward gestured with his hand. "I want to taste you."

Charlie's movements were hesitant at first, and Edward worried that he was pushing Charlie too soon after their long separation. When he stopped near Edward's head, he glanced up to see worry in Charlie's eyes. He ran a hand softly up the back of Charlie's thigh, barely brushing his ass before dropping it down again.

"If you've decided you're not ready after all, we can simply lie in each other's arms. The feel of your skin next to mine would also give me pleasure."

Charlie shook his head vigorously. "It's not that. It's that I fear I'll spend too quickly."

Edward let out a small chuckle, brushing his hand up Charlie's leg once more but allowing it to stay cupped on one ass cheek. "Then I'll make you spend again. Let me taste you now. I've missed your bitter salt too much."

The flush decorating Charlie's torso and the blush upon his face stoked Edward's lust. He grasped Charlie's ass with both hands, leaning up on one elbow as he did. Too anxious to start with soft licks, he swallowed around Charlie's rigid length, then ran his tongue along the velvet hardness as he withdrew to capture the preliminary drops of seed.

Charlie gasped then moaned, clutching at Edward's hair as his cock swelled on Edward's tongue. Three more strong pulls was all it took before Charlie emptied his balls down Edward's throat. Edward sucked some more, draining his lover before lapping at his softening member. The moment Charlie swayed on his feet in the aftermath of his climax, Edward wrapped one arm around his waist and the other behind his knees, encouraging him to collapse by his side on the bed.

He gathered Charlie to him, the rapid flutter of Charlie's heart an insistent beat against Edward's chest.

"I'm sorry." Charlie tipped his head back to look at Edward. "You were too good."

Edward took his mouth, pressing his tongue inside to let Charlie taste himself. Everything about Charlie was exquisite and he wished for the day when he would know his own worth. Edward wanted to be the one who led him to that realization.

Edward angled back to lock gazes with Charlie. "I'm going to soften you up so I can enter you. I know it's been a long time. Are you afraid?"

Charlie shook his head, even as he tensed and clutched at Edward's arm — his response at odds with his body's reaction. Edward rubbed noses with him.

"I have a paste I can use and I'll taste you there too. I'll go very slow."

Charlie's eyes were wide, his lips parted. "Taste? You mean...?" Charlie's shaft twitched against Edward's thigh.

"Yes, Charlie love. I want all of you." Edward patted Charlie's hip. "Roll over while I retrieve the softener from my jacket."

Charlie said nothing, merely following Edward's instructions. Edward had never done what he was about to do to Charlie, but he'd thought of it over the years while living a life of regret and longing at the Normandy estate. He'd ached to know every part of Charlie intimately. To see, touch and taste him everywhere. The relief he'd experienced upon discovering that Charlie had been with no other man during their separation had sealed his resolve.

After getting the petroleum jelly, he paused to stare at the lovely man lying on the mattress, displaying the most enticing of backsides. Charlie's ass was round and pert, complementing the bottom of Charlie's long, sleek torso perfectly. Edward set the jar of paste on the floor near the foot of the bed. He encouraged Charlie to open his thighs then pushed his legs farther apart. Charlie's breath had accelerated, but then again, so had Edward's.

Edward crawled up the bed then situated himself on his belly until his head was at Charlie's rear. He trailed his fingers across Charlie's gorgeous ass, Charlie sighing as he did. Charlie's dick was smashed beneath his body but his balls were exposed, available for Edward to suck first one then the other into his mouth. He used his tongue to explore the orbs in their lightly haired sac, Charlie squirming, little cries falling from his lips.

After lapping at Charlie's balls, Edward scooted up, dragging his tongue along the strip of skin leading to his entrance. Edward parted Charlie's cheeks, exposing his hole. The skin of his crease was darker than the rest of him, framing an even darker opening made up of Charlie's enticingly wrinkled skin. Edward lapped vigorously at the pucker, hardening the tip of his tongue to check the resistance of the muscle guarding his passage.

Charlie had clenched up initially, but as Edward increased the fervor of his ministrations, he relaxed. His noises rose in volume, but as had always been the case with their lovemaking, he muffled his cries in the pillow. After licking at Charlie's hole until he quivered beneath him, Edward stiffened his tongue again, prodding Charlie's entrance with the tip. It popped in, Charlie crying out as Edward fucked him with the small, wet appendage. Charlie rutted against the bed, Edward grasping his cheeks in a strong grip and holding Charlie down to keep him from wriggling away.

He's mine.

Edward wanted Charlie for always, loved him so much that it left an ache in his heart from the enormity of it. He retreated from Charlie's backside, Charlie responding with a whimper.

"That's my love. I'm going to open you even more with my fingers so you can easily take my cock."

Charlie groaned, and Edward had to admit that he felt a certain amount of pride at how he affected his lover. Edward snatched up the jar of moistener, opening it quickly to scoop out some paste. Charlie was still relaxed from Edward's oral attentions and he submitted beautifully to Edward's invasion of his hole. Edward sought out the knot inside his lover's passage that he knew gave pleasure. The moment he rubbed the bundle of nerves, Charlie jerked beneath his touch.

"Please! Edward, I'm ready for you. I want you inside me before I spend again."

A smile tugged at the corners of Edward's mouth, Charlie's desperate entreaty filling him with even more desire. He removed his fingers then stuffed a pillow under Charlie's belly. After pushing Charlie's thighs even wider apart, he positioned himself between them, sweat beading on his upper lip at the thought of burying his hardened flesh into Charlie's soft channel.

Edward spread Charlie's opening with his cockhead, groaning as he struggled to fill his snug passage. He draped his torso over Charlie's back, the movement driving him even deeper into Charlie's body. Edward noted the grimace on his lover's face, so he stilled. He nibbled across Charlie's shoulders, then brushed his mouth across them.

"Should I stop?"

Charlie pressed his lips together then answered, "No. Kiss me."

Edward obliged, taking Charlie's mouth, exploring him with his tongue as he picked up a slow pace of thrusting into his lover. The kiss grew in passion as did their fucking. Charlie accepted Edward's cock into his body, pushing back to meet him with every urgent movement of Edward's hips.

Edward's completion was near and he rutted frantically. He broke the kiss to suck in a lungful of air, grabbing Charlie's hands and twining their fingers together. He punched into Charlie over and over, holding on to the man who was his heart. Charlie's passage fluttered around him, and he froze, pumping his seed into his lover until he was dizzy from it.

He fell to his elbows but didn't let go of Charlie. He needed him more than he ever had, needed to know that he could have a life with love. Charlie was that love and he could never be parted from him again.

Chapter Seven

"Yes, liquidate that one too. Have the money wired to me immediately. I'd like to have it as soon as tomorrow. Good day then." Edward hung up the phone right as his father entered the breakfast room.

"Money? Are there debts you've incurred that I should be aware of? I don't need any surprises, Edward."

Edward angled his body toward his father. He knew he was in his rights to ask the same question of him, but he'd already determined not to dwell on the failures at Piedmont. He only wished to focus on building a future with Charlie. If the farm could be saved, he'd see what he could do. But a rather disturbing conversation with his brother William after his first night with Charlie had led him to believe that things were near hopeless where his father was concerned.

I wonder how long he was gambling away the assets of the farm before mother went?

"No debts. Just gathering some funds to put toward some business speculation."

His father harrumphed before settling into his morning routine with the *Daily Racing Form* at the breakfast table. Without favoring him with even a glance in his direction, his father continued. "If you're so anxious to spend your limited funds on a business, you need look no further than your own birthright! Lord knows we could use a strong influx of cash." His father peered up at him from over his spectacles. "If you took the Richmond girl's hand, her family's worth would most certainly help the Piedmont Farm cause." He grunted. "She's not as attractive or as rich as Alice, but she's about as good as you're going to get—what with the stain of divorce and all."

Edward regarded his father with a tight smile. "I've never even met the woman." He held up his hand as his father opened his mouth to speak. "Nor do I wish to. It's been less than three months since Alice and I separated. It wouldn't look good."

His father slammed his fist down on the table, sloshing his coffee in the porcelain saucer as a result. "That bitch you married has already announced her engagement to that poncey Sheridan fellow! Why shouldn't you find someone of your own? Instead you hide here at the farm doing God knows what."

Edward rubbed his forehead. His current conversation was the main reason he avoided his father as much as was feasible. Fortunately, since Edward had returned to the farm, his father had been busy traveling with Lord Blue half of the time.

"Father, I don't think Jon Sheridan is living off of Alice. He has money in his own right."

"Ha! He was probably lurking about the whole time you were married, trying to find a way to her heart. Or her cunt. Or both!"

Edward flushed. His father's coarse nature had always embarrassed him. Albert had been careful around their mother, but had no problem unleashing his true self on his sons. He was still aghast at the way he'd spoken to Alice on their last evening together. Edward had sent her flowers and an apology, but as he'd expected, she'd never responded.

"Be that as it may, it's over and done with."

He cleared his throat, careful not to sound too anxious. Charlie was waiting for him at the paddock near the small stable to show him how well Shadow was doing. The horse had begun to make a believer out of Edward. Under Charlie's loving guidance, he was already galloping on the short training track. The next time his father left town, they planned on taking him to the larger track to let him breeze an eighth of a mile.

"Anyway, I'm going to check on a few of the horses out at the small stable, see how —"

"Don't bother."

An unnamable fear clutched at Edward's chest. "Why is that?"

His father didn't even trouble himself to look up. "I'm getting rid of the last of those horses. I sold them and they're being picked up tomorrow. I can't waste any more money on their care." He flipped a page of the paper. "That groom has to go too. Never should have promoted him from stable boy. He spends too much time fawning over those creatures, doesn't see them for their true value."

Even if Edward could draw enough air into his lungs to speak, he knew he couldn't. The rage that consumed him over his father's callous disregard of everything and everyone around him would be impossible to control if he were to utter a word. Instead, he turned on his heel and marched from the room. By the time he'd descended the steps from the door off the main kitchen, he was in a full run to the stable where Charlie awaited him.

He wasn't typically given to grand displays of emotion over business affairs or his father's rantings and ravings. But he'd hit his breaking point. He needed a few more months at the least to secure a reasonably priced location where they could take Shadow, along with purchasing a few more horses to begin their venture together and settling his debt with James Normandy. However, his father was forcing his hand and he wasn't sure what to do.

His other concern was Charlie. He'd be devastated if he lost Shadow. And if he didn't have his job, where would he go?

I won't let my father destroy everything. Not this time.

As he rounded the back of the stable, he spotted Charlie in the paddock adjusting Shadow's bridle, cooing to him as he always did. It broke Edward's heart, knowing what he did about both Charlie and Shadow's fate. But his resolve remained. There had to be a way to fix the mess his father had made.

Charlie spotted him, waving enthusiastically, an excited smile on his lips. Edward drew closer, swiping a hand across the top of his head in the hopes that he didn't appear too frantic. When Charlie met him at the fence, the expression projected back to him was one of concern. Charlie frowned at him.

"What's wrong, Edward?"

We're so attuned to each other. I could never hide myself from him.

"Charlie love, I need you to listen to me." Edward glanced around to assure himself that they were quite alone, and that his father hadn't been possessed with the urge to follow him out to the stables. "We need to step up our plans." He cringed at the expression of fear coming from Charlie's eyes. "No matter what, remember that I love you and that we'll be together. But…it's Shadow."

Charlie's eyes widened as they filled with tears. "What? What about Shadow?"

Edward's stomach twisted. *Damn my father.* "He's been sold."

"*Sold?*" Charlie spat on the ground. "To who? I haven't seen anyone here, no one's been by to look at any horses. He's lying."

Red filled Charlie's cheeks, the water in his eyes finally spilling over. He swiped at his face then turned from Edward.

"Charlie, please listen. He's not lying, so we have to decide what to do next. You see, there's something else."

Charlie whipped his body back around, his eyes filled with fear. "Please no. Don't tell me you're marrying again. I can't…"

He wobbled on his feet and Edward grabbed his arm to steady him.

"No. What did I just say? I love you and I'm never leaving. But my father's letting you go. He's firing you."

Charlie's lower lip trembled but instead of more tears spilling, he breathed heavily through his nose, his fists clenching then unclenching. "Good. I can't stand to be here with him anymore anyway. But he's not taking my horse and he's *not* taking the man I love."

The vehemence with which Charlie barked out his words startled Edward. He was stunned at first, but then it became clear to him how much he still viewed Charlie through eyes that were colored with the beginnings of his lover's adulthood, when Charlie was still learning his way in the world. The Charlie who stood before him had not only survived heartbreak, loneliness and abandonment, but he'd also advanced in his trade to the point where Edward knew he had a good and strong partner.

"That's my love. We can figure this out together. I don't know how yet, but we'll get Shadow back. I won't let my father destroy the life we've been planning together."

Charlie nodded, a new resolve in his eyes. "Wait here. I'll be right back."

Before Edward could respond, Charlie had sprinted back to the stable. As he waited for him to return, he regarded the stallion in the paddock. Shadow appeared powerful, his glossy black coat shining under the rays of the sun. He was no longer the runty yearling that hadn't been very impressive. If Shadow kept advancing the way he'd been under Charlie's care, Edward had no doubt the thoroughbred would be a contender.

Charlie came bounding back, breathless as he reached Edward. He cradled a beat-up and rusted coffee can in his arms. "Here." He shoved the container at Edward. "Give this to your father. There's eight hundred and seventeen dollars in it. That should cover the cost of all four horses and then some."

"How...? My God, Charlie. Have you saved every penny you've ever earned?"

"No. Just as much as I could. I've saved some since I first arrived. But after my family left, then you left—I was determined to keep as much aside as possible." He lowered his head. "I'd planned on adding it to whatever you had." He peered up at him. "I wanted to contribute to starting our new life. Do my part."

Edward pressed his lips together, nodding his head. "I understand. But you know I never expected it, right?"

"I know. But you can give it to your father, right? We can keep Shadow from being sold?"

Edward's gut twisted, his anger at what his father had done rising anew. "I'm sorry, Charlie, but no. A deal has been struck. But I'll find out who's purchased him and I'll do whatever I can to convince them to sell him back."

Charlie's face twisted into a grimace, and Edward knew his lover was doing everything he could not to dissolve into tears again.

"Thank you." He took a deep shuddering breath. "I know you will." Charlie petted Shadow's nose, and he twitched his ears, flicked his tail. "What about everything else?" Charlie regarded him. "I have nowhere to go except the flophouse in town. When will we be able to get a place of our own? Will we—" Charlie's voice cracked. "*Will* we be able to get a place of our own?"

Edward wanted to crush Charlie to him. He didn't dare—not when they were out in the open. It didn't matter how alone they seemed to be.

"Yes, love. We will. No matter what else happens, I promise we'll be together."

Charlie nodded. "I believe you." He held up the coffee can again. "Take this. Use it to buy back Shadow if possible then put the rest toward our new place or whatever you feel we need. I love you, Edward. Wherever you go, I'll be there."

Edward accepted the metal container, but wrapped his hands over Charlie's and held them there. "I love you with all that I am, Charlie. I won't let you down."

Chapter Eight

Shadow was gone. Charlie had said his goodbyes to the regal stallion then gone back to his quarters to pack up his things. He'd been unable to stay and watch the buyers come and take away his horse.

He is my horse. No one else's.

Old man Carruthers had delivered the news that Charlie already knew. He'd had no reaction when the head groom had told him he had to be gone by the end of the day. Carruthers' attitude had been as if Charlie hadn't lived and slaved away at Piedmont Farms for eight years of his life. As if everything he'd done there had meant nothing. The only thing that had kept him from coming completely apart was that Edward had held him in his arms all night. They'd taken a risk they never had before—they'd slept together in Charlie's bed.

He sighed as he stuffed his remaining pieces of clothing into the old canvas duffel bag he'd used when he'd carried his belongings with him from his family home. There were a few small holes near the bottom where a mouse had chewed through the heavy fabric.

Must've been a strong mouse.

His lip trembled as thoughts of Shadow entered his mind again. He was small, but he was strong and filled with fire. Whoever bought Shadow would either make a fortune off him or waste his talent. But more than anything? They'd never love him the way Charlie did.

He jerked his head up at the sound of footsteps crunching in the hay outside his door. There was a light knock.

"Charlie? Are you in here?"

His heart lifted the way it always did at the sound of his lover's voice. "Yes, Edward. I'm still here."

Edward entered his room and Charlie was startled at how drawn and exhausted his face was. Sadness radiated from his eyes, the glisten of tears evident from the small ray of light shining through his one dusty window. He held his arms open. Charlie launched himself into Edward's embrace, clinging to him, terrified that he might never hold him again.

Edward stroked his back and whispered soothing words to him, assured him of his love and that everything would be fine. Charlie set his emotions free, crying it all out on Edward's shoulder. When he felt as if he was under more control, he dug in his pocket for his handkerchief then wiped his face. He gazed up at Edward. "I'm scared."

Edward caressed his cheek then petted his hair back off his forehead. "Don't be. I have a plan. But you have to really trust me. I might be gone for as much as two weeks."

"Wh-what? But..."

Charlie furrowed his brow. He'd be all alone in a strange place. The flophouse had a reputation for being rough. He'd never had a father or big brother around to show him how to fight, how to defend himself. Edward pressed several bills into his hand.

"It's a good plan, but it'll take time and some maneuvering. Here's some of your money in the meantime. Did you get your last wage?"

Charlie swallowed hard. It had been the final insult. "Carruthers told me that I owed Mr. Piedmont the five dollars from the twenty-five I'd already been paid for this week."

Edward tensed under his touch, his jaw clenched tight. At last, he took a deep breath then spoke. "He's despicable." Edward crushed his mouth against Charlie's, pushing through the seam of his lips to sweep his tongue inside, kissing him with a desperate intensity. "I'll be taking you into town in the motorcar. I've secured lodgings for you at the dry goods store under the pretext that you're in need of employment."

Charlie's stomach clenched, the tears rising again. Would Edward take the opportunity to get him settled into a new life, but then leave him behind when he left town?

Edward kissed him again, framing his face with his hands as he did. When he pulled back, the expression in his eyes was one of love and affection. Charlie was ashamed at how quickly he'd allowed himself to believe the worst of Edward. He was just so very tired and uncertain of what would happen next.

"So I should work there until you come for me?"

"Yes, love. Say nothing. As far as anyone knows, you've happily begun a new life in town."

"But what will happen when you do come for me? What will people say?"

Charlie smiled then placed another light kiss on his lips. "Let me worry about that. We're going to have everything we dreamed of. A home. Race horses. A life together. We're going to have it all, Charlie love."

* * * *

Edward sat in the study of his rooms in the east wing of the estate going over some figures and verifying he had all his documents in order. It had taken him longer than he'd planned to get everything worked out and he ran the risk of running into his father before he left Piedmont Farms for good. His original intention had been to finalize everything while his father was off traveling with Lord Blue for another series of races. Once his father discovered what he'd done, he'd be disowned for sure, so he needed to make sure his personal business assets were protected. As it was, he and Charlie would struggle for a while until things were up and running.

If they ever get up and running.

He banished the negative thought from his mind. Not only was he confident in their success, but more importantly was the fact that as long as he was with Charlie, he honestly didn't care about anything else.

After carefully placing his remaining papers in his satchel, he checked the time on his pocket watch. It was thirty minutes before midnight. He rose from his chair, slinging the leather bag over his shoulder. He crossed the room into the bed chamber then picked up his valise. Rawley had forwarded everything else already. It'd been fortunate that his valet had seized the opportunity to accompany him. The fact that the older servant understood the nature of his and Charlie's relationship had been a pleasant surprise. Rawley favored men as lovers too.

He trotted down the stairs, excitement thrumming under his skin. His senses were alive, both apprehension and joy warring within. As he reached the bottom of the grand staircase, he froze. His mouth went dry as the front door flew open, his father's silhouette framed by the lantern at the entrance.

"Good God. What in the name of hellfire are you doing at this hour all dressed up and toting your belongings as if you're going on an excursion?"

Edward searched his mind for a plausible excuse. He had none. "It's quite a long story, and I do need to get a move on. I'll tell you all about it later." He continued forward, about to brush past his father when Albert blocked his way.

"You most certainly will not. I demand an explanation for this nonsense immediately!"

Anger bubbled up to replace the anxiety of being caught by his father. "I'm thirty-two years old. It isn't necessary for me to explain my actions to you. Now if you'll excuse me, I need to be on my way."

His father grabbed his arm at Edward's second attempt to push past him. Edward shrugged his hand off, but Albert continued to block his exit.

"What are you up to, boy? I'd better not find out you've cleaned out the family coffers and are running off in the middle of the night with my riches."

Edward gasped. That his father's first assumption was that he'd steal from him was not only insulting, but led him to another realization about the man. His father's mind had gone to such an awful place because it was the type of thing he would've done.

"How dare you make such an accusation against me!"

His father crossed his arms in front of him. "How dare I? How dare you! This is my estate and I have to protect it at all costs!"

"By gambling away its assets? Decimating it to the point where it may be lost to you completely?" Edward's fury could no longer be held back. "And what about your continued insistence that I invest in *my* birthright? There won't be one, will there, Father? Not when you've spent every last dime on your pursuit of gambling and young maids!"

Edward shoved his way past his father, the promise of freedom before him. He threw his bags into the back of his convertible, then jumped into the vehicle. His father shouted curses at him, warned him never to return, shrieked that his brother William would inherit everything.

As Edward barreled down the driveway of what had been his home for the majority of his life since birth, he finally allowed himself a smile. He was leaving behind his past but embracing a much better future. Charlie waited for him.

Chapter Nine

Charlie fidgeted with the strap of his duffel. It was a couple of minutes before midnight and he was ready to crawl out of his skin. Edward would be there soon and they would begin their mysterious new life together. He'd sent Rawley over with a message for him to be ready, but that was the extent of the information he had.

Headlights shone through the window and he leaped up. He hadn't wanted to wait outside in case someone questioned why he was lurking about so late. He'd already left a note and most of his wages for Bill Johnson, the man who'd been kind enough to hire him and give him a place to live. He peered through the glass and spotted the Rolls-Royce Silver Ghost convertible that belonged to Edward.

His heart jackhammered—his excitement was so strong he thought he might faint. Charlie hoisted his duffel bag on his shoulder then rushed out of the door to meet Edward.

He really came for me.

Even though he'd felt guilty over his worries that Edward would never come back, he couldn't deny the relief he'd experienced when Rawley had delivered Edward's message. It had been almost three weeks since he'd last seen or spoken to his lover and he'd begun to fear the worst.

"Jump in, Charlie. We have to hurry!"

He did as Edward had commanded, surprised at how vehement he'd been. As they sped away, gravel spraying from under the motorcar's wheels, Charlie tried to imagine what was so urgent that had the typically even-tempered Edward so flustered. He waited patiently as he raced down the road, Edward's gaze intent on the highway and his fingers gripping the wheel.

Once they left the town limits, Edward visibly relaxed, his shoulders easing. Charlie glanced at him. Edward let out a sigh then removed his hand from the wheel to clutch Charlie's.

"Charlie love. I have so much to tell you."

* * * *

Charlie stirred, his sleep disrupted by the car coming to a stop. It was morning, but he knew it was still very early. He pulled his newsboy cap off his eyes then set it back on his head.

"Charlie love? We're here."

He glanced over at Edward, the exhaustion clear in his eyes, but happiness was there too.

"Where are we?"

"Berkshire, New York. We're near Ithaca, just west of the Catskills."

A large wooden two-story farmhouse stood before them. It was painted a brick red with white trim, a solid white porch wrapping all the way around the structure. As he took in more of the view, he noted a matching barn off to the right. Beyond that was a small stable, even smaller than the one he'd lived in at Piedmont. To his eyes, though, it was the most beautiful one he'd ever seen.

The buildings were surrounded by what looked like acres of green, as well as some woodland in the distance. Charlie wondered how much land there was that they could call their own.

"This is our new home." Edward placed his hand on Charlie's arm. "It's not as grand as I'd hoped for, but I had to move fast, liquidate as much of my stock and other concerns as I could."

"It's grand to me." He was in awe and almost bouncing on the seat. "I think it's the most magnificent farm I've ever seen." Charlie turned to see Edward grinning at him. He was relieved to see his lover so happy. Edward had been burdened with too much worry for so long. "Did my savings help?"

"Yes they did, Charlie love." Edward unlatched the car door then pushed it open before stepping out onto the dirt driveway. "Come along. I have something else to show you."

He scrambled out of the vehicle, more excited than he could ever remember being.

Our home.

Edward suddenly broke into laughter then grabbed Charlie's hand, tugging him in the direction of the stable. "Hurry, Charlie!"

He laughed too, his joy spilling from him as they jogged past the barn. They rounded the corner, and he stumbled at the sight before him. Edward caught him, pulling him flush to his side. Happy tears fell down his cheeks as Edward laughed more, the sounds punctuated by small sobs.

"How did you do it, Edward? How did you get Shadow back?"

"Come say hello to him and I'll tell you all about it."

Charlie knew the moment Shadow had spotted him. The stallion whinnied, nodding his great head as he danced in the paddock. He trotted to the rail as Charlie approached. Charlie climbed on the first rung to lean over and wrap his arms around the beast's neck. He inhaled deeply, the smell of horse filling his lungs, the coarse hair of Shadow's lush mane tickling Charlie's nose. He whispered to Shadow, telling him how sorry he was that he hadn't been there, how he'd never leave him again and how much he loved him.

Edward's hand rested at the small of his back, a reminder of the care and support he knew he'd always have from the man he loved with everything in him. After petting Shadow some more, he jumped down then grabbed Edward around his waist.

"Where was he? Who had him?"

"I snuck into my father's study and found out the name of the man who'd purchased him and the other horses. It turns out that he recognized what my father and our trainer never did, which was exactly what you'd known all along. He saw a champion. But in order to get Shadow at a low price, he bought all the horses under the guise of using them as pleasure horses for his grandchildren."

"But if he thought Shadow was a champion, why did he let you buy him back?"

"Ah yes. This is why having a brother who's a lawyer can come in handy at times. William traveled with me from Boston to this man's farm and threatened legal action because according to the way our trust is designed, once we reached the age of twenty-five, the farm and all of its assets belong equally to me, my brother and my father. William and I own two thirds of Piedmont, which includes all the horses, and since we didn't consent to the sale—that meant it was void under the law. I simply returned the money he paid originally, then Shadow and the other horses became ours." Edward smiled down at him. "That's where your money went."

It was all so incredible. "What about the rest of Piedmont?"

"I want to cut my ties with my father. In the note I left, I forfeited my share of the estate. But I also included legal documentation that William drafted for both of us stating that we give up all rights and walk away completely."

Charlie frowned, not sure why the brothers would do such a thing. "Don't you want your inheritance?"

"It would've made things easier, yes. At least it would've seemed that way initially. But sometimes easiest isn't best. The way things are going, our father could run up so many debts against the estate so that when he passes, William and I could be ruined by trying to pay it all back. This way, not only do we not have any claim on the estate, but it doesn't have one on us either."

"Goodness. You've thought of everything."

Edward chuckled. "We have our own home and you have your horse back. That's all that matters."

Charlie tipped his head back and offered his lips. Edward kissed him with a fierceness that stole Charlie's breath. When they finished the kiss, they stayed close.

"I was so sad when you left, but you found Shadow and you found our home while you were gone from me. Thank you so much."

Edward cupped his cheek. "I should be thanking you for coming to live with me. I love you dearly, Charlie, and I'm so grateful that I get to spend every day and every night with you from now on."

Edward took him in a strong embrace and they held each other in silence for several minutes. The moment was broken when Shadow neighed loudly.

They let go of each other, laughing.

"What is it, boy?" Charlie climbed on the rail again, offering Shadow some stray bits of alfalfa that lay in the dirt. The stallion jerked his head to the side as if insulted by such a paltry treat.

Edward patted Charlie's ass, something they never could've done back at the farm. "I believe he's anxious to continue his lessons. You have a champion to train, Charlie love."

Epilogue

Charlie carefully positioned Shadow's latest trophy on their oak mantle. If he won his next big race, the stud fees alone would pay for the upkeep of their farm, as well as the rest of what they owed to the Normandy Estate. But Shadow wasn't the only contender they had anymore. Another horse had caught Charlie's eye at a nearby farm. He'd visited the yearling several times before deciding he had to find a way to acquire him. After discussing it with Edward, they'd offered two of the other Piedmont horses for the one that Charlie desired. The man had agreed since he wasn't in the racing business. To him, it had seemed like a terrific deal in his favor.

After arranging everything above the fireplace the way he wished, he stepped back to take it all in. It was springtime again and they'd been in their own home for almost nine months. Nine, glorious, joyful months with his Edward. There'd been a lot of hard work to get everything up and running, and the winter had been tough, but he wouldn't change a thing. Everything about it had brought him and Edward closer together as partners — and that was all he really cared about.

He started as strong arms wrapped around him from behind. Edward propped his chin on Charlie's shoulder.

"How's my Charlie love tonight?"

Charlie wrapped his hands over Edward's and allowed him to sway them both. "I'm wonderful, especially now that you're here."

Edward let out a soft chuckle. "I've been here all day."

Charlie shook his head, his scruffy hair brushing against Edward's shirt. "Not *here*, here. Not holding me."

"Mmm. Holding you is all I ever want to do. But perhaps tonight I can do a little more?"

Charlie curled his fingers around Edward's, his cock filling at the promise in Edward's words. "Should we go upstairs?"

"I'd rather light a fire and take you in front of it. It will be too warm for that soon."

"What?" Charlie twisted his head to see if Edward was teasing him. "What about Rawley and Hilda?"

The valet was the only one who lived there, but the housekeeper spent six days a week at the home and never left until after she'd prepared supper.

"Rawley is visiting his sister and her family for the next few days, and I gave Hilda some time off with pay."

"With pay? We can't afford that."

Edward squeezed Charlie's middle then nipped at this earlobe. "Oh yes we can, Charlie love. I signed the first agreement for Shadow's stud fees today so I want us to celebrate." Edward turned him in his arms until they faced each other. "You've worked very, very hard this year. You've mucked stalls, repaired fences, exercised and fed the horses and trained Shadow to become a true champion. You've done the work of three men." Edward took a light kiss. "And you've loved me and filled my heart to bursting. You deserve every happiness. I'm very proud of you."

Tears stung Charlie's eyes, blurring his vision. He buried his face in Edward's chest, too overwhelmed to respond. Edward lowered his hands, stroked down his back then cupped his ass. Soon, they were rutting against each other, their breath mingling as they explored each other's mouths with lazy kisses.

After they'd made love on blankets in front of a blazing fire, Charlie lay back in Edward's arms. All he'd ever really wanted was to have Edward's love. The horses were a balm to his heart, but Edward was the other half of his soul. When Edward had left to marry, he'd thought he'd never be near him again. He snuggled closer to Edward, and Edward tightened his embrace.

He was home. Their home, together.

THE SECRET OF DELVILLE WOOD

Helena Maeve

Dedication

For Sue, the best editor and cheerleader a writer
could ask for.

Chapter One

"Is there something you wish to tell me, *mon chou*?"

Silas had thought the sitting room empty. He whirled around when that familiar, smoky voice trilled out of the shadows.

The wingback by the silent hearth was inhabited by a silk and rhinestone lampshade number, which revealed more than its fair share of long, pewter-dark legs. Their owner's silhouette resolved in the dark, looking more like Silas than any other resident of this little corner of Scandinavian paradise.

Beatrice Lazare tipped forward, grinning. "I didn't scare you, did I?"

His heart still relaxing its fervent drumming, Silas mustered a shallow smile. "You're a riot."

She was also up well past bedtime, although in Silas' experience, jazz singers weren't exactly known for keeping reasonable hours.

Even her chuckle was melodious. "Drinking on the sly, are we?" She clucked her tongue. "What will our hostess think?"

"Tell her and find out." His good mood wavering, Silas resumed his straight shot to the sideboard. Beatrice could be pleasant company in small doses, provided she was sober and her sharp wit focused on a target other than Silas. Fulfilling neither condition, this run-in was best cut short.

The crystal decanter clicked against the rim of a clean glass. Silas had to concentrate to avoid spilling Ms. Eckdahl's liquor in the dark. "Then again, what our hostess doesn't know can't hurt her."

"You rake… Oh, no," Beatrice tittered, when Silas began to splash the Norwegian *akevitt* into another stem glass. "None for me."

"It's not."

Beatrice's T-strap heels met the oak floor with the click of castanets. "Ah, *bon?*"

Pulsing clouds of Chanel No. 5 heralded her approach. Silas feigned indifference as she draped herself over the sideboard like she might have done a grand piano, sending glasses and decanters wobbling on their silver trays. With the staff dismissed sometime before midnight, no one had been left to tidy up when the household guests had finally retired.

"Go on," Beatrice wheedled. "You can't leave me hanging. Who is it, the ice queen or the ingénue?"

Silas fanned his fingers around the bowl of both glasses, raising them elegantly out of her reach. "Neither."

"Ms. Eckdahl herself, then?"

A note of disbelief had entered Beatrice's voice. Silas knew it was petty to take pleasure in thwarting her nosiness but couldn't resist. "*Bonne nuit*, Beatrice."

Her inquisitive, coal-black eyes warmed the back of his neck as he rounded the corner into the hall. Moonbeams dribbled through the oval skylights, splashing the grand staircase in a fractured blue-white halo. Despite the relatively short climb to the first floor, Silas only narrowly avoided catching the carpet runner with his unlaced Oxfords. He toed the bedroom door closed with his foot.

"You'll never guess who I saw downstairs—all alone, which I'm sure you'll admit a little odd…"

Whether Ms. Eckdahl had appointed her star guest the largest guestroom in her home to make a point, or that was simply the luck of the draw, Silas was unable to say. As Axel's companion for the night, he appreciated the accommodations either way. A man could easily dance a waltz around the broad expanse of the room, and the mahogany armoire by the door would have provided more than enough space for his trousers and dinner jacket, if he'd been bothered to hang them up.

The pristine Scandinavian order that had reigned when Silas was first introduced to Axel's lodgings had suffered slightly in the interim. Exchanging the glasses from hand to hand, he picked his way through the scatter of leather wingtips and hastily discarded trousers, undergarments and neckties, all while shedding his recently borrowed lounging robe. The breadcrumb trail tugged his gaze to the bed—a generous four-poster draped with a fringed burgundy canopy and white sheets rumpled by recent diversions.

"Or, if you'd prefer we don't talk at all," Silas offered as he bent to run the fingertips of his free hand over the pale jut of an ankle peeking from under the covers.

There was no reaction. Not a flinch or a laugh.

"Axel?"

Propped upright against the headboard, Axel did not so much as meet his gaze. Countless newspaper photographers had snapped his likeness over the years — wild-eyed with the euphoria of victory, smudged with the mud of the racetracks, worn but happy. Always happy.

The washed-out black and whites of the London dailies would have been hard-pressed to render his currently vacant stare.

A frisson shot through Silas, his fantasy of their time together abruptly cut to ribbons. Was this how it began? Regret, quickly morphing to guilt and self-recrimination? He had lost lovers to post-coital penitence before. The prospect did not appeal.

"Darling, what…"

Trembling, Axel raised fingers that had clutched at him in the throes of ecstasy and pointed, past Silas, to the window.

Fretting about peeping toms now was a matter of closing the barn door after all the horses had fled, but Silas buried his irritation and turned to close the drapes.

He froze mid-motion.

Electric lamps flanked the bed, their buttery glare blotting out the birches outside but doing precious little to conceal the body swaying minutely from the second-floor balcony, a rope around its neck.

* * * *

The victim was Virgil Morrow, sole proprietor of Morrow Stables and proud owner of one-third of Delville Wood, recently titled as the swiftest thoroughbred in Sweden.

As he was by no means a small man, hoisting Morrow back into his second-story bedroom took the combined efforts of Silas, his hostess and the least pleasant of all her guests. Between the three of them, they managed to pull Mr. Morrow onto the balcony tile but no further.

"I can't get this blasted thing loose," Ms. Eckdahl lamented. "Someone get me scissors!"

"Don't think there's much point." Silas held two fingers to Mr. Morrow's neck and shook his head.

Beside him, Ms. Eckdahl swore.

"Is—is he dead?" echoed from inside the room. "Oh, heavens!"

Silas looked up to find the young Ms. Conway hide her blotchy red face in her hands. Mrs. Conway, standing beside her, startled as though woken from a trance. After an awkward few moments, she patted gingerly at her stepdaughter's narrow shoulders in a pathetic attempt at soothing. They were both so pale and blonde, and dressed down to shapeless white nightgowns, that they looked ethereal in a way they had not when armored in stiff cloche hats and red lipstick.

Still panting with exertion, Wesley Pollard took an exaggerated step over the body to comfort his fiancée.

"For God's sake, Mrs. Conway, she shouldn't be here—"

"We heard a commotion," protested Mrs. Conway.

Wesley ignored her. "Come along, Imogene dear. Let's get you back to bed." His gallantry was slightly tempered by the scowl he shot his future mother-in-law, who for reasons that Silas could not fathom, flinched under his stare.

"Suppose I should telephone the police," Ms. Eckdahl suggested, yanking his attention back to the grisly task at hand.

"Probably best," Silas agreed.

Ms. Eckdahl gave his shoulder a companionable squeeze then departed to her task, giving Beatrice a wide berth in the doorway. Their resident songstress had evidently heard the fuss upstairs and come to investigate.

"What happened here?"

Silas rubbed a knuckle into the grit of five o'clock shadow on his cheek and offered her a shrug. "Poor bastard hung himself with the canopy sash... At least it was quick."

"Sure about that?" Heedless of the immodest slit in her many-tailed skirt, Beatrice crouched down. The red of her fingernails shone like blood against the braided cord.

"Bruises," Silas surmised, then peered closer. The purple shiners were uneven, distributed around the sides of the neck rather than the front and back, where the rope would have squeezed Morrow's throat.

"Yes," Beatrice hummed. "Bruises."

Their eyes met. She was the first to look away.

Unease coiled like a reptile in Silas' chest, retreating only when he glimpsed the butler hobbling into the room, his jacket askew. He must have dressed in a hurry. "Ah, Mr. Holmgren! Have the police been called?"

At sixty-eight years old, Holmgren was well past his prime and stubbornly committed to his position as Ms. Eckdahl's butler and right-hand man.

"Not yet, sir," he answered, his English heavily accented. "Some trouble with the phone line... Ms. Eckdahl is trying again."

Beatrice climbed elegantly to her feet. The late hour and the shock of seeing a dead body seemed to have no impact on her. "Our champion must have a weak stomach," she mused. "I don't see him anywhere." Her moue of bemusement slipped as she locked eyes with

Silas. "Oh, don't tell me *you* shipped him off to bed already. *Killjoy.*"

Being reminded of Axel shook the last fretful embers from Silas' thoughts.

"You can hardly blame him for —"

"No, no. I won't argue with you." Beatrice put up her hands. "I'm quite chastened."

Her sashaying retreat left Silas feeling inexplicably wrong-footed. He made to follow after a beat, but something about leaving Mr. Morrow in such a dismal position seemed altogether unchristian. The rope around his neck was impossible to pry off without scissors, but the other knot, secured to the balcony rail, offered better prospects.

"Pull on the other end," Holmgren suggested.

"Like this?" Silas obediently tugged the short end of the cord and the hitch instantly came undone.

"Evenk knot," Holmgren informed him with a sigh. "Must've learned it in his stables."

"Must have." Silas nodded his thanks and rose.

The whole house seemed trapped in a strange twilight between excitement and exhaustion. The lights on the landing had all been switched on despite the late hour. Every bedroom door stood slightly ajar. Here and there, Silas caught the odd flash of movement on his way down the hall but tried not to linger. From the first-floor landing, he peered into the foyer below.

A smoldering cigarette propped between two fingers, Ms. Eckdahl was waging a fruitless battle against the dial of the candlestick phone. The table upon which it sat gave a rattle.

Getting through to police in Katrineholm was proving a challenge.

Ms. Eckdahl didn't seem to notice him. Silas walked on.

He smothered the absurd urge to knock on his own door. He had worried, briefly, that explaining his discovery of the body might trigger questions. Luckily, the rest of the household had been far too absorbed in the tragedy to wonder why Silas might have been visiting Axel's room at such a late hour. Moving Axel to his own bed had been no less imprudent, but Silas couldn't very well leave him there alone.

He let himself in unannounced.

The sight that greeted him made his heart sink. "You're still up."

"It's Virgil, isn't it?"

Silas had hoped to save this conversation for the morning. He nodded. "I'm sorry."

Axel propped himself up against the mound of pillows at his back. Though he looked a far cry from the languid, sweat-sheened creature Silas had left in bed when he'd gone to fetch a nightcap, Axel was still nude, his blond hair tousled, as though he had spent the last hour or so pulling at it.

On impulse, Silas reached out a hand to comb the fair strands away from Axel's forehead. "It appears like he might have been drinking." The bottle of aquavit on Morrow's bedside table certainly implied as much.

"Damn him."

Raw hurt edged Axel's growl. It was reason enough to forgive the less than charitable sentiment.

"Police should be here by morning," Silas added.

It couldn't take longer than that. Katrineholm was only two hours north by automobile and Stockholm not much farther.

"Why?" A wrinkle ribbed Axel's brow.

"To take him away. And, I suppose, to confirm the cause of death."

The memory of Beatrice gently guiding his hand and his eyes to the bruising that didn't quite match the necklace of rope around Mr. Morrow's neck pulsed through Silas. Normally he wouldn't have kept the secret, but Axel was sufficiently distressed.

Shedding his robe, Silas bent a knee to the mattress and scooted down to lie beside him instead. "This isn't how I hoped to finish our evening."

Axel smiled wryly. "No, I expect not."

His fingers were gentle on Silas' cheek. Silas caught them and brought them to his lips. They tasted faintly of aquavit.

Axel must have indulged the nightcap without him.

"I don't think I can—"

"I know," Silas said, arresting apology before it could be uttered. He and Axel had only been to bed together once, tonight, but that was enough for tenderness to bloom between them.

Lowering their joined hands, Silas pulled Axel against his flank, skin to skin, and kissed him lightly on the mouth. "Sleep, if you can manage it."

He felt more than saw Axel's eyebrows hitch in astonishment.

"You're not kicking me out of bed?"

"No."

After the evening's events, to dispatch him back to his own room would have been cruel. Virgil Morrow had been instrumental to Axel's winning streak. His latest crowning glory in the Täby Galopp was as much the old man's achievement as it was Axel's. Morrow owned Delville Wood. Axel rode him. Together they made the impossible seem achievable.

Silas told himself that to be a shoulder to cry on was better than nothing. As with most men, Axel was sure to come to his senses once the loss of his prime sponsor was felt to its fullest extent. In the meantime, Silas could revel in his soft skin and delectable mouth, and not dwell on the inevitable.

Chapter Two

Morning dawned gray and somber over the manor. A gentle breeze stirred the deceptive waters of the Sågträsk, the gales streaming in through the open French doors. Out on the deck, a white tablecloth fluttered like billowing sails between the guests gathered around the breakfast table.

"It was the drink that did him in," Wesley proclaimed with a sneer. His knife shaved off a generous glob of butter, which he slathered haphazardly onto his bread roll. The surface shattered like kindling when he sank his perfect teeth into the roll — another one of Mrs. Holmgren's culinary chef d'oeuvres.

"Do you really think so?" Ms. Conway breathed. Despite the warm June winds, she wore lace gloves that concealed her hands from fingertip to elbow. A sliver of pale upper arm showed where the sleeve of her low-waisted frock tapered at a sharp angle.

In his first days at the house, Silas had worried that his wardrobe would be too simple for the company. Now he strolled out of the shadows of the sitting room with all the confidence of a peacock. His linen trousers and shirt were no less neat than Wesley's, despite lacking the couture of Saville Row tailors. His boat shoes were on par with Ms. Conway's *paysanne* sandals.

Beatrice alone put them to shame in her feather shawl.

"Good morning," he greeted, taking the empty seat beside her.

"Is it really?" Mrs. Conway rubbed her temple. "I couldn't sleep at all, after…"

Wesley thinned his lips. Beside him, Ms. Conway picked up her teacup with a shaking hand.

"After all that," her stepmother concluded. "Mr. Berggren was just telling me he suffered the same insomnia."

Silas locked gazes with Axel. He hadn't heard him leave the bed, much less gather his clothes and disappear to his own room. Axel must have done it, though, because by the time Silas had woken, the whiff of aquavit hanging over the room like a stubborn ghost had become his only companion. He had washed down the dregs of last night's thwarted revels in the small sink beside the wardrobe.

If only it was as simple to wash away regret.

"And he didn't even come galloping at the first sign of trouble," Beatrice crowed, her lips a perfect, rouged oval around the end of her spoon. Like most Frenchwomen Silas had known, she preferred *café au lait* to plain old tea.

"You yourself were there, as I recall," he countered. *And behaving rather oddly.*

Unperturbed, Beatrice smiled. "Virgil owed me twenty kronor. I had every intention of getting my money back."

"Who can think about money when a man is dead?" Mrs. Conway gasped.

The outburst was somewhat farcical. The third Mrs. Conway had married into the family of a wealthy if unremarkable man only two weeks after first making his acquaintance.

Silas hadn't thought to inquire why Mr. Conway hadn't seen fit to accompany his wife and daughter on their Scandinavian holiday. To hear Ms. Eckdahl describe him, he preferred gentlemen's clubs to boating and tennis.

According to Beatrice, he also preferred the sort of entertainment that men like Mr. Conway believed to be unsuitable to wives and daughters.

"Perhaps that's the French way," Wesley muttered, drawing himself up a little straighter. "Ah, but I forget myself. You're not *from* France, are you, Ms. Lazare?"

Silas had found himself on the receiving end of those beady blue eyes before and had emerged with his pride only slightly tarnished. He bristled impotently to see the same presumptuous interest directed toward Ms. Lazare.

"Yaoundé, in Cameroon," Beatrice shot back. "But then I believe I don't have to tell *you* that, Mr. Pollard. Tell me, does the Ministry know you intend to invest in a foreign protectorate?"

Wesley's eyes widened, briefly, before the grille of public school education came down hard over his features. "I'm sure I don't know what you mean."

"Do you not? I must have you confused. There are so many blond boys at the Raleigh…"

Ms. Conway frowned, her bloodshot eyes narrowed against the glare of the sun. "My father is a member of the Raleigh."

"Has anyone seen Ms. Eckdahl this morning?" her stepmother interjected, before a potentially indiscreet reply could be offered.

Heads shook around the table. Silas confessed to having spotted her trying to get through to the police the night before, but kept to himself her apparent agitation. To the casual observer, Ms. Eckdahl was little more than the product of her late father's war chest—well-heeled and unattached, and blessed with a devil-may-care attitude. Silas had no desire to spoil the mirage by mentioning Ms. Eckdahl's private troubles. Her other guests suspected nothing. Together, they arrived at a consensus that she must have slept in this morning, to make up for yesterday's shock.

After breakfast, the party broke up speedily—Ms. Conway to accompany her stepmother on a walk by the lake, Beatrice to take in the sun on the small stretch of shingle beach at the foot of the gardens.

Silas had hoped to have a chance to speak to Axel in private, though what he planned to say was by no means clear, but Wesley summarily co-opted his lover for a game of tennis.

Having seen Axel with a racket in hand upon his arrival at the house, Silas half expected a refusal. The memory pulsed through him. He recalled the way the driveway curved around the rose garden, passing under a brass archway with burnished finials, and looping tightly around the grass court. One of Axel's volleys had gone wide, the citron-yellow cannonball nearly shattering the Packard's windshield just as the picturesque mansion had come into view. Silas' first glimpse of the white, immaculate walls would forever be colored by that heart-pounding reception.

He remembered, too, how Axel had come bounding through the hedges mere moments later, uttering profuse apologies in his native Swedish, then upon realizing that Silas was quite at a loss, switching to halting English. Silas had later discovered that Axel wasn't at all unsure of himself in the language so Silas had assumed — and had promptly brushed away the assumption — that Axel simply believed *he* might not be so versatile, given the shade of his skin. It was a slight easily forgiven, when weighed against alluring athleticism and an eagerness to make amends.

Grace, after all, was not one of Axel's assets. Whatever finesse he displayed in the saddle was utterly absent when he stood on his own two feet, yet it took little prompting for Axel to acquiesce to Wesley's invitation.

Silas bottled the small flash of jealousy that accompanied the observation.

Left to his own devices, he prowled the grounds on his own, then returned to the house and continued his exploration of the past days at a languid pace. It did not surprise him to discover that beneath the thin veneer of extravagance lay peeling paint and crumbling stone walls, gardens left to grow wild and dust gathered on every available surface.

Ms. Eckdahl preferred hobbies to housekeeping, and her manner was too capricious for the routine of managing such a grand house. Her invitation had come out of nowhere. Silas still recalled telephoning to verify that she had meant the letter for him and not some other Londoner by the same improbable name.

A thousand miles of frigid North Sea crackle through the receiver, the sound interspersing with her laughter. "Are there many Silas Onumas in England?"

"Not to my knowledge, but — "

"You came highly recommended." If the past few minutes have confirmed anything, it is that Ms. Eckdahl doesn't believe in wasting time on pleasantries. Her speech is a Vickers Gun of sharp questions. She sounds older than the twenty-six years the newspapers give her. "Of course, if you cannot make it..."

Silas squeezes the candlestick receiver in a sweaty palm. His minuscule flat overlooks St. Paul's, the dome mushrooming over the squat rooftops around it like a billowed skirt. "I confess I've never been asked to treat a patient in another country before."

Perhaps Ms. Eckdahl expects more enthusiasm than that because her silence stretches, a cord pulled taut. "It's not your work as an alienist I'm interested in."

"Ah."

"I can wire you the money for the crossing, Mr. Onuma. If you would only — "

"Money is not the issue," Silas says, the lie rolling smoothly off the tongue. His sparse furnishings and empty pantry tell a markedly different story, but he will not be some bird's monkey. He has the telephone, for God's sake. He makes a small but tidy living.

He has survived twelve years without trading in his pride for his next meal. He won't begin now.

Ms. Eckdahl sighs. "Then what is the magic word?"

Her invitation lies open on Silas' desk, scribbled in a frantic hand and stamped in Stockholm, a week ago. It is a curious thing, yes, but Silas hears the disdain in Ms. Eckdahl's voice and knows she is no believer.

Why, then, would she contact an occultist?

"I thought I might find you up here."

Silas snapped out of his reverie at the sound of Axel's voice. The stable door framed him like the gilt edge of a Christian icon. With his mousy haired tousled and sheened with sweat, he might have been an angel freshly descended from heaven for a bit of rough and tumble with the wicked mortals.

"And *I* thought you and Wesley were chasing each other on the court."

Grass stains dappled the elbows of Axel's shirt where he must have slid in futile pursuit of Wesley's vicious serves.

He shrugged, gaze ticking toward Delville gnawing on a bale. "He gave me a sound seeing-to and agreed I should stick to horse-riding."

"Probably wise."

"And you?" Axel jerked his chin to indicate the house behind them, the second-floor balcony jutting out like a perilous ledge.

A quick gander through Morrow's room had revealed that not much had been done to mend last night's disorder. The sheets remained a tousled mess, the French doors gaped open onto the vacant balcony. Mr. Morrow had been removed to a settee by the window, thank God, and police would have to make do with that minor tampering once they deigned show up.

"I...suppose I'm feeling a trifle morbid," Silas deflected, glancing back at Axel. He couldn't very well confess that he'd gone to revisit the scene of the crime.

Axel clucked his tongue in mock reproof. "Even with this beauty around?" He gave Delville a scrub along the neck, his hand extraordinarily pale against the inky coat. "I'm shocked at you, Mr. Onuma."

"Careful. Keep singing his praises and it'll go to his head."

"As it well should. He's a champion... Aren't you?"

Delville butted his head against Axel's hands, whickering in acquiescence.

It was impossible not to find their evident affection for another charming. Silas bit the inside of his cheek to corral a smile. "Shall I leave you two to enjoy each other's company? I fear I'm becoming a third wheel."

"You can come in, if you'd like," Axel offered.

"A generous offer."

He narrowed his eyes. "You're not afraid of horses, are you?"

"Afraid? No. Sensibly cautious?" Silas inclined his head.

"Oh, don't be such a ninny. Here," Axel said, reaching for his hand. "He won't bite."

Silas' first instinct was to retrieve his arm, but he marshaled the attempt before it dimmed Axel's good humor. He'd been so affected by what had happened that to see him smile again felt like a hard-won achievement. And Delville didn't bite.

He sniffed a little around Silas' coat once he came close enough before promptly losing interest and returning to his meal.

"Did the police come yet?" Axel asked, releasing Silas' hand.

"No... Though I'm not sure what good it will do to bring them now. If there was any evidence of Mr. Morrow's final moments, I'm sure it's already been trampled underfoot."

A shadow flickered onto Axel's features. Just like that, the light in his eyes was extinguished and he looked tired and flushed once more. "I've asked Holmgren to put the geyser in motion. I'm in dire need of a bath."

Despite the pendulum swing of their conversation, Silas cocked an eyebrow. "Be sure to ask Holmgren to assist you. We wouldn't want you to slip..."

"I believe Mr. Holmgren has other duties to attend to."

Silas bit his tongue. In London, he inhabited a world of long looks and versatile silences. He could read a conversational volte-face for the terse refusal it was.

But perhaps something was lost in the translation, because just as he turned to leave the stables, Axel launched one final salvo.

"Although I notice *you* don't seem to be doing anything of note..." Sunlight caught the green-gold twinkle in his eyes, as worthy an invitation as any.

Silas fell into step before the offer could be retracted.

As any man of his persuasion, he knew the ways of clandestine rendezvous in dark alleys and shadow-edged parks. He was patient, giving Holmgren enough time to set Axel up in the first-floor bathroom, then checking to make certain the coast was clear before he knocked.

In the handful of seconds it took Axel to flip the lock and let him in, Silas' pulse reached a gallop. His cock had already firmed by the time he'd pressed Axel against the closed door and kissed him soundly.

"You don't waste any time," Axel gasped, laughter brimming in his voice as Silas tasted the long column of his neck.

"Men in *déshabillé* shouldn't be throwing stones," Silas quipped.

He slid his hands down to knead the warm swell of Axel's arse, bringing their cocks into contact through layers of fabric.

Axel was already erect, his nipples peaked beneath the flat of Silas' tongue. "Get this," he growled, "*off*." He gripped Silas' jacket with fists better used to clutching reins and shoved it past his shoulders before tackling his shirt buttons.

Undressing had been a feverish, dizzying affair last night and the sunbeams dancing on clouds of steam in the bathroom did little to temper his enthusiasm this morning. He barely desisted when Silas guided him to the edge of the tub and kneed his thighs apart. Triumph was brief, though, because in the next instant Axel had a hand around Silas' cock and was taking him into his mouth with uncanny eagerness.

"Slow," Silas choked out, locking his knees against the surge of want that lanced through him. He wanted nothing more than to knot his fingers in Axel's curly hair and ride that lovely mouth until he found release. He resisted the impulse. Not all men were like him. Not all of them enjoyed being bent over, stuffed full. Treated roughly.

He knew he'd made the right call when Axel pulled back, coughing, and took to mouthing at his sac.

"That's it," Silas encouraged. "There's no hurry."

The door was locked. The household was busy. Careful not to dislodge him, he bent to curl a hand around Axel's neglected length and felt his moan all the way in the pit of his stomach.

If Axel hadn't been in such a hurry to leave, they might have spent their morning doing nothing but this. Yes, their fellow guests might have counted their absence at breakfast suspicious. Yes, explaining it away wouldn't have been easy.

It hardly mattered when Axel could be coaxed into such lovely sounds, his cock slick with arousal and pulsing in Silas' hand.

"Get in the bath," Silas urged, staggering a little as he straightened.

Lips red and eyes foggy with want, Axel looked set to tackle him to the floor and return to his ministrations. He looked, Silas mused, positively brutish.

The moment passed. Some measure of common sense prevailed.

Water lapped close to the edge of the tub as Axel swung first one leg, then the other over the rim, and lowered himself.

Silas was far less nimble in following suit. He blamed the shimmering bathwater for the strange doubling that occurred as he straddled Axel's hips and took him in hand. He was sore from last night's frolic and the water only did so much to ease the way, but it hardly mattered.

Axel's fingers flew from the edge of the tub to dig bruises in his hips. The back of his skull met the enamel rim with a dull thud. "Oh, oh—"

"Yes..." A little pain was par for the course. Silas relished the sharp burn as Axel filled him to the brim, then rocked back, easing off as far as the narrow gap between their bodies allowed without losing the delicious burn of friction deep inside.

Air knifed in and out of Silas' lungs, no longer the priority. Axel couldn't be counted on to keep still, his control slipping before he'd even started in earnest.

Rather than disappointment, Silas felt a wave of tenderness sweep through him as he curled a hand around his own cock and tugged. Trying to match his strokes to Axel's thrusts was only possible for a handful of seconds. Axel drove up sharply, gritting his teeth. His face contorted as pleasure threatened to overwhelm.

"Yeah," Silas goaded. "Go on. Go on, love..."

He welcomed the sharp sense of clarity that ignited when Axel dug his fingers into his hips and came with shuddering, gasping pulses. Being on his knees last night, he'd missed the way Axel's eyes fluttered shut and the tendons in his neck pulled taut. He hadn't felt the overwhelming urge to kiss him, much less been able to.

Unhindered, Silas tipped forward and slammed their mouths together, drowning both his cries of completion and Axel's panted, coaxing pleas. He spilled between them within seconds, striping his hand and Axel's chest, the slick of release washed away in an instant.

"How's that," Silas wheezed once he could speak again, "for a sound seeing-to?"

Axel's grin was the precursor to sharp teeth dragged against the shelf of his collarbone. "Oh… We can do better than that."

Silas laughed, euphoric, and propped his chin on Axel's shoulder. A sharp hiss of pain stopped him short.

"I hurt you? Let me see—"

"It's fine," Axel muttered, but the angry purple of a fresh bruise on his shoulder was impossible to ignore.

"What in the… Did the tennis ball hit back?"

Axel shifted to press his shoulder blades resolutely to the edge of the tub. "I'm fine. For God's sake, don't fuss. I get bruised all the time. Probably acquired it any one of the hundred times Delville's thrown me off."

He tried to make a joke of it, but his tone was too harsh. Silas regretted bringing it up.

"You're right," he relented, sliding to rest against the opposite end of the tub, his legs open around Axel's. "I'm sorry."

"I'm hardier than I look."

"I know."

Axel curled both hands around Silas' ankles. "Besides, you don't seem to mind it when you're the one hurt."

"You noticed." Silas had bedded men who'd blanched when he asked them to be a little rough. He'd been pleased to discover Axel wasn't one of them.

Even now, he prowled toward him through the water with a devilish smirk. "*You* are not that easy to ride, either."

"At least I don't throw you out of saddle," Silas volleyed. His cock twitching with the last tendrils of his orgasm, he obediently tilted his head up for a kiss.

He took pains to avoid brushing his fingertips to the bruise on Axel's shoulder as their bodies slid together beneath the surface.

He was twice as mindful about ignoring the stubborn voice at the back of his mind that insisted the bruise had not been there when he'd pried Axel from his clothes last night.

Chapter Three

The bathwater had long cooled by the time Silas and Axel disentangled themselves. Cautious to avoid outstaying his welcome, Silas dried and dressed himself with some alacrity, determined to ignore the tantalizing pink of Axel's freshly scrubbed skin so close within his reach.

"I'll see you downstairs?"

In seeking to conceal the fragile hope in his voice, he must have come across as careless. Axel's expression shuttered before he smoothed away all emotion behind a too-bright smile.

"No doubt we'll cross paths."

Silas hesitated, his hand on the doorknob. "You might come by my room tonight," he suggested, "for another...nightcap."

He hadn't offered the first time around, and finding Axel's door open had been a pleasant surprise. It was ungenerous to expect an encore.

"I might," said Axel, buttoning his shirt with great concentration. A smile dimpled his cheeks.

Silas let himself out with the throb of anticipation pulsing away in his bloodstream. The carpet runner muffled his steps. The house itself seemed to be holding its breath.

In the foyer, he spared a glower at the grandfather clock. It was nearly lunch. Could the police have come and gone already? Silas tipped against the banister and peered up into the helix of the grand staircase. If officers had taken over the second floor with their investigation, they were the quietest bobbies Silas had ever known.

"Mr. Onuma?" Holmgren stood in the library door, flanked by two mounted stag heads. "May I help you, sir?"

Silas straightened. He had long lost the habit of telling servants the truth. "Any idea where I might find Ms. Eckdahl?"

"I have not seen her."

"Hasn't she come down for breakfast?" Silas asked, distracted from his fib.

"No, sir."

A bolt of electricity raced down his spine. "Have you checked on her? Perhaps she's ill —"

"She's not," said a familiar voice, the French accent laid thick.

Silas glanced up. Beatrice had not changed since breakfast. Her feathered shawl caressed the balustrade as she descended.

"I looked in on her a moment ago. The bed has not been slept in."

Silas shot Holmgren a searching look, dreading the old man's confirmation. His unease took root as Holmgren admitted that *he* hadn't made the bed.

"Is the car gone?" Silas asked, resorting to the obvious alternative. If the phone didn't work, Ms. Eckdahl might have decided to brave the darkened country roads and alert the police in person.

"I will check," Holmgren assured them and, moving with the swiftness of a much younger man, made for the front door.

"I'll ask the others if—"

"There is something else," Beatrice whispered, and before Silas could lend action to words, grabbed his sleeve. Her gaze darted nervously around the many halls and doorways that fed into the entryway. Satisfied that they were alone, Beatrice reached into her satin wristlet. "I found this upstairs."

She deposited a red ribbon tied around a lock of straw-blond hair, the curl smooth and rounded like a fingernail. It fit snugly into Silas' palm. Without further explanation, he couldn't tell what he was supposed to make of it.

"You found this in Ms. Eckdahl's room?"

"Don't be silly. It belonged to Monsieur Morrow."

Silas' bemusement veered to disbelief. "What were you doing in Morrow's room?"

Beatrice shrugged, the portrait of nonchalance. "Same as everyone else—I heard a commotion last night. I went to see what all was going on."

"And you happened to find this."

"*Etrange, non?*"

Silas ran the pad of his thumb over the soft strands. The lock of hair might have belonged to anyone. Scandinavia didn't lack for blonds. "Mr. Morrow had an admirer."

"I found it by the bed, where the rug was pushed aside."

So much for post-coital bliss. And to think minutes ago he had been thrilling with the prospect of his next tryst with Axel. Silas let out a long breath. "Speak plainly, Ms. Lazare."

"My father was a doctor before the war. When the French came and punished those who would not denounce our German masters, there were many suicides by hanging." A small, awful smile drew itself upon Beatrice's rouged lips. "All sporting the same curious contusions…"

The suggestion was altogether preposterous. Silas would have refused to consider it if he hadn't seen the bruises with his own eyes. He brushed the lock of hair against his lifeline. "Contusions like our Mr. Morrow?"

Beatrice inclined her head. "Must I speak plainer than that?"

"Mr. Onuma, Ms. Lazare!" said Holmgren, panting as he jogged back into the house.

Silas' heart leaped. Here was the police, surely, come to take the whole miserable matter off their hands and restore the household to the less contentious pursuits of cutthroat tennis matches and illicit passions. The expression on Holmgren's grizzled features nipped his optimism in the bud.

"It's Ms. Eckdahl. She is… She is…"

Not dead, Silas was relieved to discover once he'd wrenched the car door open, but well on her way.

"This would be the culprit," he surmised, snatching up a bottle of aquavit off the passenger seat. His foot encountered another next to the gas pedal.

The Packard gave a protesting creak and judder as he shifted back, sending Ms. Eckdahl's head lolling like a marionette's.

"Get her inside," Beatrice ordered. "Holmgren, call for a doctor."

"The phone doesn't work, Miss."

"Hence why Ms. Eckdahl thought to drive to Katrineholm," Silas grunted, laboring under his hostess's weight as he eased her out of the driver's seat.

Ms. Eckdahl was no waif and Silas lacked the upper body strength of men like Wesley Conway, but with Beatrice and Holmgren to help, they succeeded in getting Ms. Eckdahl indoors. Beatrice took over then, briskly delivering commands to the household staff and ushering everyone else out of the room.

Just before the sitting room door closed behind him, Silas caught a glimpse of Beatrice palming Ms. Eckdahl's awfully pale cheek with an affectionate hand and murmuring to her softly.

He ran into questions before he could make sense of what he had seen. Mrs. Conway wanted to know if there had been another suicide. Wesley scoffed, arguing that they weren't bloody epidemic.

Ever obliging, Ms. Conway went ahead and fainted before Silas could get a word in edgewise. With the sitting room already occupied, her stepmother and fiancé helped Imogene to a wicker chair in the conservatory, where the smell of potted eucalyptus gradually restored her to full awareness.

Silas hovered in the doorway, contemplating a quiet retreat back to the sitting room. He refrained, both out of respect for Ms. Eckdahl and regard for her wallet. She was still his employer, by a fashion. It would not do to upset her.

He startled when a hand pressed lightly between his shoulder blades.

Axel retrieved it at the flinch. "Sorry."

"Don't be," Silas said, voice lowered to a whisper.

"What happened? Is Pia—"

"All right for now. She'll have the mother of all headaches when she wakes, but..." He gave Axel a rundown of what he had seen, and how, only to discover, as silence settled over the conservatory, that he had acquired a larger audience.

"So the police don't know about Morrow?" Mrs. Conway gasped.

"The telephone doesn't work."

"That's hardly a reason to drive a woman to drink." Not to be outdone by her stepdaughter's frail constitution, Mrs. Conway dabbed her brow with a lace handkerchief. "How unbecoming!"

"I doubt she was provoked by a defective telephone." Silas turned to Axel, wishing he could think of some way to mention the lock of hair Beatrice had found and at the same time reluctant to bring it up before the others. "Were she and Mr. Morrow close?"

Axel opened his mouth, scowled, then closed it again when he noted the avid looks being turned their way. "Not particularly."

"Her late father and my husband owned the other two thirds of Delville Wood," Mrs. Conway put in, as though Silas didn't already know. "Imogene here is like a sister to dear Pia. They used to write each other all the time. Dear Mr. Morrow would play postman…"

Her addendum *did* come as a surprise, for all that Ms. Conway appeared not to register her stepmother's hand on her knee. For a brief instant, she cut her eyes to Axel, then glanced away again.

"Someone ought to tell Holmgren to water these plants," she murmured. "And throw away those day lilies."

Silas tracked her gaze to the desiccated flowers. He hadn't paid it much mind before, but everywhere he looked in the sunroom he found rusted leaves and crinkled blossoms, the soil cracked and hard like the hills of his homeland. He cleared his throat. "Morrow didn't have any children of his own, did he?"

"He never married," Mrs. Conway confirmed.

Wesley greeted this with a snort. "We all know why *that* is."

"Beg your pardon?"

Not one to flinch easily, Wesley raised his gaze to Silas', cigarette glowing amber between his fingers. "Shall I enlighten you, Mr. Onuma?"

The butchery of his surname was nothing Silas hadn't heard before. "If you would." From the corner of his eye, he spied Axel shifting his weight.

"Virgil Morrow," said Wesley with a great deal of relish, "was an unapologetic nance."

* * * *

No one disputed Wesley's charge. In the hours that followed, it seemed less and less likely that a romance could have bound Ms. Eckdahl to a man twice her age. Silas' theory floundered as a result.

"I can't believe none of you drive," Beatrice said, a curl to her lip. "I will go myself—"

"No, you're the only one with a lick of medical knowledge," Silas argued. "I'll do it. How hard can it be?"

Holmgren shook his head. "Harder than it looks, sir. And I know Ms. Eckdahl would want you here when she wakes." His watery blue eyes bore into Silas'.

He knows.

"Very well," Wesley drawled, rising from his seat at the dinner table as though surrendering to the pleas of an adoring audience. "It'll have to be me."

On cue, Ms. Conway reached for his hand, curling gloved fingers around his wrist to retain him. "Wes, no!"

"You can't think to leave us here *alone*," her stepmother protested, equally scandalized.

Silas hitched his eyebrows. To hear them speak, Ms. Eckdahl's mansion was perched on some distant corner of the continent and not a mere two hours' drive from Stockholm. Yes, the rugged terrain and sparsely populated countryside made it appear quite isolated, but civilization was not so far away as to be unreachable.

Smugness etched onto his patrician features, Wesley patted his fiancée's hand. "Don't fret. I'll be back before morning."

"That's a bold estimate," Beatrice murmured, softly enough that no one seemed to hear but Silas.

"Something the matter with the Packard?" he asked.

Beatrice huffed. "Depending on who you ask, we've a ghost on the premises."

"Ms. Eckdahl is awake?" Silas asked before he could think better of it.

Astonishment softened Beatrice's expression, only for disbelief to swiftly take its place.

"Dessert and refreshments will be served in the conservatory," Mrs. Holmgren said from the doorway. She looked much like her husband — haggard and overtired, and not best pleased with this latest upheaval.

She was paid little heed. Mrs. Conway and Ms. Conway followed Wesley out of the dining room like a pair of ducklings, still clucking at him to reconsider. Silas made to follow them out, but Beatrice seized the sleeve of his dinner jacket, arresting the attempt.

"Come with me."

Her red-painted fingernails might as well have been talons in the fragile cotton. Silas has no choice but to oblige. He was escorted to the sitting room across the foyer. The sideboard beckoned with the promise of liquid courage, but Axel was already there. He turned at the click-clack of Beatrice's T-strap sandals, a glass of aquavit halfway to his lips.

"How do *you* know about Pia's suspicions?" Beatrice demanded of Silas.

While she might have been indifferent to their spectator, Silas didn't have that luxury. "I suggest you ask Ms. Eckdahl herself—"

"Oh, yes. I will wake her just so she can worry herself silly!" Beatrice folded her arms across her ample bosom. "You don't know anything about horses, do you?"

In his peripheral vision, Silas became aware of Axel lowering the glass, of him glancing between Silas and Beatrice as though wishing to intervene.

"I know no more than you," he demurred.

"I'm not here for that."

Then why? Silas bit back the question. People like them had made their way across the continent for centuries peddling a version of themselves palatable to a public yearning for distraction. Beatrice had cornered the market on francophone jazz with a whisper of sub-Saharan sensuality. Silas' means were no less cynical than hers.

As he watched her eyes widen in understanding, he knew his cover had been blown.

"*You're* the occultist."

Axel's glass met the sideboard with a click. "The what?"

Both Beatrice and Silas turned to him, she scowling at the interruption, Silas wracking his mind for some explanation that would soothe the hurt in Axel's voice.

"You told me you were an investor..." Axel had never looked more like his racing newspaper stills than he did then, scowling and cross, confronted with a fraud.

"Pia mentioned hiring a medium," said Beatrice. "I should have guessed that'd be you. A long way from the delta, aren't you?"

Silas dug his fingernails into the meat of his palms, but there was no denial, no excuse he could offer. Ms. Eckdahl had dragged him out of London by teasing his curiosity with her brash manner. She'd paid his crossing and picked him up from Stadsgården Port herself. And she had agreed to keep his true purpose at the house a secret because Silas had told her it would make be easier to investigate the strange happenings she'd mentioned to him without her other guests peering over his shoulder.

She was not the first to finance his flight with an interest in gifts that could have cost him his life in Nigeria.

Axel gave a mirthless guffaw. "Pia neglected to mention she found spiritualism."

"She didn't," Beatrice retorted, her denial brooking no opposition.

It fell to Silas to explain. "Ms. Eckdahl believed that she was being...haunted." He licked his lips and tried not to feel as though he was betraying her trust. "She had received what she believed were messages from the beyond—letters from her late father, that sort of thing. She asked me to investigate and rid her home of any...negative energy." He was only too aware of how ludicrous he sounded. In some parts of London, a black man spreading around this kind of talk would be well on his way to a thrashing.

Sweden wasn't so different, if the raw anger in Axel's eyes was any hint.

"And did you?" Beatrice wondered.

"No."

"Because you're a charlatan," Axel gritted out.

Silas flinched. *So much for spending the night together, you and I.* It had been enjoyable while it'd lasted.

"I'd like to see these letters, if you have them," Beatrice said.

"They're in my room." He could fetch them, but to do so would be to turn his back on Axel without even attempting to justify his half-truths.

He hadn't lied except by omission, yet the distinction didn't seem to count for much.

Axel downed the aquavit in a single swig then slammed the glass down. His shoulders drawn bullishly around his ears, he stalked out of the room without a single glance to Silas.

"Ah," murmured Beatrice.

"You know," Silas started, only for the emotion in his throat to choke him.

She slid her arm through his. "I do. But, *mon chou*, you would have had an easier time with the ice queen."

Chapter Four

Stripped of her makeup and propped up against the silken knoll of pillows at her back, Pia Eckdahl looked more mutinous than ever. She had waged a commendable effort for the chance to speak to Silas in the drawing room downstairs, but Beatrice had prevailed in the end.

Their resident songstress gloated now from her perch on the lounge chair by the window, long legs tucked under her and one of the feathers from her shawl tickling her cheek. She seemed right at home in Ms. Eckdahl's bedroom.

"You can't truly believe someone took Virgil's life," Ms. Eckdahl said, once the smattering of proof had been laid before her.

"It's more realistic than his sudden fondness for heights, isn't it?" Beatrice hitched her penciled eyebrows. "I seem to recall he suffered terrible vertigo."

"I'm not sure a little thing like that would stop a man intent on taking his life."

"Do you suppose a ghost did it, then?" A note of asperity entered Beatrice's voice, thwarting Silas' timid hope that perhaps she'd keep his secret.

Her lips firmed into a thin line of displeasure, Ms. Eckdahl spared him a glance. "I thought we agreed on discretion."

"When I insisted on silence, I was unaware that you had divulged your intentions," Silas shot back. Anonymity had been his only request. It made no practical difference — he would be leaving Sweden at the end of the month anyway and his short-lived affair with Axel had little chance of outlasting his stay even if they somehow mended fences — but still it registered as a betrayal. He chased the thought. This was business. "In any event, I'm inclined to agree with Ms. Lazare." If only because he very much doubted the existence of the supernatural in this house.

Or, indeed, anywhere else.

"A lock of blond hair, a room so messy it could easily have been the scene of a struggle," Beatrice recounted, counting each piece of evidence on her fingers. "What else?"

"The knot." The bedpost gave a creak when Silas uncrossed his arms and reached up to tug lightly on the canopy cord. The system was a simple one. The heavy velvet draperies that might have obscured the sleepers hung down in stiff lines of braided silk, their ends flared like a flapper's skirts. "It came undone easily enough, but somehow held up his weight — "

"It was a simple hitch," Ms. Eckdahl said, examining her nails. "One of the first horsemen and women learn."

Beatrice frowned. "I thought you said Virgil wasn't fond of horses."

"Didn't he own Delville Wood?" Silas asked, bemused.

"He does. He *did*," Ms. Eckdahl corrected herself. "He was about to lose his third."

"To whom?"

Ms. Eckdahl raised her shoulders listlessly. "Whoever had enough to buy in. You must understand, when my father and Mr. Conway first joined him in buying the horse, Delville was a long shot. But now? With his latest victory in the Galopp, Delville has become Sweden's top contender. No one bets against us anymore and those who bet with us... Well, we're a safe wager for many."

"And yet Mr. Morrow was in danger of losing his share." *How is that possible?* The intricacies of equine gambling still eluded Silas' understanding.

"He had debts, both in your country and over here," Ms. Eckdahl confessed. "What little he made from Delville Wood, he invested in harebrained schemes to make more money. Regrettably, they had a habit of failing."

In her reluctance, Silas read the first hint of an upper-class education. Despite her apparent frivolity and her love of jazz, the milliner-turned-industrialist's daughter had attended a girl's school in England and had studied under Sweden's top docents. And like all well-bred young ladies, she didn't discuss money.

This was particularly fascinating to Silas, for he knew that upon graduating, Ms. Eckdahl had neither married nor gone into trade as so many Swedish ladies of her generation. Eight years since coming into her father's fortune, she seemed to be doing just fine managing his investments.

Silas tapped a knuckle against his chin. "It seems unlikely that his creditors would send a loan shark *here*."

"What about the lock of hair?" Beatrice offered. "Could be a jilted lover, no? Some lovely, young creature he led on..."

"You French," Ms. Eckdahl huffed affectionately. "You think everything's about love."

Stiffening, Beatrice shot her a haughty stare. "Everything *is*."

"Or hate," Silas heard himself say. He squirmed beneath their inquisitive stares and cleared his throat. "It's almost midnight. I should let you rest."

"Yes, I expect we'll all have some explaining to do come morning."

Silas shammed a smile. "Only if Mr. Conway doesn't lose his way in the dark."

Beatrice rose from the lounge chair. "I'll see you out."
You're staying?

The question was best left unspoken. Silas bid his hostess goodnight and followed Beatrice to the door. He wasn't sure he understood what might possess a woman like Ms. Eckdahl to develop a fondness for an émigré jazz singer, but the complex world of female affinities had always been a mystery to him.

The hallway took a lazy turn from Ms. Eckdahl's bedroom to his on the other side of the property. While her windows overlooked the gravel-strewn driveway and the long stretch of road connecting the house to distant Katrineholm, his own opened onto the lake. A casement window at the far end of the meandering corridor lent just enough light for Silas to pick his way without stumbling.

His heart leaped when a door suddenly opened on his left. Blinding light streamed through, filling his vision with white.

A man's silhouette materialized before him. Silas' eyes couldn't make sense of the apparition fast enough. Soon it was upon him, seizing his lapels with both hands and dragging him forward.

Any resistance Silas might have offered vanished beneath the pressure of Axel's bruising kiss.

"What..." Silas gasped. "Axel, wait."

"Quiet," came the harsh command.

It might have been a conjurer's trick but Silas was powerless to refuse him. He abruptly surrendered all thought of speech and gave himself over to Axel's capable hands in the guise of willing prey.

He went as bid, lurching first into one doorjamb, then the other, before they finally reached the bed. His fists never straying far from Silas' shoulders, Axel shoved him down and pinned him to the mattress with his slighter frame.

What he lacked in height he more than made up for in sinewy muscle. His evident arousal dug into the crease of Silas' thigh, ramping up the electricity building between them. Without Silas noticing until it was done, Axel squeezed a hand into his trousers and curled his callused fingers around Silas' cock.

Pleasure knotted in the pit of Silas' stomach. His breaths hitched, an embarrassing sound spilling from his throat before he could bite it back.

Axel kissed him again and again, making short work of his trousers and shoving up his shirttails and dinner jacket. He all but knocked the air out of Silas' lungs in rolling him to his belly. Bedsprings gave a protesting squeak beneath them, but neither Silas nor Axel heeded them.

Dimly cognizant of Axel wrestling with his own clothes, Silas gripped the sheets and tried to make himself relax. He yearned for Axel's usual chattiness, his constant stream of praise and wonderment, his effusive moans when Silas did something he enjoyed particularly well. But there was nothing, only harsh-bitten groans and the rustle of fabric accompanied the familiar slide of soft, hot flesh between his arse cheeks.

Axel wasn't even aroused.

The discovery hit Silas like a cannonball. Axel's grip on his nape had slackened. Silas found it possible to turn his head, shoving aside the bitter urge to go along with this for one last chance to have Axel.

"You...you don't want this."

Axel went stock-still. "What?"

"I like it a little...tumultuous. But not you." Axel's fervor was born of enthusiasm. He laughed in bed. He reveled in his ecstasy. The marks he bestowed in the heat of the moment were by no means hateful.

Axel eased his hands to the bedding, straddling Silas with little purpose. His breaths on the back of Silas' neck were barely labored. "What would you know," he snarled, "about what I like? You think you're the only one with secrets?"

Regret soured in Silas' bloodstream. "I'm sorry." He curled a finger around Axel's thumb, relaxing into the mattress. "You can have me, if that's—"

"Who *are* you," Axel interjected, his voice thick with hurt, "that you'd offer yourself in exchange for my forgiveness? What kind of man—"

By way of answer, Silas tightened his hold on Axel's thumb and pulled it back.

It wasn't enough to break the digit, but the sharp curl of pain that must have raced up Axel's wrist shook his infuriating mastery.

Before Axel could right himself and pull away, Silas caught hold of his chin. "I'm sorry I deceived you. Truly. But I offer you my body because I want you. If you want more, you'll have to ask for it." The corner of his mouth threatened to rise in a seditious smile. Silas curbed the gauche impulse. "Respectfully."

Disbelief plain on his face, Axel searched his eyes. Whatever he found there was enough to have him gather his strength and shove free of Silas' grip as though touching him had suddenly become poisonous.

"You mock me."

"You're the one who dragged me in here," Silas pointed out, propped on his elbows. His shirt and jacket were gone, trousers and underwear bunched around his knees. He rolled them down, grimacing when that left him wearing only his socks.

What little comfort there was in noting that Axel was no better attired faded when Axel began doing up the buttons on his shirt.

"Do you object to my profession on Christian grounds," Silas wondered, "or purely for moral reasons?"

"I'm told my persuasion doesn't allow much room for morality."

Although the pair of fashionably ornate lamps on either side of the bed limned Axel in gold light, his features remained shadowed. It was impossible to tell if he was sneering or sincere.

"*Our* persuasion, you mean," Silas corrected. Throwing his lot in with Axel's didn't seem to earn him any points, so he went on, "You knew about Morrow, didn't you?"

"Yes."

"Were you two...?"

Axel looked up sharply.

"Were you sleeping together?"

"What business is that of yours?"

A moment ago, Silas had been face down in the sheets for keeping his work too neatly shelved away. It would have amused him to bring up the irony if Axel hadn't looked so distressed.

"Beatrice found a lock of hair in his room. We believe it might have been a treasured possession, seeing as it was preserved with ribbon." He paused for effect. "Did you know anything about that?"

Slowly, Axel dropped his hands from his shirt buttons. The top three demurred undone and the flash of pale skin that showed through the gap was particularly tantalizing. "I didn't give Morrow a token of my affections, if that's what you're asking."

"It wasn't."

"Then what?" Axel snorted. "Do you know — you're starting to sound as though you suspect *I* might have something to do with his death!"

"Of course not," Silas retorted, meaning the full force of his denial. "I know you're not capable —"

"I thought we agreed that you don't know me."

"Not for lack of trying." Aware that it was a cheap shot, Silas nevertheless canted his head to one shoulder and smirked. "I *am* naked in your bed. What more can a man do to get your attention?"

Axel's eyes narrowed, but the rosy blush in his cheeks gave him away.

"You don't think much of playing it safe, do you?"

"Safe doesn't get me what I want," Silas murmured.

"And what's that?"

"You. Finishing what you started. Wesley could be back any moment..." And for all their combined brazenness, Silas had no desire to brave a tryst under the nose of some stodgy police captain.

Much to his relief, Axel seemed to agree. He paced a slow circuit around the bed before hitching a knee up and sliding into Silas' lap as though in echo of their soapy romp in the bath.

The heady sensation of Axel's bare thighs on either side of his hips was incentive enough to set aside their quarrel, but the spark that had ignited Axel's temper was slow to burn itself out.

"Tell me one thing," he growled. "Are you scamming Pia?"

"I'm not clairvoyant." Silas ran a finger down the dip between his collarbones, popping buttons as he went. "But I can tell you that I haven't taken her money yet." Outside the all-expenses vacation, his hands were quite clean. "Her ghosts are still very much running wild."

Axel let out an exasperated sigh. "There's no such thing as ghosts."

It might have been possible to settle for the catch in his voice if Silas' pride hadn't been pricked. He reversed them gently but without a word of warning.

See how you like being on your back for a change.

A great deal, if the insistent swell of Axel's cock was any sign.

Silas smirked down at him. "There's no such thing as ghosts, Morrow wasn't your lover...and you know nothing about his admirers. Does that sound about right?" He punctuated the question with a slow roll of hips, his length sliding against Axel's to the tune of a delicious little moan.

"I didn't—didn't say that."

Silas nipped at the shell of his ear. "Tell me."

Axel made a sound halfway between a sigh and a choked plea. Silas bit down harder, rocked his hips more forcefully. Tendrils of pleasure chased their way up his spine as friction built and built between them—

until he stopped, one hand knotted in Axel's sandy hair and the other pinned to the mattress.

"Tell me."

"You're extorting me in bed?" Axel huffed, incredulous.

"All information has a price." And Silas could tell Axel wanted to share this, the words all but hovering on the tip of his wicked tongue.

He was easy to read, an open book of frequent grins and good-natured japes. There was something princely about him, even in anger. Even now.

Silas palmed his cheek, his own skin so dark against the rosy pink of Axel's blush. "Just tell me this. *Was* it an admirer?"

Axel's lashes fluttered as though to conceal his dilated pupils, the want to evident in his gaze.

"No," he said and craned his neck to press his mouth to Silas'.

One kiss became two, became half a dozen. Silas soon lost his train of thought, his reptilian brain taking over as the world narrowed to the warmth of Axel's skin against his, the slick of his arousal easing the grip he took on them both. The bed groaned beneath them as Silas sped his strokes, greedy to see Axel surrender himself to the sweet agony.

He didn't have long to wait. Axel came with a dazed gasp, his body curving spasmodically into Silas' as he pulsed through the aftershocks. He was still trembling, trying to catch his breath, when Silas took himself in hand and spent in thick streaks all over his chest.

Heedless of the mess, Axel twined their fingers, using his thumb to tease out the last of Silas' release. "You...you said something about letters."

"What?" Silas wheezed, struggling to pick up the thread of a conversation he hadn't realized they were still having. He could hardly be expected to think with Axel tormenting him like this.

"Earlier, with Beatrice. You said—"

"Ms. Eckdahl's letters, yes." *Now* he remembered. Trying to ignore Axel's ministrations was impossible. Silas brought their joined hands to the mattress by Axel's head and dismounted. His legs could barely hold him. "What of them?"

"Could I take a look?"

"Why the sudden interest?"

"Because," said Axel, a faraway look in his eyes, "of Delville Wood."

Chapter Five

Drowsy with sex and spent rage, Axel fell into a deep sleep sometime around one in the morning. Silas lay beside him and enjoyed the steady rise and fall of his chest. He couldn't resist stroking Axel's bare forearm, where the shirtsleeve fanned open and fine gold hair tickled Silas' fingertips.

Axel looked so serious in slumber. Far from peaceful, he scowled and gnashed his teeth, which occasionally peeked between the Cupid's bow of his lips. His features smoothed now and again around a hollow smile, before the frowns returned, and the routine was set in motion once more. Without his stony, feline eyes to question Silas' intentions, there was little need to look away.

A man might well spend a lifetime trying to pierce the veil of his dreams, Silas mused, and it wouldn't be ill-spent.

At length, lulled by Axel's even breaths, Silas began to doze.

He had long mastered the ability to sleep anywhere — a steamship journey from Lagos to Cardiff was just the thing to cure a lifelong case of insomnia—and Axel's bed was far more comfortable than the mission-house cots of his youth. But before he could truly succumb to blissful oblivion, a peal of sound caught Silas' ear.

The noise came again, softly, with the muffled screech of floorboards overhead.

Silas peered up. Ms. Eckdahl's house was old and creaky, susceptible to all the usual foibles of ancient properties. Wooden boards routinely snapped and echoed with even the quietest tread. Yet the room above Axel's had belonged to the late Mr. Morrow. And the ruckus showed no signs of abating.

If that's a ghost, it ought to learn some manners.

The thought shot through Silas entirely without mirth. At Axel's prompting, he had spent a good hour describing the letters Ms. Eckdahl claimed to have found recently—all written in her late father's hand, all involving eerily familiar details about her, her family and her family's wealth.

In return, Axel had divulged more than Silas had ever cared to know about Delville Wood. The prize gelding was pictured everywhere in Ms. Eckdahl's house, from black and white photographs to oil paintings in ornate frames, to extraordinary renditions in that new style that rendered everything geometric and borderline disturbing.

Tableaus of varying artistic merit festooned the stairwell walls, where the portraits of her ancestors might have hung. Silas hadn't paid much mind to the oddity before, but then he hadn't known just how valuable Delville Wood was to the Eckdahls and Conways, and the late Virgil Morrow.

The same Virgil Morrow whose bedroom door stood open, revealing the wavering of a shadow within.

There is no such thing as ghosts.

Silas curled his hand around the door handle and pushed his way inside before he could rethink the impulse.

A gasp, a flash of movement, and the singly lit lamp beside the bed fell upon its side, mosaic shade thrown off-kilter. Ms. Conway flinched away from the noise, backing up into the nearby dresser.

"Oh, Mr. Onuma!" She pressed a hand to her chest. "I—I didn't hear you. I was just... I was, uh..."

Silas waited her out, but no further explanation followed.

Ms. Conway busied herself with righting the lamp. Her cheeks bloomed pink in the fractured halo. Her hair was a corona of blond strands spilling untidily over her nightgown.

The longer he stared, the more uncomfortable Ms. Conway seemed to become. As she folded her arms across her chest, Silas was suddenly glad he'd thought to button his shirt up all the way before he'd left Axel's room. Ms. Conway had nothing to fear from him, but the poor girl didn't know that.

"I believe," said Silas, taking pity on her, "that you were looking for this." From the inside of his trouser pocket, he produced the lock of hair and placed it on Mr. Morrow's bed. Someone—Silas imagined Holmgren or his wife—had righted the sheets since last night's discovery.

The police weren't likely to be too pleased with that.

Ms. Conway's mouth twitched, as though laughter threatened to work its way free of her throat. Perhaps fearing such a reaction might make her appear guilty, she marshalled her expression into something approaching her fiancé's native haughtiness. "I'm sure I don't know what you mean."

"I understand Mr. Morrow was something of a swindler. Did he threaten to expose you?"

Ms. Conway's silence spoke volumes.

"I didn't realize it when your stepmother first mentioned his help in ferrying your letters between Stockholm and London. But then I found out Morrow made his wealth by learning other people's secrets... Stumbling on the true nature of your friendship with Ms. Eckdahl must have been quite the victory."

Chin trembling, Ms. Conway said nothing

"He promised you his silence, I assume. And perhaps he would have kept his tongue if his finances hadn't demanded that he go back on his word. I imagine he threatened to tell Wesley or your stepmother...maybe even your father." Who, if word around London was to be believed, was an old-fashioned war veteran with little affection for blacks, Indians or inverts.

"I didn't kill him," Ms. Conway blurted out and violently pushed away from the dresser. Her agitation was understandable, but she didn't make for the door.

The quivering of her lips tugged at Silas' heartstrings. He was in no position to condemn or absolve. He only knew that Morrow hadn't tripped off the balcony with a noose around his neck by chance.

"I wanted the damn letters back," Ms. Conway admitted. "That's all... That's all it was. He was asleep when I came in. I thought he'd passed out drinking. I — I tried to be quiet, but he must have heard me."

"He caught you red-handed."

She flinched at the charge, but the same faraway look in her eyes remained. "He was *livid*. We fought for the letters. I may not be very strong, but he'd been drinking." Ms. Conway looked down at her knotted fingers. "I had him by the neck. I don't... I don't remember how. He was scratching me." The backs of her hands indeed sported the marks of the struggle.

That explains the gloves. Silas took no pleasure in that particular piece of the puzzle.

Ms. Conway whirled around to face him. "But he was still breathing when I left, I swear! I couldn't kill a man. I didn't—"

"I believe you."

Astonishment seemed to stun her. "You...you do?"

"If we'd found Mr. Morrow strangled in his bed, I might have doubts. But you're not strong enough to drag him to the balcony, much less over the rail."

Ms. Conway's relief convulsed out of her in a sob. "Oh, thank God... Wesley would—he'd leave me. If he knew."

Wesley Pollard's continued regard didn't strike Silas as much of a reason to rejoice. "He won't hear it from me," Silas assured her. "Does Ms. Eckdahl know? About Morrow's blackmail." *About your feelings for her.*

It took Ms. Conway several attempts to get herself in check. She swiped her fingertips beneath her eyes to brush away tears she hadn't shed.

"Of course not. Why bother mentioning it? All that nonsense was *eons* ago. An adolescent fixation, nothing more... I'm not unnatural." She seemed to take great pleasure in the assertion, but that didn't stop her snatching up the lock of hair as though Silas might rescind his offer.

"Those letters can't have been too bad, then," he mused, "if they were just nonsense."

Morrow, who was a homosexual himself, had been well placed to gauge the precise value of such correspondence.

A small, cruel smile twisted at Ms. Conway's lips. "Didn't Axel tell you? Morrow had a talent for embellishing. He could turn a scrawny little warhorse into a champion with a few strokes of a pen... A dockside whore into a sportsman."

"What?"

"I *thought* that might interest you." Her last piece of incriminating evidence clutched firmly in hand, Ms. Conway brushed past Silas on her way out. "Axel was a nobody when Morrow found him. Now he's Pia's guest of honor and nobody blinks an eye when he takes the help into his bed."

The muscles in Silas' jaw slackened. It was nothing he hadn't heard before, but women like Ms. Conway were usually too proper — and too wary — to insult him to his face.

"I would be careful, Ms. Conway." Silas took a step toward her. Then another. "Or did Pia neglect to mention she counts a witch among *the help*?"

The pleasure he took in seeing Ms. Conway blanch was entirely beneath him, but it was as real as the roar of engines echoing through the silent house.

At last, Wesley had returned with the police.

* * * *

Dawn broke over the lakeshore slowly, the sun's rays barely cleaving the mist that had settled during the night. Ensconced on a wicker settee, with a blanket draped across their laps, Beatrice and Ms. Eckdahl sat holding hands. Behind them, the distant echo of policemen and household staff whispered through the fog.

"I don't understand," Ms. Eckdahl confessed. "Why would Virgil torment me so?"

"For the same reason all men do ill onto others." Silas picked up a flat stone from the shingle beach and tossed it. "He needed the money." The stone bounced off the surface of the lake like a boomerang, skipping three times before sinking with a quiet *plop*. "It's an unpopular thing, to fight on the losing side in a war."

Ms. Eckdahl met his gaze, her expression wary. "Excuse me?"

"Your father was a German officer before turning his coat."

"No, he was a spy for —"

"The British." Silas picked up another stone. "He claimed to have been a spy for the British all through the war. But that's not true. Morrow confided in Axel, who told me... Your father transferred his allegiance two years into the war, when he and a couple of venal Englishmen joined forces in robbing a number of wealthy French families." Axel hadn't filled this part in for Silas, but the picture he'd painted did not present a rosy outcome for the unfortunate victims. "Their pockets full, all three were supposedly wounded at the Battle of Delville Wood and sent home to England, to heal. By the time they were well enough for the front, the war had already ended. Our three friends bought a horse to commemorate their lucrative stint and parted ways.

"Two made their fortunes on opposite shores of the North Sea. A third was less lucky and began dealing in blackmail and fraud. With Axel, it was the matter of his origins that forced their partnership to continue long after it stopped being mutually beneficial." Silas allowed himself a smile. "And I'm sure if I were to dig a little deeper, I would discover all sorts of unpleasantness that Mr. Morrow graciously unearthed and claimed to keep secret for your guests."

"He never blackmailed *me*," Ms. Eckdahl protested, but her voice, much like her certainty, seemed to waver.

"He couldn't chance it with you."

"Why?"

"Delville Wood incriminates him, as well as your late father. If you called his bluff, he would have been exposed. Morrow sought to avoid that with his...letters from the beyond, a trick he picked up during his convalescence and used to further dupe his victims."

"I don't believe this," Ms. Eckdahl blurted out. The blanket fell from her lap as she rose, her gait unsteady.

"I'm sorry," Silas started, only for a raised hand to cut him off.

Ms. Eckdahl staggered away, clutching her sides. The fog swirled around her in gray vapors.

"She'll be all right," said Beatrice.

Silas tried but couldn't quite find it in him to share the conviction.

"What about the rest?" Beatrice asked. "The lock of hair?"

He waved a hand. "The token must have belonged to another of target of his foul conduct."

"And the bruises?"

Silas had yet to find a way to brand those as accidental. "By now they will have faded. I doubt the police will notice."

It was not the answer Beatrice had been gunning for, but she didn't press the point. Their eyes met and held for a long beat, before she too rose from the settee.

"I'm almost sorry that it wasn't a ghost," she murmured in passing.

Silas smiled at her retreating back. The fog made an indistinct blur of her hourglass figure and Ms. Eckdahl's broad-shouldered frame. Just before he turned away, Silas saw them embrace far more intimately than friends, even female ones, might do.

He picked his way up the beach to the sloping lawn and up the curled lip of stone steps to the house. Holmgren was just seeing the police out when Silas stepped into the foyer. One of the officers turned at the sound of his footsteps and saw him. A seed of anxiety blossomed in Silas' chest, but the officer only touched the brim of his cap and bid him good day.

Out here, no one knew of Silas' predilections or his dubious career. No one cared.

Well. Perhaps one man.

Silas' feet led him up the stairs of their own accord. He had slept so little last night that a kip was in order, yet a not so rational thought kept him climbing. He was outside Morrow's door before he knew what he was doing and past the threshold before the blurry form on the balcony had resolved into the solid shape of a man.

"He's gone," Axel said, twisting to face Silas. The sleeves of his white shirt were pushed up to his elbows to reveal tanned forearms, his waistcoat unbuttoned. Rather than shabby, he looked well-groomed and polished, like a freshly whittled blade, diminutive but not harmless.

"Glad to see the back of him?"

"Would it be cruel to say yes?"

Silas shook his head. By all accounts, Morrow had not been a pleasant man.

He stiffened when Axel leaned against his flank, but the pressure lingered and slowly he let himself relax.

"How did Pia take it?" Axel wanted to know.

"You mean the news that an old family friend was hounding her in the most despicable way possible? Surprisingly well, actually."

"She'll be all right," Axel said, unknowingly parroting Beatrice's words.

In lieu of answer, Silas brushed his lips to Axel's temple. They stayed like that, entwined, unseen, the fog cocooning them like a balmy cloak. The world itself seemed to dissipate around them.

"I woke up last night and you were gone," Axel murmured. "Where did you go?"

"I heard the cars."

"Oh. I thought you'd left before that." Axel sighed and straightened, seemingly unwilling to dig deeper. "I don't know what we'll get up to in this weather. Doesn't seem like a day for tennis."

"We could go back to bed," Silas suggested.

Axel let his gaze journey down the length of Silas' body and licked his lips. "I might be persuaded to consider that."

"Lead the way."

He spun on his heel, graceful and swift, animated by the same eagerness Silas had found so flattering two nights ago, one floor below, under a ceiling that resonated with the slightest hint of movement.

Air fled Silas' lungs.

Ms. Conway didn't have the strength to drag Morrow across the floor and stage his suicide, but Axel did. There was little chance Axel had missed the commotion overhead. He would have heard Ms. Conway's struggle.

He would have known how to secure Morrow's noose with an evenk knot.

That bruise on his shoulder wasn't Silas' doing.

Axel turned, lanky but not weak, his body brimming with tight-laced strength. A wrinkle creased the valley between his eyebrows. "Silas?"

Their eyes met. If the slightest hint of culpability hovered in Axel's gaze, Silas missed it. The balustrade gave an almighty crackle and disintegrated beneath Silas' fingers.

A hollow opened behind him. Gravity sank its claws into his flesh.

There was a moment of chagrin, the shame of having been so utterly gullible, then horror. The steep fall awaiting him. Silas opened his mouth to scream.

The sound snagged in his throat as he was braced, suddenly, above the abyss. Axel's warm breath buffeted his cheeks. Time seemed to slow, as understanding, then calculation dawned in Axel's eyes.

He knows.

With both hands anchored in his shirtfront, Axel hauled him back onto the ledge. "Watch it!" he gasped. "Are you all right? Silas, good God!"

"Fine," Silas managed. His heart hammered viciously in his throat.

"You gave me a start! Lucky I was here, eh?" A small smile quivered on Axel's lips, but relief was only half of the myriad emotions flashing across his face.

He searched Silas' gaze as though the answers he needed were hidden there.

"You *are* all right, aren't you? For a moment there, I thought..."

Silas curled a hand around his slender neck. Axel's pulse throbbed beneath his fingers. His Adam's apple bobbed when he swallowed. And, slowly, Silas' view of him reconfigured.

No wonder Axel had been so cross with Silas for lying. What man wanted to see his own flaws mirrored in his lover? There was no avoiding it. Like called to like and Axel, too, was a survivor.

"I'm sorry," Silas whispered. "It won't happen again. It won't ever happen again."

Their kiss was no harsher, no sweeter than any they'd shared over the last handful of days. But standing there, on a crumbling architecture of bones and lies, it was a promise.

Slowly, the fog began to lift and Axel kissed him back.

KEEPING THE LUCK IN

L.M. Somerton

Dedication

For Sue with Love

Chapter One

Pip heaved yet another barrowload of mucky straw from the stable. He walked backward, finding it easier to pull than push, and almost collided with one of the other stable hands.

"Oops, sorry!" He put the barrow handles down and rested for a moment, hands on thighs.

Carrie grinned at him. "I can't believe you keep coming back for this hard labor every summer, Pip."

Pip grinned back. As always, Carrie's smile was infectious. "Unlike you, I need the money. I have student loans up to my eyebrows and my new job doesn't start until September."

Carrie pulled a piece of straw from Pip's hair. "I'll let you take me for a drink tonight and you can tell me what it's like to be a fully qualified vet. I want to hear all about this job, just to make sure it's good enough for you, you understand. Now you don't have to study every minute of the day, we can check out the talent at the same time. You've been practically celibate for the last three years."

Pip shook his head. "Are you ever going to stop trying to set me up? Our taste in men is poles apart and you know full well I haven't had time to get out and meet people."

Carrie wrinkled her nose, making her freckles merge together. "You just need re-educating and I'm the girl to do it. I'll come and find you around six. Make sure you have a shower and change because I'm not taking you out dressed like that."

"What's wrong with what I'm wearing?" Pip peered down at his mud-stained navy jodhpurs and ratty T-shirt. His ankle boots were caked with mud and straw.

"You look hotter than I do, that's what the problem is. Wear something unflattering, I don't need the competition." Carrie flicked her bright orange hair and pouted. "It is so unfair that you're prettier than I am. My butt swells to huge proportions in jodhpurs."

"It does not." Pip rolled his eyes. Carrie was attractive in a curvy, girly kind of way and she knew it. "You're just fishing for compliments. Now get out of my way, I have shit to shovel."

"And that's why you spent five years at vet school." Carrie stuck her tongue out at him then flounced off.

Pip got back to dragging his barrow out to the manure pile. The cobbled yard didn't help his progress, and by the time he'd dumped his load, Pip was sweating. He paused and wiped the back of his hand across his brow. It came away mucky, telling him that he most likely had something brown and disgusting streaked across his forehead. He shrugged. Dirt was a fact of life in the yard and as the summer help, he got all the worst jobs that the regular hands wanted to offload. Mucking out wasn't too bad. It was good exercise and a way to keep trim without forking out for gym fees. Pip patted his flat stomach. "Not exactly Mr.

Universe, but I'm happy with flab free. Who needs giant muscles anyway…?" His voice trailed away as he caught sight of the most delicious eye candy emerging from the forge. "Oh God. Rory Ironstone. And he's carelessly lost his shirt. I think I'm in heaven."

Pip stared hard, not wanting to miss a second as the blacksmith-cum-farrier paused at the water trough and splashed water over his face and heavily muscled, lightly furred torso. Pip's cock hardened in appreciation. He yanked his shirt down a bit, trying to cover the very obvious bulge that skin-hugging riding trousers did nothing to conceal. A moan escaped his lips. "Oh God, he's beautiful." Pip sank his teeth into his lower lip. He knew Rory was gay. Had known the delicious, dream-inspiring morsel of information for going on three years. Ever since he'd started work at the yard one summer. Carrie had relayed that juicy fact. She knew everything about everyone. Pip was far too shy to do anything about it and he doubted that Rory had ever even noticed him. Pip never had cause to go to the forge, and Rory didn't venture into the stables very often, at least not when Pip was around. They were kept apart by their work.

Rory finished his impromptu bath and headed back to the forge. Pip sighed. Now his studies were over and he no longer had the excuse of long hours poring over his books, he craved companionship. Rural Wiltshire wasn't exactly a haven for gay men, let alone the kind of man Pip hankered after. Rory was perfect, but Pip got tongue-tied talking to anyone new. If he attempted a conversation with Rory, he'd just make an idiot of himself.

Pip wheeled his empty barrow back to the equipment shed. He parked it against the wall where nobody would trip over it. That job finished, he headed toward the tack room where a pile of saddles and a tin of leather polish awaited him. The work was dull, but at least he'd get to sit inside in the shade. The sun was beginning to make his head hurt. He almost made it to the door when he heard someone shout his name. Well, not his name *exactly*.

"Hey, Pipsqueak!"

Pip rolled his eyes. "Calvin. What have I done to deserve this?" He waited, fake smile fixed on his face as Calvin Henderson-Dobbs, the senior resident groom, strolled toward him. If only Pip had the nerve to call him Dobbin to his face. That was what all the other stable hands called the jumped-up, obnoxious pillock behind his back.

"Glad I caught you, Pipsqueak. I've got a job for you." Calvin, full of self-importance, his face flushed, stood with his hands on his hips.

"I already have work to..."

"Whatever it is, it can wait. This is more important," Calvin interrupted.

"Of course it is," Pip muttered.

"I'm taking Orson's Legacy out on the gallops for a potential buyer to view but Royal Midnight Wind has an appointment for new shoes at the forge. You can take him over there for me."

Pip swallowed. The horse Calvin referred to was not known for his sweet temperament. Even the prospect of spending time with Rory couldn't tamp down the shiver of trepidation that ran the length of Pip's spine. Calvin was already walking away.

"Wait! Calvin...are you sure there isn't anyone else?"

"Why, Pipsqueak? Afraid the big mean horsey will bolt and drag you across the yard? Some vet you'll make," Calvin sneered. "Just do as you're told and stop whining."

Much as Pip wanted to feed Calvin a knuckle sandwich, there was an element of truth in his words. Pip's new job as junior vet with Wiltshire's biggest equestrian practice would mean handling horses regularly, even though he would principally be picking up the small animal part of the business. Pip loved horses — he just didn't have a whole lot of experience handling highly strung thoroughbreds. Most had their own grooms familiar with their eccentricities but the owner of the racecourse housed his own horses there, as well as a few guests waiting for the farrier. The regular grooms were used to dealing with a range of animals. Pip, during his short summer stints, occasionally did some grooming but was otherwise firmly restricted to the most menial tasks.

"What are you waiting for? Get your backside round there now," Calvin snapped. "And try to remember that the horse is worth a hell of a lot more then you are. Don't damage him." Calvin stalked away, nose in the air.

"Nice to know where I stand on Calvin's scale of worth. Somewhere between worm and manure." Pip shrugged. He only had to put up with Calvin's crap for a few more weeks. Pip strolled to the end of the yard and followed the cinder track to the residents' stable block. He walked the gauntlet of curious expressions and twitching ears as all the horses nosed at him over their stable doors. He paused and patted a few of them, murmuring calming words and stroking velvet-smooth necks. It was a privilege to work among so many stunning animals, and Pip could appreciate their strength and grace. He got to the final stable on the block.

"Hey, Windy, how are you doing?"

An indignant whinny told Pip exactly what his charge thought of the nickname.

"I know I know…it's undignified but I will *not* be using your full name, it's far too much of a mouthful." Pip leaned against the stable door and allowed Windy to snuffle all over him. "Of course, I can think of something much better to fill my mouth with. I'd bet a week's wages that Rory Ironstone is hung better than you are." A head butt followed an outraged snort.

"Hey! Stop that. I'm sure all the mares around here would love nothing more than to get up close and friendly with you. When they put you out to stud, you'll get all the frisky tail you can handle, believe me. Your sex life is going to be a lot more fulfilling than mine will ever be." Pip sighed. "I'm baring my soul to a horse. I have serious issues. Well, at least Calvin got your bridle on already. Are you going to behave for me?"

Pip slid the bolt on the stable door and swung it open. He took hold of Windy's leading rein and waited for the horse to calm. He patted Windy's neck and stroked his flank. "Such a good boy. Now, let's go and get you some new shoes." Pip stepped forward and to his amazement, Windy followed. He didn't have to tug or cajole. Windy held his head high and ignored his stable mates. Pip let the horse set the pace and kept his fingers crossed that nothing would go wrong.

* * * *

Rory eyed the stallion being led toward him with suspicion that came from long and sometimes painful experience. He'd shoed the beast a month earlier and there were still traces of yellowing bruises on his hip where the bad-tempered creature had lashed out. Rory had quick reflexes, otherwise he might well have ended up in the hospital with broken bones.

"Should have known better than to trust that idiot Calvin to keep Beelzebub calm. Boy has the attention span of a goldfish on crack." Beelzebub was not the horse's true name but Rory had decided he needed a more fitting moniker than Royal Midnight Wind. Rory snorted. The names of thoroughbred racehorses never failed to amuse him.

"Have to admit, he *is* a handsome devil." The stallion was pure black. There wasn't a single interruption to the color of his sleek coat. He had a haughty, regal way about him and killer lashes that got the ladies cooing every time. Rory tried to catch a glimpse of the groom escorting that morning's customer but could only see the top of a tousled blond head. Rory stood six feet five inches in his bare feet. To him, the entire population seemed short, but this guy had to be miniature.

"Could be a girl of course, shouldn't make assumptions." But it wasn't. Beelzebub's minder was male, maybe five feet four if he stood on his tiptoes, and cute. Very cute.

"Ooh boy." Rory puffed out the breath he hadn't even realized he'd been holding. The little man pushed every single one of his lust levers. "Please God, let him be gay," Rory muttered, glancing up at the cloudless sky. "How can he not be when he's the perfect size to tuck under my arm?" Rory allowed himself a mental image of the groom bouncing on his ample cock, lips parted in a silent scream of ecstasy. "He'll definitely have to ride me, I'd just squish him otherwise, he's so teeny." Rory grinned. He adored lying back while an athletic partner impaled himself and got all sweaty and excited.

Rory gave himself a shake. It wouldn't do to be daydreaming while he worked. Beelzebub would know instinctively if Rory wasn't one hundred percent focused and would take full and painful advantage. Rory slid open the wide forge doors and checked his equipment. His preference was to hot shoe. It was a more time consuming process but usually resulted in a better fit than cold shoeing and fit was vital for a racehorse.

An iron ring he'd forged himself was set in the wall close to the doors. The groom looped the lead rein through the ring and patted the horse's sweating neck.

"There, there...don't be a baby, Windy. You're going to get a pedicure and shiny new shoes. You have to be nice."

Rory choked back a laugh. *He's calling a three hundred thousand guinea horse Windy. I think I'm in love.* He grabbed a bag of tools and took it out to the yard. The horse gave him the evil eye but didn't kick or dance around so Rory got into position and nudged its front leg until he could rest the hoof on his thigh.

"I'd appreciate you keeping him as still as possible, lad. What should I call you?"

"Pip. Everyone calls me Pip." The young man peeked from beneath a floppy fringe.

Rory used his pincers to remove the old shoe, then trimmed the hoof wall with his favorite nippers. He used a knife on the sole and frog of the hoof.

"Do you understand what I'm doing, Pip?" Rory couldn't resist explaining. "Shoes don't allow the hoof to wear down as it naturally would in the wild, and it can become too long. The coffin bone inside the hoof should line up straight with both bones in the pastern. If I don't trim the excess, the bones will become misaligned, which would place stress on the legs of the animal."

Pip didn't say anything, but he edged closer and paid attention.

"I'll measure the shoes to his feet and then bend them to the correct shape. The mark the hot shoe makes will show me how it lies."

"It doesn't hurt him, though, I know that," Pip whispered.

"Not at all, but I do have to take care not to hold the hot shoe against the hoof too long because the heat can damage it."

Rory worked methodically, and to his amazement the stallion remained calm as Pip gentled him. He resized each shoe on the anvil, then cooled them in water before nailing them in place. Once the nails had been completely driven in, Rory cut off the sharp points then used a clincher to bend the rest of the nails so they were almost flush with the hoof wall. The last stage was to use a rasp to smooth any rough edges.

Pip maneuvered himself around so that he could watch while Rory hammered each shoe into shape. Rory's tanned skin glistened in the light of the gas furnace and his muscles bulged as he worked. Pip cooed sweet nothings to Windy to keep him calm but his attention was firmly fixed on a thoroughbred of another breed. Pip imagined Rory picking him up and pressing him against the wall. He was so strong, Pip was certain they could get up to all kinds of athletic things and there would be no risk of getting dropped on his arse. He shifted uncomfortably, his eager cock demanding freedom.

"I'm going to have to find an empty stable for a little me time," he muttered.

"Sorry, what did you say?" Rory cooled the final shoe and there was a hiss of steam. Pip wondered if he could pass off his heated skin as the result of his proximity to the quenching barrel.

"Nothing... I mean I was talking, but to the horse. He doesn't like being ignored."

"Ah, I see."

Pip ducked his head so he didn't have to meet Rory's gaze. Pip couldn't lie to save his life — something that had not served him well when making up excuses for late papers at college or with his mother, who could see through his fibs instantly.

Rory straightened up and gave his lower back a rub. "Right, you walk him around the yard so that I can check his gait."

Pip bobbed his head, unlooped the lead rein then did a slow circle. Windy followed, nudging at Pip's shoulder.

"That's good." Rory stood with his hands on his hips.

Pip increased the sway of his hips a little and hoped the comment was for him as well as the horse.

From the corner of his eye, Pip caught a movement. He glanced up to the forge roof.

"Oh no. No, no, no, no, no..."

A squirrel, fluffy tail twitching, stared at him with evil intent in its beady little eyes. Pip held Windy's lead rein a little tighter. The squirrel scampered the length of the roof then took a dive down a drainpipe worthy of any trained stunt animal. It peeked from the pipe opening then shot across the yard, barreling underneath Windy's body. With an outraged neigh, the horse reared, pawing at the air. He turned in a rapid circle, dragging Pip with him. Pip yelled as his wrist was yanked and twisted. It was all he could do to hang on. He couldn't allow the horse to bolt. Windy shunted backward and kicked. His brand new hooves made violent contact with the forge door. Wood splintered and the frame shuddered. The horseshoe fixed above it parted company with its nail and fell with a clang. The noise enraged Windy even more. Pip narrowly avoided flying hooves and tugged on Windy's leading rein. He maneuvered him toward the wall, speaking in soft tones, repeating calming words over and over. His persistence paid off. Windy's eyes stopped rolling and he steadied.

"There, there. What a fuss over nothing. You're okay." He walked Windy to the trough and let him drink, taking the opportunity to check him over. "Not a mark on you. Thank God."

"Are you okay?" Rory's deep voice sounded behind Pip.

He swiveled around. "He's fine. No damage."

"I didn't ask about the horse, Pip, I asked about you."

"Oh. Oh! I'm good. I'm going to get Windy back to his stable and settled." Adrenaline coursed through Pip's system. "Sorry about your door." Pip walked Windy away, taking deep breaths. "Wow, that was close. I'd rather get my thrills some other way, you know."

As he got Windy settled back in his stable with his scheduled bucket of feed, Pip relaxed.

"He cared about me." Realization dawned. "He didn't just see the horse, he saw me too." Pip closed the stable door and bolted it firmly. He winced at the tug on his wrist. He rubbed at the dirt on his skin and flexed his fingers. A closer examination revealed that the joint was swollen and signs of a bruise were beginning to emerge. Registering the damage immediately increased his awareness of pain and a throbbing ache spread up his arm.

"Damn it. I do not need an injury right now. Stupid squirrel." Pip leaned against Windy's stable and a huff of horse breath hit his face.

"I know. You're sorry. It wasn't your fault. Just a stupid accident. Better go and find some ice. Fuck, it's going to be a long day."

Chapter Two

Rory watched Pip disappear around the corner.

"Damn that boy has a fine set of hindquarters. Maybe I should go check he gets that nag stabled safely." Rory sighed. "Nope. He's shy. Don't want to scare him off." He examined the forge door instead. Two central planks were in splinters, which, considering they were made of solid oak, was impressive. Royal Midnight Wind had one hell of a kick on him. "Thank God he didn't make contact with Pip. Sweet little man would have been sent flying halfway across the racetrack."

Rory lifted the door from its hinges and set it against the wall. He fetched some tools and set about making temporary repairs that would last until he could get his hands on some replacement oak. As he hammered a couple of pine planks into place, his mind constantly drifted to Pip's pretty face and slender body. "Gonna need to take a dip in the water trough," he mused as his cock hardened. "Fuck!" Rory cursed up a storm as his hammer connected with his finger instead of the nail he was targeting. "Concentrate, you idiot." He sucked on the throbbing digit and immediately imagined Pip sucking on it instead. Those lush lips needed to be wrapped around appropriate appendages. Losing concentration again, he kicked over his tin of nails.

"Damn it!" There was another delay while he diligently hunted down the nails. If one got left behind to injure a horse, he'd never forgive himself.

He re-hung the door and noticed the missing horseshoe.

"Uh oh. How much bad luck is that going to bring?" He cast around on the ground and found it a few yards away. He brushed some dirt from the metal, enjoying the feel of the rough iron. He'd unearthed the shoe as a kid playing with a metal detector on the outskirts of the racecourse. He could still remember the excitement of rushing into the forge to show his father and how proud he'd been to see it hanging above the door. His dad had even let him hammer in the nail to keep it in place as he'd explained why it was lucky.

Rory rubbed at his battered finger and tried to decide whether or not he was superstitious. He'd walked under several ladders without mishap. The stable cat was a fat, ginger furball, not black. He did recall throwing salt over his shoulder on occasion but his bathroom mirror had been cracked for years and it didn't seem to have had any impact on his life. Surely one dropped horseshoe couldn't be a problem.

He fetched a step stool, grabbed his hammer from the ground then selected a sturdy nail. He kicked the stool into place and climbed up carefully. "If that fucking squirrel makes a reappearance…" Rory glanced around before positioning the horseshoe. He knocked a nail through one of the piercings in the metal and into the wooden doorframe. He tugged on it, making sure it was firmly fixed in place. "That won't come down again in a hurry." Pleased with his work, Rory stepped down from the stool. A stray nail penetrated the sole of his boot, stabbing into his foot. He yelped, lost his balance and tumbled backward, landing heavily on his ass.

"Well fuck it all to hell." Rory rolled back and lay flat out. "Better me than a horse." Above him, on the edge of the forge roof, a small furry face peeked from the guttering. With a flick of its tail and chattering madly, the squirrel scampered away.

* * * *

Cradling his injured wrist, Pip walked around the back of the main stand. He pushed open a door marked 'staff only' then ascended the stairs to the administrative offices. He rarely ventured to this part of the course. The stable hands had their own small break room and shower block so there was no need to venture into the squeaky clean, air-conditioned management suite. However, the accident log had to be completed and the track owner's secretary was a trained first-aider. Pip knew better than to attempt to conceal his injury. Private health cover was one of the main benefits of his job, extended even to the lowly temps, and it depended on accurate reporting.

He peered down at his filthy boots and mud-stained jodhpurs. Something inside his tatty T-shirt scratched his skin. He yanked it up and pulled a sharp stalk of straw out of the cloth.

"Pip Ryder, as I live and breathe. Are you stripping on my stairwell?"

At the affronted exclamation, Pip yanked his shirt down.

"Oh don't cover up on my account, sweetie. I don't get much entertainment up here you know." Iris

Ormerod winked and fluffed her immaculately coiffed French pleat.

Pip's cheeks burned. "Iris, you're shameless!"

"And *you* have dragged half the yard up the stairs." She shook her head and waggled a finger at him. "You young men are all the same. Messy pups, the lot of you."

"Sorry, Iris." Pip hung his head.

"Now I know you didn't come in here just to mess the place up. Come into my office and tell me what you need. Take your boots off first, though."

The advantage of his slip-on boots was that they could be toed off with relative ease. Pip didn't think he would have been able to manage laces and knots because his wrist throbbed in earnest and the joint was getting stiff. He pushed his boots into a neat position against the wall and followed Iris into her office. The room smelt of lavender and beeswax. Every piece of solid oak furniture gleamed. Pip traced the grain of the desktop with his fingertips, enjoying the smooth warmth of the wood.

Iris gave him a critical once over. "So what have you done to yourself? And does it require tea and sympathy?"

The room lurched crazily and pretty little stars flashed before Pip's eyes. "No... I... Oh!" Pip's knees gave and he fell backward...into the embrace of the chair that Iris had swiftly moved into position to catch him. He took a few big gulps of air and dropped his head between his knees, fighting down the urge to vomit. Iris would never forgive him if he threw up on her immaculate carpet. At the very least she'd have him on his hands and knees scrubbing out any stains. *Oh God, where the hell is my mind wandering?* Pip risked raising his head and found that the world had settled back into its proper place.

"You're lucky I've just made a pot." Iris held out a cup of tea. It really was a cup too, with matching saucer. Gold-rimmed and covered in tiny pink roses. Pip reached for it and managed to grasp the saucer firmly. He rested it on his lap so he could use his good hand to lift the cup.

"Ugh! Sugar. Are you trying to kill me, Iris?" He almost spat out the sickly sweet liquid.

Iris snorted. "Drink it up, you ungrateful boy. You need it."

Pip twisted his lips into a grimace but did as he'd been told and swallowed the drink down in a couple of gulps. Iris retrieved her crockery.

"Don't you trust me not to break it, Iris?" Pip said in his best hurt-puppy voice.

"No, I don't. Now, I suppose I need to dig out the accident log?"

"I'm afraid so." Pip extended his swollen wrist. "One of the horses tried to get away from me. Damn near dislocated it."

"Oh my goodness. I think you might have to take a trip to the casualty department. Or should I be calling it the ER these days?"

"That won't be necessary. Honestly. It's just a sprain — there's nothing broken. The swelling will go down in a few days, I just need to get some ice on it."

"And who made you a doctor?" Iris added the date in the first column of the accident book.

"Not a doctor, but I *am* a qualified vet, Iris. I do know a bit about sprains and strains. Seriously, don't worry. I'll be fine." He distracted Iris by imparting the details of his tussle with Royal Midnight Wind. She wrote everything down, frowning all the while.

"Calvin, that useless waste of space. There's no way he should have handed that horse over to you. He knows full well how difficult to handle that one can be."

"It was all the squirrel's fault really, Iris." Pip batted his eyelashes shamelessly. "Could I have another cup of tea?"

Muttering under her breath, Iris sorted out a second cup, without sugar this time.

"Sit there and drink it while I go and find a cold pack. I think the first-aid kit stretches to something a bit better than a bag of frozen peas."

While Pip waited for Iris to return, his thoughts drifted to Rory. The big farrier was absolutely gorgeous. "So far out of my league he might as well be on another continent," Pip sighed. "Still, there's no law against dreaming about all those flexing muscles." Rory had shown such affinity for Windy, every touch firm but gentle. "What I wouldn't give for him to touch me like that."

Pip was away with the fairies, lost in his daydreaming when Iris came back. She jolted him out of his thoughts by wrapping his wrist in a freezing cold pack.

"The gel in this thing should stay cold for a good couple of hours. Long enough to take the swelling down a bit. No more work for you today, Pip. How are you getting home?"

Pip sighed as the soothing cold penetrated his limb. "I've got my bike, Iris. Oh damn! I'm supposed to be going out with Carrie tonight too."

"Carrie will understand and I'm going to run you home in the car. You definitely aren't safe to be on the road with that injury. Let me grab my purse and we'll go and find all the people we need to let know that you're leaving. I want to have a word with Calvin before we go."

Pip decided on a course of self-preservation that involved nodding and making sounds of assent. Iris on a roll was not to be trifled with. An hour and a half later, Pip was comfortably ensconced in his lounge, dosed up on painkillers and giggling at the pleasant memory of Iris scolding Calvin while he'd done a fair impression of a guppy. Pip dozed for a bit and let the drugs do their work. Once the pain had faded sufficiently, he dragged himself into the shower to wash away the scent of manure and sweaty horse.

By the time he was dry and had struggled into an ancient T-shirt and faded sweats, his wrist had begun to ache again. The doorbell interrupted his mental debate between television and an early night. Pip groaned. "No! I am so not fit for company right now." He dragged himself down the hall and opened the door anyway. Carrie marched past him.

"Look at the state of you! How are you ever going to snag a bloke dressed like that?"

Bewildered, Pip closed the door and followed Carrie to the kitchen. A tantalizing aroma drifted in her wake.

"Either you've invested in an ultra-modern new perfume or you have fish and chips in that bag."

"Full marks for observation. I came to the conclusion that gay or not, you're still a bloke and therefore incapable of taking care of yourself when not completely healthy."

"Unbelievable. Stereotyping like that should be against the law. Not all men are hopeless patients."

"So tell me what you were planning on having for dinner?" Carrie grabbed two plates from the draining board and began to unwrap the slightly greasy paper packages.

Pip's face heated. "Um...beans on toast?"

Carrie pulled open a cupboard. She rummaged amongst the scant selection of tins and extracted the empty wrapper of a sliced loaf. "Well as you have no bread and no beans, that would have been a challenge."

"I just haven't had time to go shopping." Pip's attempt to defend himself and, by association, men in general, ranked as pathetic at best.

Carrie raised a disbelieving eyebrow. "Make yourself useful and find the ketchup. You do have ketchup?"

Pip sighed. The thought of fish and chips was enough to defeat any idea he might have had of throwing Carrie out on her ear. His kitchen was far too small for a table and chairs so they took their meal through to the lounge and sat in front of the telly, plates balanced on their knees.

"Will you be able to carry on working?" Carrie asked around a mouthful of chips.

"Don't have much choice." Pip shrugged. "I really need the money. I'll have to buy a car before I start my new job and I haven't been able to save very much yet. I only want an old banger. Something that I won't need a loan for. It only has to last six months. Once I've passed probation my new practice will prove transport." He crunched on a piece of batter, savoring the greasy delight. "This is sooo good!"

"Tell me I'm the best friend ever," Carrie demanded.

"You're the best friend ever."

"I might be able to help out with the transport situation. My brother's heading off on a round-the-world trip and he wants to sell Daisy to help towards the cost of the ticket."

"Daisy?"

"His Mini. It's white with a giant yellow flower painted on the roof. It would suit you down to the ground and he's not asking very much. It runs fine."

"Carrie, could you explain while you feel a car with a flower painted on it would 'suit me'?"

She waggled a chip at him. "It's small, like you. It's temperamental. Also like you. And it needs higher than average lubrication." She grinned.

Pip threw a burnt piece of batter at her. "Cheeky cow."

"All I said was that it burns oil a bit too fast. It was your pervy mind that turned it into something else. And on the subject of pervy minds, a little bird told me that you spent time with Rory Ironstone today."

"Who?" Pip feigned ignorance knowing that it would do him no good. Carrie rolled her eyes.

"Six feet six-ish, muscles on his muscles, gorgeous... Am I ringing any bells yet? Attaches shoes to horses. That should be a big enough clue even for you. Now leave off and dish the dirt! I've paid in advance with your supper."

Pip instantly lost his appetite. His stomach tightened into a knot and his mouth dried enough that his tongue stuck to the roof of his mouth.

"It was nothing. Just work. He barely noticed I was there."

"That's not what I hear." Carrie smirked.

"Who have you been talking to? Not Iris... So it must have been Calvin. Surely you don't believe a word that worm says?"

"Not usually, but in this case the green-eyed monster was showing its face so I decided he might actually be telling the truth for once."

Pip wanted to remain aloof and show no interest, but he couldn't help himself. "So what did he say? Did Rory mention me?"

"He gave Calvin a bollocking for putting you at risk. Half the yard heard him apparently. Calvin reckoned there would be no way he'd be that bothered unless he wanted to get in your pants."

Pip licked his lips nervously, tasting salt and vinegar. He wondered what Rory would taste like. "I'd love him to get in my pants."

Carrie giggled.

"Did I say that out loud?"

"You did. Not that I blame you. Rory is grade-A beefcake in anyone's book."

"He's not a piece of meat, Carrie," Pip reprimanded.

Carrie ignored him. "Do you think his dick is in proportion to his body? Wow. You'll be walking bow-legged once he's had his way with you."

"Carrie!"

"Don't pretend you're imagining holding hands and skipping off into the sunset, Pip Ryder. I know you too well."

Pip groaned. "And on that note… Thank you for supper, it was lovely but I'm going to bed. The painkillers are making me a bit woozy."

"More like you want to snuggle down and dream of Rory's enormous—"

"Out!" Pip hustled Carrie toward the front door. He gave her a one-armed hug. "I'll see you at the yard tomorrow. I might need you to hide me from Calvin. He's bound to give me the most painful jobs to do."

"I've got your back, honey. Leave him to me. Oh, and I'll come by and give you a lift in. I know you left your bike at the yard." Carrie grinned as she waved and walked away.

Pip shook his head, glad that she was on his side.

Pip ignored the mess of chip papers in the kitchen and dragged himself up the stairs. He hadn't invented his fatigue—he really was exhausted. It wasn't just the downward slide from the adrenaline rush or the pain from his injury. Months of intensive study, then his finals, followed by an immediate return to hard physical labor at the yard had combined to take their toll. He shivered and decided to keep his comfy old clothes on in bed. After quickly scrubbing his teeth, he slipped beneath the covers, grateful for his old-fashioned sheets and blankets combination. Donated by his grandma, the beige wool wasn't exactly the height of fashion, but it did keep him toasty warm. Pip wriggled around until he found a position that was comfortable for his injured wrist then closed his eyes. The darkness was soothing. His sigh was more of relief than contentment as he drifted into his dreams.

Chapter Three

Rory stretched and listened to the pops as his vertebrae realigned. He groaned his relief. All morning he'd dealt with a steady procession of highly strung customers, and that was just the grooms. In the main, the horses were no trouble at all. The resident stable lads worked their arses off to keep everything running smoothly but with a major race meeting the following day there was an atmosphere of mild panic. Normally, Rory enjoyed all the frantic activity that came with a stable block bursting at the seams but today, nothing was going right.

Though he had a sweet thatched cottage in the nearby village of Nether Wapping, conveniently next door to the Nag's Head, Rory had elected to spend the previous night in the tiny bedsit above the forge. It was serviceable enough and he usually slept on site when there was a race meeting because of the extra-long working days. There was a bed, kitchenette and a tiny shower room. That was it. Nothing luxurious but adequate for Rory's needs.

Usually, everything functioned perfectly. That morning had been a complete car crash.

"Should be against the law to start the day without coffee," Rory muttered. He'd set the percolator going while he'd got in the shower. There had been no hot water, so he'd shivered through a freezing wash then toweled down in a frenzied half-dance as he'd attempted to get warm. Just as he'd stepped through the door to the main room, the coffee pot had exploded, sending shards of glass and lukewarm coffee everywhere. The previously plain, whitewashed walls had gained an interesting abstract pattern in what Dulux would probably name Mocha Kiss or some such nonsense.

Hunger ensured the clear-up was somewhat cursory. Then, his normally reliable toaster had seen fit to convert his bread into something resembling charcoal and there had been no time to get anything else. Then the rain had started.

Rory gazed up at a malevolent gray sky. "Gonna be a downpour sooner or later." So far the rain had been limited to a light but steady shower. Enough to make everyone damp and grumpy but not enough to delay his appointments. The horses didn't seem to mind getting wet but the grooms were loath to stand in the rain to hold their charges still when there was a warm forge to shelter in. As a result, Rory had been shoved and nudged. He had a bruised shoulder from unexpected contact with a wall and a scuffed knee from a jerking hoof. He was cold, wet and hungry. His arms and thighs ached.

Rory hung his 'Back Soon' sign on a convenient nail then went inside, sliding the forge doors closed behind him. There were tins of soup upstairs in the flat. "Surely

I can manage to heat a bowl of minestrone and cut some bread without doing too much damage."

He stomped up the wooden staircase, impatient for food and a mug of hot tea. There was a loud crack. Rory's weight shifted as the stair beneath him gave way. He got a great view of the ceiling as he toppled backwards. The world spun in crazy circles. His arse made contact with unyielding wood and he tumbled down the short flight in a mess of flailing limbs. His head hit the flagged floor and after a brief moment of blinding pain and intense white light, everything went black.

* * * *

Arriving at the racetrack in Carrie's battered but surprisingly comfortable Volvo estate, Pip wondered if he could just spend the day hiding out in the car.

"I'm sure nobody would notice if I showed my face for the morning meeting then disappeared again," he said.

"You wish," Carrie replied without sympathy. "After yesterday, Calvin will have his beady little eyes fixed on you, for sure. Now get out of the car or we'll be late."

"But it's raining."

"No, really? I hadn't noticed." Sarcasm dripped from every word. Carrie got out of the car and slammed the door shut. She stomped around to Pip's side and yanked his door open. "Out."

Pip levered himself up, taking care not to put any weight on his injured wrist. He had it well strapped but it was still painful, something he hadn't confessed to Carrie. If he didn't work, he didn't get paid. Simple as that. He followed Carrie to the small break room shared by the stable lads and grooms. Bill, the head lad, was about to divvy out the morning's chores. It always seemed odd to Pip that a man in his forties should still be referred to as a 'lad' but that was the way it worked. Bill was a good guy, fair and hard working. He rotated the worst jobs whereas Calvin who occasionally stood in for him always picked on Pip.

Just as Bill started speaking, the door swung open and Iris strolled in.

"Morning, Iris, something I can do for you?" Bill asked with a lecherous grin.

"In your dreams, sunshine," Iris snapped, though her lips quirked into a smile. "But you can loan me Pip for the day. I have a huge mailing to get out and I need someone to stick labels on envelopes."

"Is that all right with you, Pip?"

Pip was amazed Bill had asked at all. He nodded. "Of course."

"Off you go then."

Pip scurried after Iris before his luck changed.

"Do you really have a mailing to deal with Iris?" Pip asked once they'd got outside.

She chuckled. "Actually, I do. I don't need any help but I guessed you wouldn't do the sensible thing and take the day off. This is my good deed for the year. There's no way you should be wielding a pitchfork or pushing barrows with that injury."

"I should pretend to be all tough and manly," Pip said. "But I can't tell you how grateful I am. My bloody wrist is killing me."

Iris shook her head. "Men."

Pip spent a couple of hours helping Iris. He was warm, dry and Radio 2 played undemanding music in the background. Iris chatted away as she went about her work, and Pip got the feeling she was glad of some company. They stopped for coffee and Pip took the opportunity to take in the view of the racecourse. There were no horses out but ground staff beetled around checking everything for the weekend's race meeting. The rain fell steadily and Pip's view was obscured with a gray haze. His mind drifted and he wondered what Rory was up to.

"How long has there been a forge here, Iris?"

"Longer than the racecourse, I believe. The smithy was built originally because we are on an ancient route between the Midlands and London, so there was plenty of passing trade. The course was laid down in the early nineteenth century but the forge didn't become part of the stable yard until the expansion in the 1960s. Rory's dad ran it then and I believe it had been in his family for a few generations before that. He has smithying in his blood, that boy."

"Was his dad a farrier too?" Pip didn't want to seem too interested in Rory alone.

"No, that's a first for Rory. He did his apprenticeship somewhere else and picked up his farrier skills there. It's a useful sideline. If he couldn't do it, we'd have to buy someone in and good farriers don't grow on trees."

"He'll be busy today," Pip said, almost to himself.

"He will. Why don't you take him a mug of coffee and some of my homemade cookies?" Iris gestured to a brightly colored tin next to the kettle. "I'm sure he'd appreciate that."

Pip took note of Iris' knowing smile and sighed. It seemed that he couldn't manage to keep his interest in Rory secret from anyone. Taking him a drink was harmless enough, though.

Balancing a mug of coffee on top of the cookie tin, Pip made his precarious way from the office, across the yard to the forge. Miraculously, both he and the coffee remained the correct way up.

"Damn." The forge door was closed and Rory's 'Back Soon' sign was in view. Pip debated whether or not to give up and leave. Maybe Rory didn't want to be disturbed. "I'm here now." He put his cargo on the floor and slid open one door, peering into the dim interior cautiously. He couldn't see or hear Rory.

"Hello?" There was no answer. "I'll just leave the cookies somewhere he'll find them." Pip collected the tin, leaving the coffee mug on the doorstep. He took a couple of paces inside, glancing around for a good place to put his offering.

"Oh my God! Rory!" Pip spotted Rory's prone form at the bottom of a set of wooden stairs. He abandoned the cookie tin on the nearest available surface and rushed across to him. He might be a vet not a doctor, but he still knew the basics of what to do. He checked for a pulse and to his relief it was there, nice and strong. He did a visual check for injuries but couldn't see anything obvious. Rory was breathing fine and his position didn't put him at risk of a constricted airway. Pip got up. He didn't have a mobile and the nearest phone was in the offices. He needed to call an ambulance but he didn't want to leave Rory alone. Shouting for help would work. Decision made, he headed for the door but a groan from behind him had him rushing back to Rory's side.

"Fuck, my head hurts." Rory's eyes flickered open. "Pip, is that you?"

"You should keep still, you might have broken bones."

"No, I'm bashed not broken." Rory heaved himself into a sitting position and leaned against his broken staircase. "Ouch."

Pip dropped to his knees. "Take it slow. You were unconscious. You might have a head injury." He grasped Rory's skull and probed gently, feeling for lumps. Rory kept absolutely still and didn't protest.

"I think I like you playing doctor," he said.

"I'm a vet and you have a nice goose egg back here."

"My foot went straight through the stair. The board must have been rotten. It's always been a bit creaky. There's nothing broken."

"You're lucky you didn't break your neck. It's a good job I came by."

"All my luck fell out the damn horseshoe. I'm grateful, but why *are* you here?" Rory got to his feet, towering over Pip who remained on his knees staring distractedly at Rory's denim wrapped crotch. "Pip?"

"Sorry? I... What did you say?"

Rory chuckled, the sound deep and warm.

"Why are you here?"

"Oh... I brought cookies." Pip gestured vaguely in the direction of the tin. "I knew you'd be busy today and Iris thought you might like a snack and she bakes the most amazing..." Pip lost track of his thoughts again. Rory's bulge was growing, he was certain. "Oh God. If you're sure you're okay, I should go."

"I'm fine but..."

Pip didn't catch the rest of the sentence. He couldn't think straight. He needed to get away and sort out the confusing mixture of emotions flooding through him. He launched himself through the door, kicked over the mug of coffee he'd left on the step and skidded over the rolling crockery. He fell forward and automatically put out his hands to break his fall. His injured wrist gave way on contact with the ground and he skidded along, scraping the skin from palms and knees. The pain was shockingly vicious. Tears rolled down his face. He got up then ran with no particular destination in mind.

He ended up sitting in the space beneath the main grandstand. It was damp, and a bit smelly, but he was alone.

"What the hell am I doing? I'm a grown man not some pathetic kid. What an idiot." He cradled his aching wrist. "I'm letting my imagination run away with me. There's no way on this planet that a man like Rory could ever find me appealing, especially as I just ran out on him." The rustle of grass and unsubtle throat clearing had Pip peeking from his hiding place.

"What exactly do you think you're doing under there, Pipsqueak?"

Pip groaned. "Calvin."

"Get your arse out here."

It was raining even harder. Calvin's hair clung to his face in soggy tendrils but he was wearing waterproofs, which was more than Pip had. His own clothes were soaked through and clinging to his skin.

"I needed a few minutes…"

"Bollocks," Calvin snapped. "I saw where you came from. Did he hurt you?" He took a step toward Pip, and Pip moved back.

"What? Who?"

"Rory. Did he hurt you?"

"Of course he didn't… Why do you even care, Calvin?" Pip's confusion grew by the second.

"You ran out of the forge like your arse was on fire, took a header and then ignored my shouting at you to come back. I followed you because…because I was worried about you." He sounded defensive.

"Oh." Pip had no idea what to say. Calvin had never been nice to him. Ever. "I'm fine. Honestly."

"You like him, don't you?" Calvin made it sound like an accusation.

"I…um… Yes?"

"I knew it. Bloody hell. No wonder you never gave me a second glance."

"You?" Pip snapped his mouth shut when he realized it was hanging open.

"Yes me! Is that so bloody surprising?"

"Well, yes. You never said anything. You always give me the crappiest jobs. How was I supposed to know you liked me?"

"I couldn't show any favoritism. Jesus, your gaydar must be shot to pieces." Calvin scrubbed his hands through his wet hair. "He likes you too, you know."

"Who?"

"Oh my God! Are you being deliberately obtuse? I thought you were supposed to be intelligent. Rory, of course."

"He does?"

"He watches your every move and yesterday he tore a strip off me because you hurt your wrist handling Royal Midnight Wind."

"Wasn't your fault." Pip chewed on his lip. "Are you sure he likes me?"

Calvin rolled his eyes. "Why would he be so protective if he didn't? He's probably searching for you right now. Get back to the forge and tell him how you feel."

"I don't think that's a good idea."

"It's a *great* idea. I had it. Now move that cute arse of yours before I'm forced to drag you back to the yard kicking and screaming."

Pip took a couple of reluctant steps, feeling like a complete idiot. Calvin followed right behind him. Pip looked back and frowned.

"If you think I'm going to let you run off again, you're very much mistaken," Calvin growled. "Rory will blame me if you disappear and he could crush me like a bug. I'd prefer to stay intact, thank you very much."

Pip sighed and bowed to the inevitable. He trudged back around the stand, trying to think up some kind of viable, sane reason for his behavior. Nothing came to mind.

"Rory's going to think I'm some kind of nut job," he muttered.

"Well, he wouldn't be wrong. Maybe he can kiss some sense into you or something. Oh fuck, talk of the devil..."

Rory marched toward them, hands clenched into fists. "Calvin, if you've been bullying him, I'm going to introduce your nose to my fist."

Pip got in between Rory and Calvin.

"I'm fine, Rory. Calvin was just trying to talk some sense into me." He placed his palm against Rory's broad chest and hummed his approval of the rock hard muscle. Rory grabbed Pip's hand and kissed the palm.

"Get a damn room, you two!" Calvin backed away rapidly. "I'll expect you back at work tomorrow, Pipsqueak, and there'll be no more hiding in the office, either."

Pip yelped as Rory swept him off his feet and carried him back to the forge. The whole over-protective caveman thing that Rory had going on heated Pip's blood and stiffened his cock, despite the freezing downpour. He closed his eyes and enjoyed the ride.

Chapter Four

Pip let the warmth of the forge wash over him, drawing some of the chill out of his bones. His wet clothes steamed.

"What on earth were you doing running away like that?" Rory asked as he pulled the door shut.

Even that simple act of keeping out the weather seemed caring and protective to Pip. "I don't know. You were okay and I... I just... I have no idea what I was doing." Pip's teeth chattered.

"I think you gave me my luck back and lost your own. You need someone to take care of you, Pip Ryder."

Pip shivered and not from the cold. It was too much to hope for that Rory might want to keep him.

"Let's get you out of that wet top before you catch your death."

Pip lifted his arms so that Rory could peel the sodden cloth from Pip's chilled skin.

"I have an old sweater here somewhere." Rory rummaged through some coats and aprons hanging on a row of forged hooks and pulled out a voluminous

Arran jumper. "Perfect. It might be a bit itchy against your skin but it will warm you up. Take off your jeans."

"What?" Pip's brain was having trouble keeping up.

"Wet denim stays cold for ages. Get them off. Or do you need me to help you?" Rory leered and Pip was glad he could pass off his flushed face as a result of the open furnace. He kicked off his boots then squirmed and wriggled out of the clingy trousers. Once free, he stood there in his thick woolen socks and a jumper that came to his knees and smelled of Rory.

"Well, aren't you adorable?"

Pip stuck out his lower lip in an exaggerated pout. "I'm wearing a woolly tent. That is so far from adorable."

"Not to me. And if I didn't have some work I needed to finish this afternoon, I'd have you up those stairs and in my bed quicker than you could say 'bottom fuller'."

Pip's eyes widened. "Huh?"

Rory grinned. "It fits into the tool hole of the anvil. Top and bottom fullers are used for setting down shoulders in preparation for forging tenons and for drawing or moving metal in one direction."

"I have no idea what you're talking about." Pip wanted to wrap himself around Rory's sturdy body and hold on tight. Instead he perched on a stool and examined his surroundings. "Tell me what it's like. To be a blacksmith, I mean. I can see you don't just make horseshoes."

"You really want to know?"

Pip loved the eagerness in Rory's tone.

"I do. Is there much interest from outside the racing circuit?"

"There is. Business is booming in fact. I'm trendy, apparently." He laughed. "Folk want hand-crafted artisan stuff rather than mass-produced tat." He pulled a heavy leather apron from a peg and pulled it over his head. "Some smiths go into architectural design—they make fences, window bars, hardware, that kind of thing. I do a bit of that, mainly on commission. I make some replica weapons for film companies and re-enactment groups." He pointed at a shelf where a set of lethal, pointed shapes sat in a row. "Pike heads for the local civil war society."

Pip's head filled with weapon related innuendoes but he kept his lips firmly clamped together.

"It's not all sweat and fire these days either. I use computer software programs for creating designs and I have contemporary welding kit, a laser cutter and power hammers. Some blokes prefer the traditional methods but you get great results with more modern techniques."

Pip licked his lips. "I'll bet you're good with a power hammer... Oh! I didn't mean to say that out loud!"

Rory grinned. "Well, I'd be happy to give you a demonstration. I need to get this job done then I'm all yours." He picked up some tongs, grasped a bar of metal and thrust it into the heat. "I need to get this pliable enough to work."

Pip watched in fascination as Rory heated the metal until it glowed, then twisted it in a vice. An hour of heat and manipulation with various scary tools followed before Rory was satisfied. Pip gaped at the end result— a forged candleholder in the rough abstract shape of a rearing horse.

Rory set his work aside. "It's one of a mismatched set. They'll be similar but not the same, that's part of the joy of working metal this way. Every piece is unique."

"It's stunning," Pip said.

"Like you." Rory pulled him from his stool. With a work-roughened hand on either side of Pip's head, he kissed him.

Pip's legs turned to jelly. His heart thumped and his cock jerked. Rory was gentle but persistent, taking charge of the kiss in a way that sent ripples of delight down Pip's spine. When Rory finally released him, Pip gasped for air.

"Wow!"

"Wow indeed."

Rory moved his hands to Pip's arse, cupping his cheeks and lifting him effortlessly. Pip wrapped his legs around Rory's body and held on as he was transported up the stairs and lowered onto the bed.

Pip shuffled as close to the safety of the headboard as he could get. Rory stripped off his leather apron, then his shirt. Pip couldn't hold back his grin at the sight of Rory's lightly furred chest and the fascinating trail of hair that lead downward. Rory's pecs twitched, making Pip giggle.

"I can't take it anymore, Pip, I've gotta have you. You feel something too, right?" Rory asked.

Pip nodded enthusiastically. "Oh yes."

Rory kicked off his boots and yanked down his trousers. He wasn't wearing anything underneath.

"Oh. My. God." Pip gaped. He scrambled out of his borrowed jumper, socks and underwear. He lay back against the pillows and tried to relax, but when Rory knelt across him, his massive erection prodding Pip's thigh, he couldn't restrain a twitch.

"Relax, Pip." Rory stroked Pip's skin as if he was the tiniest kitten, and Pip responded with a purr.

Rory brushed the back of his fingers across Pip's taught stomach. He moved Pip's injured arm so that it rested on the pillow next to his head. "Don't want to jog your wrist." He resumed stroking but went nowhere near Pip's cock, and Pip wanted to scream at him in frustration. Slowly he moved closer, rubbing Pip's inner thighs.

Rory wetted his thumbs and began to agitate Pip's nipples. Pip arched his back and moaned. Rory chuckled his amusement. "Like that, huh?" He replaced his thumbs with his tongue and the gentle nipping of even white teeth. His stubble scraped against Pip's skin, making him buck ecstatically. Finally, he reached down between Pip's legs and grasped his throbbing dick.

"Oh! Holy crap!"

Two strokes, maybe three, and Pip came all over Rory's hand, shuddering and gasping from the sheer pleasure of it. He barely had time to recover before Rory rolled onto his back and positioned Pip so that he straddled Rory's lap.

"I'm big enough to hurt you, Pip. Are you sure about this?"

Pip nodded frantically.

Rory twisted to the side, reached under the bed then produced lube and a condom. "Use plenty and take your time." Rory grasped Pip's hips but he applied no pressure.

Pip freed one of Rory's hands and squeezed clear gel onto his fingers. "Stretch me?"

Pip's dick was only half-hard again, but as Rory penetrated his ass with a single, slick finger it managed a jerk of delight. It hurt a little but not enough to stop Pip nodding his assent to a second digit. Rory cupped Pip's ass with his other hand, and Pip fucked himself on Rory's fingers, slowly at first then faster.

"Feels so good!"

Pip had no idea how his body was ever going to accommodate Rory's massive cock, but he couldn't wait any longer. He tugged Rory's fingers free then spent a few happy moments tormenting him as he slicked lube up and down Rory's latex-clad length. Rory returned the favor by smoothing more gel around Pip's hole.

"Take your time, baby." Rory gave Pip an encouraging smile.

Pip spread his knees wide and sank down until he could feel the blunt head of Rory's cock nudging his entrance. The first inch wasn't too bad. Pip moved a bit quicker and gasped at the pain caused by the next two. "Hurts!"

"We can stop any time you want, Pip."

There was no way in hell Pip was going to stop. He panted, relaxed his muscles as best as he could then slowly sank down. For what seemed like hours but was probably just a few seconds, Pip couldn't move.

"So full!" He gazed into Rory's stormy eyes.

Rory seemed in pain too, and Pip realized belatedly that just lying there must be agonizing for him. Pip's muscles refused to work. He tapped Rory's hands on his hips, and Rory took the hint, raising and lowering Pip in slight increments. Pip shuddered as the delicate bundle of nerves inside him was agitated. Rory growled. He began to lift Pip further, then lowered him faster so that his arse hit Rory's thighs with a slap.

Once the initial burn had faded, Pip could enjoy the intense pleasure that replaced it. He screamed, laughed and cried, letting Rory control the ride. As Rory came, he gripped Pip's cock and squeezed. With a cry, Pip came again, the release emotional as well as physical.

Rory's dick softened inside Pip as he snuggled into Rory's chest.

"Are you okay?" Rory murmured.

"Mmm," was the only response Pip could manage.

Eventually, Rory carefully withdrew, disposed of the condom then cleaned them both up. He got back into bed and pulled the covers over them, holding Pip close.

"Did you know that the horseshoe's luck may have something to do with its connection to the animal itself?" Pip asked sleepily.

"My dad always told me that it was partly to do with the crescent shape and partly to do with the iron because it was thought to be a magical material. Blacksmiths were believed to be magicians with supernatural abilities. It was said that iron could ward off demons and witches, and horseshoes were often hung on people's front doors for that reason."

"Well there is something magical about your iron rod, that's for sure." Pip giggled.

Rory gave him a light smack on the arse and he gasped.

"Oh, like that do you?"

Pip shook his head but it was an obvious lie. He tried for a change of subject. "Horse-worship was common practice amongst the early Celts." Pip tried to focus on his story but the warmth blooming on his skin was too distracting.

"Did you know there's quite an active market for ironwork with the BDSM community?" Rory's voice was all innocence.

Pip gulped. "You're not into all that kinky stuff are you?" He wriggled into Rory's touch as his arse was caressed.

"Not really, but I wouldn't mind seeing you in a set of handmade irons. Naked. Helpless to resist me."

"Oh my God!" Pip's mind filled with visuals that made him ache to be filled again. "You wouldn't…would you?"

"Oh I definitely would if this how it makes you react." Rory grasped Pip's soft dick and squeezed.

"You too sore for another go round when we've both recovered?"

"Not sore. Achy. Need you in me, Rory."

"Then it's definite. My luck is well and truly back in."

JUST MY LUCK

Ethan Stone

Dedication

Sue you are an amazing and strong woman. I'm
glad you're in my life.

Chapter One

I wasn't exactly sure why I was at the club. Well, I *did* know, but I wasn't sure why I felt the need to get laid on my first night in a new town, especially when I started my new job the next day. Regardless, there I was, at CC Slaughters observing men of various ages and sizes bumping and grinding to the beat of the techno-club music.

After finishing off my whiskey, I ordered another one from the cute, young bartender who handed it to me and winked.

"Here ya go, cowboy."

My dark, wide-brimmed hat set me apart from everyone else in the bar. Living in a large, metropolitan city was new for me, a necessary part of advancing in my career. I could've ditched the hat and boots to fit in more with the crowd, however I had never hidden who I was and wasn't about to start now. Well, I did hide certain aspects of my life but that went with the job.

Stepping away from the bar, I approached the crowd, still keeping a distance. I took a sip and leaned against the wall. Most of the guys were younger than me but that didn't stop my ogling. Younger men weren't usually my type, but after several years with a man five years my elder, I craved something different.

Not that I was looking for a relationship, not at all. One night was all I wanted. A 'Welcome to Portland' present for me before I started what could be an intense and time-consuming job. However, it had to be just the right man.

I knew it the second I spotted him. He was a smaller man, couldn't have been more than five feet tall. He moved with a smooth, graceful quality that entranced me instantly. At first he was dancing with a small group of women he was clearly friends with, then a guy with blond hair slid in behind my brunet stud. The object of my affection spun around, noticed the intruder, and glared at the guy so strongly it stopped the guy in his tracks. My guy waved him off. The other dude dropped his chin to his chest and sulked away.

The interaction made me laugh. The guy obviously knew what he wanted. The question was whether I was his type or not. He peeled off his sweaty T-shirt and the disparities between the two of us couldn't have been more pronounced. In addition to the foot and a half height difference between us, I was as hairy as he was smooth. I had wide shoulders and a chest that tapered down to muscular abs. His upper body and torso were flat. The distinctions just made me want him more.

After gulping down the whiskey for a bit of liquid courage, I took a deep breath and pressed into the crowd. I kept an eye on my target but froze when a guy with several tattoos stepped up to him. I refused to let it stop me—I pushed forward until I was right where I wanted to be.

I slid between the new guy and the man I'd targeted. The inked man objected but I stared him down until he slunk away. It took a minute before the short stud turned and realized he had a new dancing partner. His eyes were level with my chest and they widened as he took me in, scanning upward until meeting mine.

A smile formed on his lips and quickly became a wide grin. "Damn." His eyes glazed over in what I hoped was attraction.

I shifted closer and he didn't move away. We danced in rhythm to the beat, our bodies coming closer until they touched. He turned and I put my hands on his hips, pulling him against me. I was hard as a rock in my tight blue jeans, there was no doubt that he had to feel it. Apparently, he didn't mind because he kept dancing. The skin contact invigorated me, sending tingles throughout my body and creating gooseflesh on my skin. I trailed a finger down his arm, then up again. I brushed my lips across the back of his neck and he shivered in response. God, touching him was a thrill. I craved more. Wanted to do stuff we couldn't do on the dance floor.

He stopped moving, and I tried to hide my disappointment.

"Buy me a drink?"

"Hell, yeah." I took his hand and pulled him with me off the dance floor, not taking the chance that someone else would step in on the guy I planned on taking home with me. There was an empty table with two seats so I headed straight for it, scaring off a couple guys who almost got there before us with a scowling side glance and a flex of my muscles. "What are you drinking?" I asked when he sat.

"Cherry vodka and Red Bull."

"Okay, I'll be right back." I stopped and turned around. "Don't go anywhere."

He chuckled. "Don't worry, I won't."

The bar was crowded but I pushed through until I caught the attention of the twink who'd served me earlier.

"Hey, cowboy, what can I get you?"

"Another whiskey, and a cherry vodka Red Bull."

A minute later, he handed me the drinks. I gave him a ten and five and told him to keep the change. I was feeling generous.

As I returned to the table, I spotted a guy in my seat, talking to my man. When I got there I glared at him and growled just a bit. Apparently it was enough to scare the dude because he took off without a word. I handed the brunet his drink and he giggled.

"What?" I asked.

"Did you just growl?"

My face heated. "Sorry."

"Don't be. It was kind of sexy."

I sipped my whiskey, enjoying the way it warmed my body. "I'm Sam."

"Kieran," he replied.

"Beautiful name for a beautiful man."

"Oh, a flatterer."

"Just speaking the truth." I put my elbows on the table and leaned forward. "I mean it, you're gorgeous."

He blushed as if he didn't often hear compliments. Then his face turned serious. "I hope this isn't because of my height."

"Huh?" My brow furrowed.

"Some guys have a fetish for short guys. They call me a *pocket gay*. I've been with a few of them and it's not my thing. I want guys to like me but not just because of my height."

I shook my head. "I understand. I get it because I'm so tall. Don't even start with me on the jokes. I've heard them all."

"It's in reverse for me. My least favorite is, 'How's the weather down there?'"

"Yes! My god, at least be original."

Kieran grinned. "What's a tall person's worst fear?"

"A ceiling fan," I answered.

"What do you call a short guy with three legs?"

I didn't know the answer.

"Horny." Kieran laughed loudly and I did the same. "I hate when guys assume that just because I'm small I *only* bottom. It's not true."

I nodded. "Yeah, I get it too. But I like to bottom as much as topping. Depends on who I'm with."

"So we're both versatile. I think we're going to have a very good time tonight."

I coughed on the drink I'd just taken, set the glass down then wiped the spittle from my face.

"Sorry, was that too forward? I figured we should get to the point. I wanted to fuck you the moment I laid eyes on you on the dance floor. And when I felt your hard-on rubbing my ass...damn that turned me on. Hope you don't mind."

"I don't mind at all. I thought I'd have to work a little harder to seduce you, but I have no problem with being direct." I stood and extended a hand. "You ready to go now?"

He took my hand and pulled me into a mouth-devouring kiss, forcing his tongue past my lips. After breaking the kiss, he pulled out his phone and snapped a photo of me before I could do a thing about it.

"What was that for?"

"I'm about to leave with a man I just met," he replied. "I'm sending it to my friends so if something happens they have your picture. Just a safety measure. You have a problem with that?"

I shrugged. "Not at all. Rather smart, actually."

He followed me to my car and once inside we kissed again. He was one damn fine kisser, gentle with just the right amount of tongue. I carded my fingers through his hair and gently tugged, eliciting a sexy moan from Kieran. The sound sent a volt of electricity right to my crotch. I wanted to take him right then and there, but doing it someplace other than a car would be far more enjoyable.

"You okay to drive?" he asked.

"Yeah, not even close to drunk."

He rubbed the outline of my cock with his palm. I tugged him closer to deepen the lip-lock but stilled his hand. "Careful, you don't want me to come in my jeans, do you?"

"As sexy as that sounds, I don't want you wasting your load."

"Then you better let me go so we can get to my place." I put the key in the ignition, turned on the car and set the controls to unfog the steamy windows we'd created with the hot embrace.

He sat back and clasped his hands together. "Yes, please hurry. I can't wait to have my wicked way with you."

Thankfully, I didn't live too far away and we arrived ten minutes later. As I walked up to my front door I noticed Kieran texting again.

"Sending my friends your address. Just in case…"

"I got it. Good to know you're safe. I assume you play the same way."

"I have condoms. I don't use them for oral, but I'm fine if you want to. But they're required for any anal sex."

I unlocked the door, allowed him to enter then shut it behind me. "I'm with you."

He attacked me with such vigor that I stumbled backward. Leaning down to kiss him hurt my neck so I grabbed his ass and lifted him up. He was light and it was easy to keep him aloft.

"Damn, that is so sexy," he moaned between kisses. "You're so fucking strong. I don't normally enjoy being with guys who are so big. I don't like being overpowered, but being held by you feels different. You wouldn't hurt me."

"Never. You're stunning. Graceful, smooth, sexy."

He nibbled on my ear and my entire body shivered. I licked and sucked his neck, careful not to leave marks.

"Put me down," he ordered. "I want to be naked. See you naked. I've been imagining it since I first saw you."

I gently set him down then tore off my shirt.

"Oh my god," he murmured and ran a hand through my chest hair. He kissed a pec and caressed a nipple.

"You don't mind the body hair?"

"Hell, no, I love it. So fucking sexy. And your smell. Masculine and musky."

"I stink?" I lifted an arm and tried to get a whiff from my armpit, but didn't smell anything.

"It's just your scent," he said. "Not BO."

I nodded and continued to strip. I leaned against the wall and pulled my boots off before unzipping my pants and yanking them down. I felt self-conscious with Kieran peering at me, licking his lips as if I was a piece of meat, desire strong in his gaze. I stepped out of my pants and ran a hand over my chest, down my stomach and to my cock, still hidden in my briefs. Even unseen, my dick was outlined by the cotton.

Kieran inched forward and lightly caressed my length. He dropped to his knees then looked up, meeting my gaze as he pulled my briefs down until they were at my ankles. My dick angled out less than an inch from Kieran's mouth. Our eyes remained locked as he gripped my dick and brought it forward to his lips. I nearly lost it when he wrapped his mouth over my wide, flared head and sucked it in.

I ran my fingers through his messy brown hair and fought the urge to thrust forward. His tongue felt magical on the underside of my shaft. The suction was tight but not too tight. He was playing with me, not out to get me off. I was okay with that—I wasn't ready to come quite yet. Not that I wouldn't be able to get it up a second time, but one of us was going to fuck the other and that was when I wanted to shoot.

He pulled back with a loud slurp and stood. After wiping some saliva off his lips, he opened his pants and dropped them. He was commando so I was treated to the wonderful sight of his length, long and hard with a drip of pre-cum. I grabbed it and stroked once.

"Ohhh," he groaned, closing his eyes and leaning his head back. "Damn, Sam. I haven't been this turned on in a long time."

"Ditto," I replied. It was true, though I couldn't explain it. I lifted him again so I could feel his skin on mine. Our cocks rubbed together, a nice slide and massage. He controlled the kisses, sweeping his tongue into my mouth. I turned so his back was to the wall, allowing me to hold him with one hand on his ass. I caressed the side of Kieran's face with my free hand.

Breaking free from the lip-lock, he breathed heavily in my ear. "I know we had the talk about assuming I was a bottom because I'm short, but…"

"Tonight you want to be fucked?"

"Yes, so much, Sam. I need your dick in my ass."

I exhaled. "Thank god."

Clutching his ass again, I shifted so I could carry him to my bedroom.

"Wait," he said. "Could we do it like this?"

He wanted me to fuck him as we stood. I'd seen it in porn but I'd never done it in real life. "Yeah."

"If you get tired, let me know and we can stop."

"Honestly, Kieran, I don't think it'll be long. I have a feeling that once I'm inside you, I won't be able to hold back."

"I'm on the edge, too. No worries."

"I'll have to set you down to put on a condom."

"No! I don't want to lose the contact." He handed me a foil wrapper he must've grabbed when he'd dropped his pants. "If I wrap my arms around you, can you slip on the rubber?"

I chuckled. "Well, I can try."

He hugged me tightly with his arms and legs and I released him. I opened the package with my teeth and pulled out the lubed condom. It wasn't easy to reach around and slide it on without the benefit of seeing it, but I managed.

"Got lube?"

Keiran shook his head. "Forget it—the condom has some slick on it. It'll be enough. Just go slow." He leaned back against the wall, his hands still clasped behind my neck. He shifted up as I gripped my length, positioning it against the entrance to his small body. I thrust forward as he pressed down, my dick entering him in a snap.

"Oh, damn," he cooed.

I froze, wanting to drive forward, but knew Kieran's body needed time to adjust. I ran one hand down his throat to his chest, stopping to pinch and rub each nipple. Kieran sucked in a breath then exhaled slowly as his body eased, allowing me in further.

I rocked gently until I was fully embedded.

"Shit, Sam, so fucking good. So, so good."

"Hold on, baby. I'm gonna fuck you hard."

Kieran wrapped his arms around my shoulders and buried his face in my neck. I grabbed his ass, lifted him a bit then let gravity bring him back down.

"Oh, fuck yes!" He cried out as I did it again and again. Each time, he slammed down harder on my shaft. His form shook and trembled as I pounded him. Trapped between our bodies, his cock rubbed against my stomach as we fucked, then suddenly his ass clenched my shaft and cum squirted onto my abs.

I tried to hold on, to extend the marvelous sensation of being in Kieran, but it was impossible. A minute after his, my orgasm ripped through me and I shot my load into the condom. All strength left me and I dropped to the floor, careful to land with Kieran on top.

Falling asleep right after sex wasn't cool, but I couldn't keep my eyes open. The last thing I remembered before dozing off was Kieran kissing my neck.

Chapter Two

I inhaled the scent of horses as I strolled around the stables. Horse shit wasn't a pleasant smell for most people, but it reminded me of home and my childhood. The fact that my new job dovetailed with horses was a lucky coincidence. I'd grown up on a farm and started handling horses before first grade. My mother had jokingly called me the Horse Whisperer Kid, but really, the magnificent creatures could sense a person's intentions. At that young age all I'd wanted to do was ride. I adored horses and would've been happy taking over the family farm. However, an incident in my high school senior year had sent me in another direction, with the blessing of my parents.

I would never have imagined my knowledge of equines would come into play with my career, but indeed it had. Not that I knew how every aspect of the job was going to work. Right then, I was on more of a scouting expedition. Checking things out and getting the lay of the land, so to speak.

"Sam? Is that you?"

Hearing my name caused me to freeze. I was new to Portland. Who the hell knew me here? Other than my boss and a few others at the office, there wasn't anyone who knew my name. Well, except for... *No way. No fucking way!* I turned and plastered a smile on my face.

Kieran. What an amazing goddamn coincidence.

"What are you doing here?" He wore a dark polo shirt, tight khakis and boots that went all the way up to his knees. A traditional male horse-riding outfit.

"Ummm..." I wasn't normally such an idiot and usually did know how to think on my feet, but for some reason Kieran had me tongue-tied.

"Did you come here looking for me?"

I chuckled. "Exactly how would I have known you would be here? I don't know your last name or anything about you."

He spread his feet and crossed his arms. "It wouldn't exactly be a stretch for you to assume I'm a jockey. Ware Racing is the biggest in the community. Maybe you decided to check out the stables, hoping to run into me."

So the random guy I'd fucked was connected to Andreas Ware, the reason behind my move. Didn't this shit only happen in romance novels? I hated lying to Kieran, but I couldn't tell him the entire truth. Not yet anyway. "Sorry, but you're not the reason I'm here."

Kieran chuckled. "Good. I wasn't sure if that would be romantic or creepy. I'm leaning more toward creepy and stalkerish."

"Agreed." I chuckled.

"So, why are you here?"

"I'm missing my horses from back home," I replied. "Drove by the stables and decided to check things out."

"Where you from?"

"California. My family has a ranch with horses. Mine is a brown and white paint I named Miko. Miss him like crazy."

"Follow me, I'll show you my baby." He strolled past me, and I remained still for a moment before catching up with him and walking at his side, still a little shocked by the coincidence and unsure how to handle it.

"This is Chestnut Majesty."

The animal was well-named. He was a striking medium-reddish shade of brown and obviously a Thoroughbred. "He's gorgeous." I reached out to pet his forehead but the horse chuffed and stepped back.

Kieran laughed. "He's not the friendliest guy around. He's from excellent breeding stock and he knows it."

"Oh, so he's a cocky guy."

"That's an apt description." Kieran clicked his tongue and reached his hand out. The horse stepped forward and allowed Kieran to stroke him.

"He's yours?" Kieran had to have money if he owned a horse like this one.

"I race him, but my adoptive father is the actual owner."

"Your father is Andreas Ware?" My eyes widened.

"*Adoptive* father," he corrected and his face tensed.

There was a story behind his words and it might work to my advantage, if I told Kieran the *real* reason I was there. However, I couldn't do that quite yet—I needed permission from my boss first.

"Well, I need to get this guy out and work him a bit. I have a race at Portland Meadows next week, the first of a national tour. It's fairly important to Andreas so I have to make sure everything is perfect. You're welcome to watch."

I shook my head. "No, I need to get going." I reached out and stroked his cheek. "Any chance we can see each other again?"

Kieran grinned. "That would be awesome."

"I'll be home tonight. Feel free to drop by." I glanced around to ensure we were alone then leaned forward and kissed him. His lips were soft and I wished I didn't have to stop. I snatched his phone and added in my number. "See you later...I hope."

I left the stables and drove to the Portland Police Bureau—I needed to talk to my boss. When I arrived, FBI Special Agent in Charge Colleen Summers was in the office she had taken over. I knocked on the open door and she looked up from her laptop.

"Hey, Sam, what's going on?"

"You're not going to believe this." I sat across from her and took a deep breath. Colleen knew I was gay but I wasn't thrilled about sharing any details about my personal life. "I met Andreas Ware's adopted son. He's a jockey for Ware."

She leaned back in her seat and crossed her arms. "Do you think you can use him?"

"Well, I might be seeing him again tonight."

She cocked an eyebrow and waited for me to continue.

"I actually slept with him last night, before I knew who he was."

Colleen chuckled. "Is that right?"

I nodded and replied, "Yes. One of those major flukes. I ran into him again when I was checking out Ware's stables."

"Do you think your *personal* relationship will aid us?"

"It's a possibility." I shrugged and scratched my neck. "Depends on how close he is to Ware. I'll play it by ear and see if I think it's safe to tell him the truth about his father."

She steepled her fingers in front of her lips. "I'll leave that up to you, Sam. I trust your judgment. We need to get close to Ware as soon as possible before Saunders Cortez gets his grips on him too strongly."

* * * *

It was around ten when my doorbell rang. I had about given up hope of Kieran coming by and was coming up with a different plan. I answered the door wearing nothing but a pair of silk boxer shorts, not bothering to think what I'd do if it was someone other than Kieran. Luckily, it was.

He started to speak but stopped to check me out, moving his head up and down as he did so.

"Umm, wow." He grinned. "Damn. I lost my train of thought for some reason."

I reached out, yanked him in and forcefully kissed him. He kicked the door shut then jumped up and wrapped his legs around my waist. "Why don't you show me the bedroom this time?"

"As you wish," I said before planting my lips on his again. I carried him to the room then tossed him on the bed. "Get naked, Kieran."

He licked his lips and tore off his clothes.

"Beautiful," I murmured. "Freaking gorgeous." I dove between his legs, licked under his balls, up the length of his shaft and traced the thick head.

"Oh, yes," Kieran groaned.

I stroked his cock a few times before swallowing around it, making him cry out again. He reached out and entwined his fingers in my hair, pushing me down as he arched his hips up. I sucked him hard, swirling my tongue as he fucked my mouth. I reveled in the forcefulness of it because it wasn't something I usually got from other men. More often than not, I was expected to be the dominant one and rarely got dominated. I loved letting go and allowing men to take me hard. If Kieran was like this during oral, he had to be even more so when it came to anal.

Pulling his dick out of my mouth, I glanced up at Kieran. "Wanna fuck me?"

His eyes lit up. "Oh, hell yes."

I stood and stripped off my clothes. "What position do you want me in?"

Kieran scrambled off the bed. "Get on your hands and knees."

I assumed the position, and he stood behind me for a moment before he spread my ass cheeks and pressed his face between them. A swipe of his tongue against my hole made me shiver then moan. The first couple of licks were gentle, then it was a vigorous rimming as he tried to push his tongue into me.

Fuck, he was skilled at licking ass. Energetic and powerful. I loved rimming as much as I enjoyed having it done to me. My ex hadn't minded when I did it to him, but had rarely reciprocated. When he had, it had been weak and hadn't lasted long. Kieran's actions were welcome and a total turn-on. I pressed my forehead onto the bed and gripped the sheets as he tongue-fucked me into oblivion, sending me into an erotic high I hadn't experienced in a very long time.

When Kieran stopped and pulled back, I moaned at the feel of his tongue on me. A moment later, he ran a finger around my hole before pushing inside.

"Oooh, so tight," Kieran murmured. "Has it been a while since you've been fucked?"

"A few months. Five, maybe six."

"That's good, for me anyway. I'm gonna love fucking you." He crooked his finger and found my prostate.

"Uhhh," I grunted and grabbed my cock, running my thumb across the slit to rub in the pre-cum.

Kieran added another digit for less than a moment before pulling them back. He patted my ass. "Don't want to stretch you too much. Want it nice and tight for my cock." He licked my hole one more time before he ordered me to scoot up on the bed. I did so and a moment later he squeezed something cold and slick on my ass and rubbed it in.

"Damn, that feels amazing." I writhed under his touch.

"Baby, you haven't felt anything yet." The deep growl of his voice turned me on so much it formed goosebumps across my flesh.

I heard the tear of a foil wrapper and glanced back as he covered his dick. He shifted closer and positioned his length between my cheeks before giving a quick thrust. He penetrated me hard and the pain was intense, but it was a pain I liked. My ass stretched around his girth and he inched forward before I'd fully adjusted.

"You okay, baby?" he questioned, and I gave him a nod.

He drove in quickly until he was all the way inside. It took my breath away and I bit my lip as the sharp discomfort eased. I loved the sting as much as the pleasure. It added to the enjoyment of the sex and allowed me to give in to my lover in a way I couldn't in my professional life.

"You liked that, didn't you?" His silky voice made me tremble.

"Yuh...yes."

"I thought you might appreciate a little pain. Good to know." A second later he brought a hand down on my left ass cheek. I hadn't been expecting the slap and it made me jump. I was a little more prepared for the second one but it still stung in a wondrous way.

Kieran pulled his length back then slammed into me, rubbing against my prostate. He gripped my hips and pounded me several times, before slowing down and giving me short and quick thrusts. Every so often he'd spank me. Not a lot and not when I knew it was coming.

"I love how your ass clenches me when I spank you," he murmured. "You feel incredible, baby, so wonderfully good."

It wasn't often I was able to truly give myself to a lover. To submit, I had to know he wasn't going to hurt me. I had that with Kieran. I might not have known him well, but I trusted him. So I didn't resist the ass pounding he gave me. I pushed back against him, giving myself to Kieran in a way I hadn't ever done with another man.

I came first, shooting my load onto my comforter. He lasted a few more minutes before pulling out, yanking off the rubber and coming on my back. I collapsed, not worrying about lying on my cum. He lay next to me. After rolling over, I pulled him close to me.

"I'm gonna fall asleep," I said. "But I'd like it if you stayed." Last time he'd been gone when I woke up on the floor.

"Okay, I'll be here."

* * * *

I woke an hour or so later and Kieran wasn't in my bed. At first I assumed he'd taken off again, then I heard the shower running. I pulled myself out of bed and ran a hand over the dried cum on my stomach. I strolled to the bathroom and called out, "Care if I join you?"

He opened the curtain a bit and grinned. "Get in."

I stepped in and let the warm water run down my body. He took the wash rag in his hand and ran it across my chest. While he cleaned my body, I put shampoo in my hair and scrubbed it. I rinsed off the suds from the front of my body and turned around. Without asking, Kieran washed my back, including my ass. I flinched when he spread my ass cheeks.

"Did I hurt you?"

"Yeah, but I liked it. I'll be sore for a bit. Trust me, I don't mind at all."

"Excellent. I can get into it when someone lets me. I'd hate to have gone too far."

I turned back around and kissed him. "I would've told you. I'm not afraid to speak up."

"Good to know." Another kiss. "That was amazingly hot, by the way."

"Agreed." I deepened the kiss, and he allowed my tongue inside his mouth.

After the shower, we dried each other off then walked naked into the kitchen. "Hungry? I have sandwich makings."

"I can't. Watching my weight."

I cocked an eyebrow. "As small as you are?"

"I'm a jockey," he said as if that answered everything. When he noticed my confusion he continued, "My weight has to stay within a pound or two. Too heavy and I can't control the horse as well."

"I see. Well, I'm starving." I got out turkey, ham, roast beef, cheese, lettuce and tomato. He snuck slices of turkey and tomato before I had my sandwich finished.

I retrieved two bottles of water from the fridge and handed one to Kieran.

I took a seat next to him at the kitchen island. "By the way, I'm Sam Shaw."

He nodded. "Kieran Jones."

"You didn't take Ware's name when he adopted you?" I asked.

"It's kind of a long story. Basically, I was ten when Andreas adopted me. I'd been in the group home three years by then and had given up hope of finding a family. Families usually want younger kids so I'd planned on aging out at seventeen."

"I'm sorry. That sucks."

He shrugged. "It is what it is. Anyway, a bunch of us went to a horse camp and I found I had a natural talent with the animals. Andreas came around a short time later. Asked me if I'd like to learn more about horses, how to ride them and how to race them. My height and innate skills made me perfect to be a jockey."

It dawned on me what he was saying. "He didn't adopt you to have a family, did he?"

Kieran shook his head. "It was pretty much a business decision. He adopted me and I began my training immediately."

"Not exactly what a young kid dreams about." I reached out and ran a hand through his hair.

"I got the best training and schooling money could pay for. I've been around the world and had everything I ever needed. Maybe I didn't have a mother and father like I wanted, but it was still better than staying in the home and being kicked out at seventeen. I'm grateful to Andreas for everything he's done for me."

I sighed and rubbed my face. I wasn't sure how he was going to react to what I was about to say but I had to do it. "I'm an agent with the FBI."

He chuckled. "Yeah, right. You already got me in bed, you don't have to lie to seduce me."

"I'm not bullshitting you, Kieran."

He froze then his eyes widened. "Oh, you're telling me the truth. You really are a cowboy cop."

"Agent," I corrected. "Special Agent Samuel Shaw."

"Oh, damn. That's kind of sexy. Did you just transfer to the Portland office?"

"Actually, I'm on a joint task force between the bureau and Portland police. Have you heard of Saunders Cortez?"

He scrunched his face. "A drug dealer down in California?"

I nodded. "He's part of a major cartel and runs the local chapter. Drugs are his main business, though he dabbles in lots of stuff. He's looking to expand his business across the country."

"Wow, didn't realize he was that large of a criminal."

"He's a very bad guy." I finished off my sandwich and licked my fingers clean. "You've heard the stories of the criminals on the east coast getting into horse racing, haven't you?"

He nodded.

"Cortez wants to do the same here on the west coast."

"How would he do that?"

"We're pretty sure he's working with the biggest name in horse racing in the state." I waited for him to realize what I was talking about.

"That would be...Andreas?"

I nodded.

"No way." He stood and walked a few steps away. "Andreas isn't a criminal. He wouldn't get in with the likes of this Saunders guy."

"Our information says otherwise." I strolled to Kieran and faced him. "Andreas likes to gamble, doesn't he?"

Kieran's face blanched and I knew the answer. "Yeah, he loves the casinos, but he has the money so he can afford to lose a little."

"He's lost a lot," I said. "But he has millions so it would be hard to go into debt. He *has* started attending some illegal poker games. That in itself wouldn't be a major deal, but it's the activities going on there where it becomes a bigger deal."

"Activities?" Kieran tugged an ear.

"Prostitution and drugs."

"Andreas would never do drugs!"

I put a hand on his shoulder and massaged it. "He hasn't done drugs. But he does like younger women. Unfortunately, some of the women were underage, sixteen in fact. He probably didn't even know they were minors at the time, but it gave Cortez blackmail material."

"How do you know all this?"

"We have a tap on his phones. We get a great deal of information, but nothing we can use to bring him down."

He shook my hand off, strolled into the living room and flopped down on the couch. I sat on the coffee table across from him and put my hands on his knees. "We have reason to believe Cortez is going to use Andreas to transport drugs across the country and possibly make money on the races."

"Andreas wouldn't let them use him like that. He takes racing seriously."

"We might be wrong, but I don't think so."

Kieran leaned back then glared at me. "Wait a minute. Is this why you came after me at the club? You want to use me to get info on Andreas?"

I shook my head. "Yes. I mean no."

He crossed his arms and scowled. "Which is it, Special Agent Shaw?"

"When I saw you at the club I had no idea who you were. I didn't know there was a connection until today at the stables."

"That's a huge coincidence."

"I know, Kieran. I was shocked, too. Remember how tongue-tied I was at the stable? I was floored to see you there."

"But you do want me to assist you?"

"I think you can find out what's going on with Andreas."

He stood and strode into the bedroom. By the time I got there he was pulling up his pants.

"Kieran, wait." I touched him, but he shook me off.

"Don't touch me, Sam. I'm not very happy at the moment."

"I understand you're hurt, but I need to know what you're going to do. I shared private information with you."

He put on his shirt. "I won't tell Andreas anything, but I think you're wrong."

"I hope I am," I responded. "But I doubt it. At least keep an ear out for anything suspicious."

He sat to put his socks and shoes on. "Like what?"

"Andreas may ask you to do something he wouldn't normally. He might even ask you to throw a race."

"He wouldn't ask me and even if he did, I wouldn't do it."

Fully dressed, he strode to the front door and opened it. He stopped to look at me for a second then he was gone.

Chapter Three

For the next two days I didn't hear a word from Kieran. Agent Summers wasn't thrilled at what had happened but couldn't blame me since I'd cleared it with her beforehand.

We weren't sure how to proceed because our first plan might be kaput too. Originally, I'd been going to use my knowledge of horses to get a job as a stable hand or horse handler with Ware and travel with them to all the races. I'd planned on letting Ware know I had ways to fix races without being caught in the hope that would bring me in contact with the cartel. It wasn't expected to be a quick assignment and I was willing to spend as many years as possible undercover.

Meeting Kieran had been a stroke of luck, but I wasn't exactly sure if it was good luck or bad. If Kieran refused to work with us he could also put the kibosh on me getting hired. Even worse, if he told Andreas about the task force, Cortez and the cartel would know we were on to them. It would set us back for sure, maybe even shut us down until we could regroup and come up with a new plan. For sure, my role as an undercover officer would be eliminated.

This was supposed to be my career-making case and now that was up in the air. I wouldn't be fired but I could be transferred anywhere the higher-ups wanted. I could end up in some small local office where I did more paperwork than anything else. Not exactly how I envisioned my career. I didn't necessarily regret telling Kieran — I believed it had been my best option. I just didn't like not being sure of what was going to happen next.

I was beginning to think I would never hear from Kieran again when he called — it had been three days since he'd walked out.

"Hey there," I said.

"Umm, hi."

"How are you doing?"

"We need to talk. Right away."

"Absolutely. Where?"

"I'm at the stables."

"Give me twenty minutes."

"Thanks," he said before ending the call.

I told Summers about the call then took off. I found Kieran standing at Chestnut Majesty's stall, stroking the animal's forehead.

He gave a smile when he spotted me but it quickly vanished. He was upset about something and I forced down the need to comfort him and make him feel better. Instead, I whispered, "I've missed you."

Kieran grabbed my hand for a moment. "Yeah, me too."

"This is so crazy." I ran a hand through my hair. "I went to the club to find a guy to sleep with for one night. But I can't get you out of my head. Even if you weren't connected to my case I'd still be drawn to you. All this other shit is just…"

"Majorly fucking weird." Kieran nodded then glanced around. "Let's talk somewhere private."

I followed him to a stall filled with several bales of straw. He sat but I remained standing.

He pulled a short shaft of straw and chewed on it. "I had dinner with Andreas yesterday."

"Is that usual?"

"Yes and no." He shrugged. "We have dinner each week but it's usually on a Sunday, not in the middle of the week."

"Did…something happen at dinner?" I questioned.

Kieran scrubbed his face and inhaled before making eye contact. "He told me to throw my upcoming race. You were right about him. I never, ever thought he would do something like that."

"Did he tell you why he wants you to lose?"

"He wouldn't be specific, claimed he had some friends betting on me to lose."

I sat next to him and squeezed his leg. "What did you say?"

He snapped his neck to face me. "I told him to fuck off. I am *not* going to throw a race, ever. I can't do that and still respect myself. This is my career, my life."

After wiping tears from his face, I pulled him close and embraced him. Kieran buried his face in my neck and wept for a few minutes. After pulling back and rubbing his face, he said, "I'll work with you to nail these fuckers. I'll do what I can, but I will not throw a race, no matter what."

"I can work with that—my bosses will too."

"I'm sorry for walking out like I did."

I waved a hand. "No worries. I understand you were confused."

"There's one thing I'm not confused about, Sam." He peered at me through half-shut lids, making my cock thicken. "I want to be with you. Can we do that *and* work the case?"

"My boss knows how we met so I don't see why she'd have trouble with it now. We'll call it keeping our informant satisfied."

He smirked. "Yes, I may have a few requests."

I waggled my eyebrows. "Such as?"

"How about a blow job? Right now."

Scrambling to my knees, I opened his pants and swallowed his semi-erect cock.

Despite having worked with horses since childhood, I'd never had sex in a stable or barn. Giving Kieran head where we could easily be caught gave me a charge and apparently it did the same for him because he came quickly. The kiss afterward where we shared his load was rough and sexy. I'd been looking for a man like him for years. I was going to enjoy our time together even if it only turned out to be temporary.

We stood and straightened our clothes before exiting the stall.

"What happens next?" he asked.

"I'll tell my boss you've agreed to work with us and we'll come up with a plan for how to proceed. Why don't you come over tonight and I'll fill you in."

"Sounds good. I might have a few more requests."

I chuckled. "And I'll be pleased to comply with every demand."

"Damn, you turn me on when you talk like that."

We kissed again before saying goodbye. I avoided glancing behind me, afraid I'd want to pull him back into a stable so he could reciprocate, but I finally did when I reached my car.

Kieran was feeding Chestnut Majesty as two men in dark clothes, a blond and a ginger, skulked up behind him. Kieran turned to face them as the blond struck out with a fist, cold-cocking Kieran. The redhead caught Kieran's unconscious body and slung him over his shoulder.

"Hey!" I hollered and ran after them.

They glanced back, spotted me then began running. I sprinted after them but by the time I got there they were in a tan van without a license plate and speeding off. I dashed back to my car and took off, but by the time I got to the street the van was nowhere to be seen. I raced up and down every nearby street with no luck.

I sped back to the station and tore into Summers' office. "Kieran's been kidnapped!"

She sat forward, putting her palms on her desk. "What happened?"

Tugging on my hair, I said, "I know it was the cartel. I don't have any doubt."

"Tell me what happened."

I still didn't answer her question, just kept pacing and rubbing my face. "Damn it, I can't believe this happened."

Summers stood and bellowed, "Agent Samuel Shaw, calm the fuck down and tell me what happened."

I snapped to attention. "Sorry, ma'am. Andreas Ware requested Kieran throw a race and Kieran refused. He agreed to work with us to get the cartel. I was leaving when I saw two guys knock him out, put him in a van and speed off. Tan, no license plate. They're probably pissed Kieran refused to play with them. Took him to force Ware's hands."

"What are you going to do?"

What am I going to do? She was the agent in charge and was depending on me to figure things out. Hell, Kieran was depending on me too. I forced my brain to stop spinning and focus. I snapped my fingers. "I need to talk to Andreas Ware. Find out if he knows about the kidnapping."

"Excellent, Agent Shaw. Now go do it."

* * * *

Flashing my badge was the only way into Ware's mansion and even then he made me wait forty-five minutes in a vast library. Under normal circumstances I would have appreciated the beauty of the setting but I was far too concerned about Kieran to relax even slightly.

"What can I do for you, Officer?"

I turned and took in Andreas Ware. He was tall and thin, apart from a slightly pudgy belly.

"Agent," I corrected as we shook hands. "Special Agent Samuel Shaw."

He nodded and sat on an antique couch with maroon cushions. I took a chair in front of him and leaned forward. "I'm not going to mess around, Mr. Ware. We don't have time."

"I don't understand…"

"I'm part of a task force investigating Saunders Cortez and his cartel."

"I don't recognize the name. I'm sorry."

Glaring at him, I snarled, "Don't fuck with me, Mr. Ware. Kieran's life depends on total honesty."

Fear flashed in his eyes. "What does this have to do with Kieran?"

I was glad he was concerned, it showed he cared — it meant he was more likely to work with me.

"I witnessed two men taking Kieran hostage just over an hour ago. I assume it's because he refused to purposely lose a race."

"How do you know all this?"

I waved a hand. "That's not important. Let's assume I know almost everything about your business with Cortez."

"Damn, damn, damn." Ware slouched and clutched his stomach like he was going to be sick.

"Mr. Ware," I said quietly, "I need your cooperation to save Kieran, but it may be dangerous."

He lifted his head and peered at me with determination in his eyes. "Whatever you need to save my son. I'll do anything. It's my fault he's in trouble."

I patted his knee. "You've made the correct decision."

* * * *

Cortez called a short time later and requested a meeting with Ware, who agreed.

Thanks to lots of prior planning, Summers was ready to respond when I declared we had a chance to possibly nail Cortez. Ware informed me how he'd become indebted to Cortez, confirming the information we had. He also told me how he'd met Cortez—at a friend's party. Cortez had personally invited Ware to his private club, meaning the criminal had targeted Ware. The old man hadn't stood a chance.

Cortez arrived at Ware's mansion thirty minutes late, an action I was sure was purposeful—a way for Cortez to assert dominance. He thought he had all the power, but in reality I was the one in control. By the time Cortez and four of his men got there, Ware's place had been bugged and surrounded by a team ready to swoop in and arrest Cortez. The plan hinged on the fact that Cortez had underestimated Ware. Up until that point, Ware had been a pushover and hadn't stood up for himself at all. Cortez simply didn't think Ware would even consider going to the cops, considering what Cortez had on him.

"Who is this?" Cortez growled and pointed at me.

"Samuel, my bodyguard," Ware replied.

"You've never needed muscle before."

Ware crossed his arms. "I've never dealt with men like you before."

Cortez offered a fake smile. "You've done well so far, Andreas. Continue doing that and you won't need a thug like him." He motioned toward one of his men and ordered them to pat me down. It was a half-assed one that wouldn't have found anything if I had been wired.

Additionally, a thug ran a device over the room looking for bugs. Too bad they were behind the times and the FBI had better toys. When they were all done *securing* the room, Cortez and a thin, Italian looking gentleman sat on the couch Ware had been on earlier, while Ware flopped in the chair I had used. I stood behind Ware with my arms crossed. Two of Cortez's other men took spots toward the back of the room.

"I was disappointed with your jockey's refusal to cooperate." Cortez's voice was honeyed but fake.

"Kieran is my son, not just an employee," Ware corrected.

Cortez waved a hand dismissively. "I felt the need to take action. Your horse cannot win this upcoming race."

Ware sat forward. "What did you do? If you hurt my son, so help me god I will…"

"You will do nothing!" Cortez's face darkened for an instant, then his phony smile returned. "Kieran is my...guest at the moment. What happens to him depends on you, Andreas."

"What do you want me to do?" Ware asked. "I've already agreed to transport your drugs and I can't force Kieran to do anything. He'll quit before he does what you want him to do."

"If you want the jockey to live, you will transport double the amount of product."

"Double?" Ware sputtered. "How do you expect me to do that?"

Cortez chuckled. "That is your problem. I'm sure you'll find a way. You'll need to hire a new rider for your horse, one who'll comply with orders."

Ware shook his head. "Fine, I'll do whatever it takes to save my son."

Cortez sat back and clapped his hands. "I knew you'd be smart about this."

"When will you release my son?"

"Not just yet." Cortez waggled a finger. "Not until after the race."

That wasn't good. I'd hoped to get a location before we arrested Cortez. Cortez probably had no intention of freeing Kieran. Cortez would continue keeping Kieran hostage so he'd have a bargaining chip with Ware. I'd have to find Kieran after the arrest, perhaps by getting one of Cortez's men to talk.

Cortez motioned to one of his men who had a large duffel bag. He brought the bag over and set it in front of Ware.

"What's this?" Ware opened the bag. Inside were bricks of white powder. Heroin, I assumed.

"This is for the first trip later this month," Cortez said. "There'll be more at the first stop."

"How long am I supposed to carry this?" Ware demanded.

"You'll have a visitor at the third location. He'll have money and different product."

"How much shit am I supposed to handle?" Ware stood. "This isn't what I expected. It's not what I agreed to."

Cortez leaped up and stood over Ware. "You'll do whatever I ask, Andreas. Don't forget, I have proof of your…indiscretions with minor girls. Plus, your son's life is in my hands. I'd suggest you not piss me off."

Ware sighed. "Okay. Please, don't hurt Kieran." He glanced back at me, and I nodded. We'd gotten everything we needed on the wire.

"It's for the best," I said, my cue to the task force that they could come in.

Ware walked around and stood near me, preparing for the impending gunfire. Doors opened and dozens of officers ordered Cortez and his men to freeze. Cortez didn't obey of course, and he turned to scowl at Ware.

"You son-of-a-bitch!" He reached into his coat and pulled out a pistol.

Within seconds, I had Ware on the ground behind me and my gun drawn. I fired once, hitting Cortez in the shoulder and knocking him to the ground. Two of Cortez's men flanked him and began shooting at the officers so I aimed and hit one directly in the chest. He fell backward and a moment later the other thug was taken out by a cop. The third and fourth of Cortez's men had spread out on opposite sides of the room, one taking cover behind a desk and the other disappearing behind a wall. I spotted Cortez clutching his wound and trying to find an exit, and I was about to chase him when a bullet whizzed past my ear. I spun around, lowered to one knee and shot the crook. Once I'd ensured it was clear to move, I beelined toward Cortez. He wasn't moving quickly, but I still took him down hard. I launched myself into the air and crashed into him. We landed on the floor with a loud *ker-thunk* and I wrenched his arms behind him. "Saunders Cortez, it is my pleasure to say you are under arrest."

After I had read him his rights, Cortez was hauled away and I surveyed what had happened during the shoot-out. Cortez and two of his thugs were taken to hospital for the injuries they'd sustained. A third man had tried to get away but had been caught by officers outside. The fourth crook, not one of the ones I'd shot, was dead from a bullet to the head. Only two officers were hurt and it was only minor injuries. Definitely could've been worse.

Summers interrogated Cortez and his right-hand man, but I didn't think either one of them would give us Kieran's location. Cortez did, however, tell us that if he didn't contact his men within an hour, Kieran was a dead man, so I didn't have long to locate him.

The only possibility was using the cell phones Cortez and his employees possessed. I was afraid to call and pretend to be Cortez because if the guy on the other end got spooked he might not wait the full hour to take out Kieran. Instead, I got a list of the numbers Cortez had recently called and we tracked the approximate locations of where they were.

A couple were out of town, but I was pretty sure Kieran was nearby. I didn't have time to find out if Cortez owned any properties and it wasn't likely he'd have many in his own name anyway. One number did bounce off a cell tower in a rural area outside Portland. My instincts told me that was where Kieran was being held.

"Take a crew and get out there," Summers ordered. "It's your best bet."

I hated not being positive, but I couldn't sit and wait. I had to do something. The area we went to was mostly farmhouses. We took five vehicles with three men in each so we could split up to check as many of the houses as possible. We were looking for anything that seemed out of order, a vehicle that didn't fit or a rundown house that should've been empty but had signs of life.

I was with a local cop named Blankenship, who had a good eye. I was probably too hyped to concentrate, but he spotted a property with a For Sale sign. There was no house, only a large two-story barn. There wasn't a vehicle near the building but there were lights emanating from the upper floor.

"That's it." I slapped the steering wheel. "I'm sure of it." I pulled my vehicle as close as possible without being seen, got out then dashed toward the barn.

"Agent Shaw," Blankenship called out, keeping his voice quiet. "We should wait for the rest of the team."

I ignored his words. It was up to me to save Kieran. I couldn't wait.

I spotted one guy surveilling the lower part of the barn, waited for him to check out the back then came up behind him, wrapped my arm around his neck and squeezed until he passed out. I lowered his unconscious body to the ground and gestured to Blankenship. He nodded, pulled out a pair of zip tie cuffs.

The inside of the barn was empty so I silently climbed the ladder that led to the next level then stopped before I got to the very top. Keeping my head low, I peered over and spotted Kieran.

He sat on a bale of hay, tied up and gagged. His captor carried a pistol as he paced, and constantly checked his phone. I retrieved my Glock from its holster and aimed for the center mass. I was about to pull the trigger when my foot slipped and banged against the ladder.

The gunman's eyes widened. He brought his gun up and fired at me. The bullet zinged past me as I regained my footing. I couldn't fire blind, the risk of hitting Kieran was too strong, so I climbed up the final rungs of the ladder and rolled behind several bales of hay. I peeked out from behind my cover and gasped. The gunman had his pistol to Kieran's forehead. I aimed and fired on pure instinct, hitting the gunman in his chest. He fell backward, landing with a loud thwack on the floor.

With my gun still trained on him, I advanced until I had his weapon under my foot. I kicked it away, kneeled and checked for a pulse. None. He was dead. He was the first guy I'd ever killed. I'd known it would likely happen sometime in my career—I hadn't expected it to happen on my first major case. I didn't feel bad, but wondered if I should have felt at least some remorse—it had been him or Kieran.

Finally, I rushed to Kieran and cut his bonds. When I tore the gag from his mouth he cried out and fell into my arms.

"Oh my god, Sam," he cried. "I thought I was going to die. I was so sure."

"Shh, baby, it's okay. You're fine."

"Thanks, Sam." He kissed me. "Thank you for saving my life."

"I assumed that would be one of your demands," I said, trying to downplay the danger.

Kieran chuckled and kissed me again, not caring that we were now being surrounded by the rest of my team.

"You are one helluva of a guy, Sam."

"I think you're pretty special too."

Epilogue

The proof of Ware's indiscretions was destroyed and no charges were brought. He hadn't asked for immunity and had been ready to do the time, but I didn't think it was necessary and Summers agreed.

In addition to the drug charges, we were able to nail Cortez with kidnapping and attempted murder. He was going to prison for a long time. He'd be out eventually, but hopefully most of his cartel would be dismantled by then. That was the task force's next project and my next assignment.

Whoever took up Cortez's spot in the cartel would likely still want to get into the horse-racing business. It had been a staple of organized crime on the east coast and criminals all over the country saw it as a way to launder money and get things done. My job was to figure out how they were getting in.

Kieran and I agreed to a relationship, even though it would be a long distance one. He traveled with Chestnut Majesty and I traveled wherever my leads took me. On our free time we tried to visit each other depending on where we were. Most of the time we managed to see each other at least once a month, but then things got busy for us both and we didn't see each other for three months.

Then everything came together. Kieran was in New York at the same time I was, though Kieran wasn't aware of the stroke of luck that had brought us together. It happened to be the one year anniversary of when we'd first met, so I wanted to make it special.

I'd colluded with Andreas to convince Kieran to go to a specific club. I hid in the shadows as Kieran loosened up with some strong drinks and eventually started dancing. He was just as gorgeous as that night one year before, moving fluidly in tune with the rhythm. Men approached Kieran and he danced with them, but pushed them away when they got too close. He was staying true to me, not that I'd had any doubt.

Finally, I slipped through the crowd, scared off Kieran's current dancing partner and moved to the music behind my lover. I stepped close, grabbed his hips and pulled him close. He yanked away and shoved me, ready to scream at me for going too far without permission. Kieran froze when he saw me and wiped his eyes like he wasn't convinced I was actually there.

Finally, he grinned from ear to ear and jumped into my arms. He kissed me, thrusting his tongue into my mouth. "You're actually here. I can't fucking believe it."

"God, I've missed you, baby."

"Me, too."

Still holding him in my arms, we danced and made out on the dance floor. Lots of people stared at us, some with jealousy while others *oohed* and *awwed* and said we were cute together.

"I have something to tell you," I said.

Kieran shifted so we were eye to eye. "Bad news?"

I shook my head. "I don't think so. I hope not."

Kieran furrowed his brow.

"I love you, Kieran Jones." It was a big step for me and for us. I think I'd fallen in love at first sight, but hadn't wanted to rush things and scare him away.

Kieran leaned his head back and laughed.

"Why are you laughing?"

"I'm just so freaking happy. Do you know why?"

"Why?"

"Because I am madly, wildly and passionately in love with you, Sam Shaw."

HORSES AND HARLEYS

Molly Ann Wishlade

Dedication

For Sue with love XXX

Chapter One

Henry peeled his eyes open and waited for his vision to clear. His mouth was furry and his head threatened to explode. He dragged open the drawer of his bedside cabinet then dug around until he found two aspirin.

Tablets swallowed, he closed his eyes and lay still, willing the medication to disperse quickly into his bloodstream. It was becoming routine, this morning-after-the-night-before suffering. He knew that it had to stop but so far he'd been lacking the willpower — or even the inclination — to end the destructive cycle.

A rustling at his side made his eyes spring open again, and he cursed as pain ricocheted through his skull.

"Shit!" He blocked out the world with his hands and took a few deep breaths.

"Hey, handsome." An unfamiliar voice penetrated the haze and Henry flicked back through his memories to try to place it.

Nothing.

Zero.

His mind was blank, his body ached with dehydration and toxins and his heart was heavy.

"How're you feeling, lover boy? That was one hell of a party last night."

Henry blinked cautiously behind his broad palms, allowing the light to seep in. If he took it slowly, maybe it wouldn't hurt. He peered at the man who lay tangled in the sheets beside him.

Who the fuck...

The interloper started to laugh. The noise was deep and throaty, the guttural chuckle of a heavy smoker. "I take it from your expression that you don't remember inviting me to stay the night? I'm George Monroe."

Henry sat bolt upright. There had been champagne. Lots and lots of champagne. In fact, he wouldn't be surprised if they had emptied his well-stocked wine cellar last night.

There had been business. Talk of horses. Upcoming races. Breeding plans.

Then there had been pleasure. Lots and lots of hedonistic, no-strings-attached, primal fucking.

And now he had the hangover from hell and an empty heart to prove it.

Typical Saturday then.

"So you want me to get you breakfast in bed?" George smiled then ran a hand over Henry's chest, causing Henry to shiver. George lingered at Henry's exposed nipple and tweaked the light brown center, encouraging it to stand erect before teasing it with a perfectly manicured fingernail.

Henry shuddered. "No. I want you to go." He slipped from under the duvet and crossed the room, cupping his naked package as he went. He located his sweat pants and tugged them on, only releasing the breath he had been holding when his cock and balls were securely covered. "I'll be downstairs. Let yourself out." He cast a glance at his bedfellow.

George pouted and slipped the sheet aside, revealing that he was completely naked. "You don't want a repeat performance?" He fondled his rising shaft.

"No. Thanks...uh...for last night. But I have plans and I'm already running late."

"Okay, Henry, your loss. I saved my number in your mobile, though, so call me sometime."

"Sure." Henry gave a small nod then left the room and made his way down to the kitchen. He opened the fridge door and stood in the blue light, letting the cool air soothe his headache and cleanse his skin. The all too familiar feeling of shame was burgeoning inside like a dark gray storm cloud. Why did he do it? Time after time after time? Each loveless encounter was meaningless, empty, pointless. It got his balls emptied all right, but he always ended up feeling sad, seedy and soiled afterward.

That was it! *That was the last one. Never again.*

He slammed the fridge door shut and the glass bottles in the door clinked together.

Love was dangerous, impulsive and painful, and there was no way that he intended on suffering the consequences of involvement again.

* * * *

Alex dug the fork into the straw again then turned and dumped it into the wheelbarrow. The repetitive action of mucking out was comforting and familiar. He'd been damned lucky to get the position as a groom. The job at Foxhill Grange had come with accommodation and a pleasing salary. And it had come at the right time too.

Alex had needed to get away from his childhood home in South Wales, and Corbridge, Northumberland, was certainly far away. Some things were best left behind.

Like grief.

He rolled the wheelbarrow into the spring sunshine then went back for the fork, which he placed against the stable wall. He wiped his sweaty brow with the back of a hand then bent to take hold of the wheelbarrow again when a deep voice stopped him in his tracks.

"Hey there! You! Hold on a moment."

Alex stood upright and stared at the approaching man. He was tall and broad with a stylish blond haircut. Everything about him was expensive, from his black leather boots to his thigh-hugging, stylishly faded denims and his soft brown leather jacket. Alex's heart picked up its pace and he swallowed hard as the man stopped before him. He had never thought of himself as short at five feet ten, but he had to raise his head to meet the man's intense gaze and he had to fight not to appraise the wall of muscle that clearly made up the shoulders beneath the leather.

"You're new here."

Alex nodded. "Started two weeks ago."

The stranger raised one golden eyebrow. "You like it?"

Alex nodded and smiled. He couldn't hide his pleasure at finding such a fabulous position, at getting a job where he could work with horses all day then sleep above their stables at night. He couldn't hide his relief that he was far, far from the town where he'd grown up and that nobody knew him here. No one could drag up his teenage nicknames or remind him of the times when he'd been pushed into the local river or tied to a rugby post by his ankles and left there until the teacher had found him. He hadn't been able to leave it all behind him as soon as he would have liked, because of his mother and because of...*him*...but when his mother had taken ill then passed away suddenly, there had been nothing to hold him back.

Alex had scoured the Internet looking for jobs and had attended a few interviews before getting the one at Foxhill Grange. He had taken most of his mother's meagre possessions to the local charity shop, given their landlord notice, packed a bag, jumped on a train then headed off to freedom, anonymity and a new life.

"Well make sure that you treat the horses better than you'd treat your own family, won't you?" The stranger stood before Alex like a soldier. He looked ready for action, prepared to take Alex down if his response was unfavorable.

Alex bit back a retort. Who the hell did the man think he was barking orders? What kind of chocolate boy was this anyway looking like he'd just stepped off a catwalk and smelling so damned fine? So fine that Alex's pulse was racing and he found himself leaning forward just to breathe deeper of the intoxicating aroma.

The stranger eyed Alex for a moment longer then suddenly reached out and ran a large hand over Alex's cheek. Alex started and saw the man's eyes darken at his reaction.

"You had straw in your hair." He held the offending object up for Alex to see.

"Oh. Uh. Thanks."

"You're welcome. Though it did kind of suit you, gave you a country cuteness. What's that word...bumpkin?" He smiled.

Bumpkin? Was he being called names already? Did he exude *kick me* vibes or was *loser* actually tattooed on his forehead.

"I'm sorry. I didn't mean to offend you—it was just a joke. I'm Henry, by the way." He held out a large hand.

Alex gazed at the hand for a moment before shaking it. It was warm and strong and it enveloped his own, making him feel at once safe and confusingly aroused.

"And you are?" Henry raised his eyebrows.

"Oh…uh, Alex." How could he stammer over his own name? Because he'd been about to offer an alternative then had realized it would be ridiculous. He worked here now. It wasn't like lying to a stranger on a train or a guy in a club who he would never see again. Henry looked like he kept active. So perhaps he was responsible for sawing down trees, mowing lawns and trimming hedges. The image of him shirtless as he pushed a lawnmower made color flood Alex's cheeks and he shook himself. *This isn't a Diet Coke advert, idiot.*

"Well it's great to meet you, Alex. Have a good day and I'll see you around." With that, Henry winked at Alex, and his already warm cheeks burned. *Blushing like a teenager!* How much of an idiot could he be? *But winking.* What kind of arrogant, dated and crappy action was that?

Alex couldn't explain it, but try as he might to be offended, he just glowed inside. Henry had winked at him. Made him blush with pleasure. It was as if he'd been noticed and accepted.

Alex watched as Henry walked away, leaving nothing behind other than the delicious waft of expensive aftershave and Alex's slowly cooling cheeks.

"You can forget all about that one." Alex was nudged in the ribs. He turned to find Mina, a fellow groom, grinning at him.

"What?"

She twirled her long brown hair around her fingers in a hypnotic movement. "He is off limits, sugar cube." She winked.

"Who is he, Mina?"

"That, my dear, is your boss! Mr. Henry *hottie* Lockhart."

The other grooms had told Alex about Lockhart but this was the first time he'd seen the mysterious owner of Foxhill Grange. He'd been warned that Lockhart was attractive but he'd not expected him to be so jaw-droppingly delectable. A man like *that* made men and women want to fall at his feet just to gain a moment of his attention. Look at how Alex had reacted when Henry had introduced himself and shaken his hand. It had knocked Alex off balance and he'd been left hot and bothered and horny as hell.

He shivered. Henry Lockhart was definitely off limits. He was also dangerous. Alex knew that he had to stay away from him. His job and reputation here were far too precious to endanger for what would probably be a fleeting attraction. Men who looked like well-built, high-ranking marines with a dash of David Beckham thrown in did not fall for men like Alex.

"Look, Alex." Mina hugged him. "You're really cute but you're not Mr. Lockhart's type. He goes for flashy and sexy, lovers with fake tans and champagne glasses glued to their hands."

Alex nodded. For a man like Henry Lockhart, Alex could only ever be a bit of rough. That pathetic old cliché. He slipped out of Mina's grasp and took hold of the wheelbarrow. "I have no idea what you're talking about. I'm not even slightly attracted to men like *that*. Besides, I've got work to do and I've already forgotten about...*him*." He pushed the soiled straw across the yard. He knew that Mina meant well. She'd been really kind to him since he'd arrived at the stables and had helped him to settle in. But she *was* wrong about this. Alex had opened his heart once and he had no intention of doing so again. Wealthy and experienced older men should come with a large red light flashing above their heads.

And for Alex they did. After all, he put it there.

Chapter Two

Henry jabbed at the wiry man who ducked and dove in front of him. Sweat and testosterone permeated the air. He threw a hard right hook that caught his trainer and made him stumble.

"Woa there, Henry!" Josh held up his sparring pads. "You want to tell me what's going on with you today? I seem to be the target for all your army training as well as for whatever bug got up your arse!" He slipped off the pads and dropped them to the floor.

Henry shrugged and held out his hands for Josh to remove his gloves. Henry had ranted to him in the past but this time, he didn't really know what to say — it was kind of complicated.

Once his hands were free, he took the proffered towel and wiped his face and neck. He'd worked up a sweat and that was good. It was what he needed. What he'd needed every day this week.

He couldn't pinpoint exactly what had gotten him so worked up. He'd made another mistake at the weekend, sure, but it wasn't the first time he'd drunkenly screwed a reality TV celebrity — even though he hated himself for it. Even though he kept promising himself he wouldn't do it again. But that had been nearly a week ago. So what was it that was eating him?

He swigged from his water bottle then spat into the corner bucket.

It was that damned groom.

Alex.

The new one with the big brown eyes and short ebony haircut, with olive skin that looked as soft and smooth as silk. Skin that Henry had immediately longed to taste.

Ever since Henry had spied the younger man at his stables, he'd been agitated. Henry didn't usually go for *that* type either. He chose the tanned and gym-toned airheads that he could pick up and cast aside. The ones who were fake from their garbled hashtag language to their whiter than white teeth. No fear of falling in love or getting hurt with them. Sex was animalistic. Primal. And once the urge was satisfied, Henry moved on and never looked back. Except in moments of regret and recrimination, that was, and he never allowed himself to indulge in that nonsense for long.

But now, completely unexpectedly, Henry had encountered a man who looked like he had something going on behind his dark eyes. Something more than just thoughts of the next bottle of champagne or gossip column. A man who seemed to care about horses as much as he did.

And Henry didn't like it at all. He wasn't interested in finding someone he could fall for.

It was good that he didn't go down to the stables that often anymore. He used to be there every day…when… Before…

His chest tightened and his throat began to ache.

He raised his hands to Josh and gestured for him to put the gloves back on. He needed to throw more punches, to keep his body and mind busy. He didn't want to think about things like racehorses and intelligent young men. That was where the pain hid and Henry had no intention of letting it resurface.

Not now. Not ever.

* * * *

Alex moved around the mare slowly, smoothing her down with the large flat brush and talking to her in soft tones. The chestnut beauty was not a racehorse and she had been purchased for more domestic purposes. The stables homed several well-bred racehorses and a few riding horses, so it would be easy to assume that the owner had a love of riding.

He just couldn't work it out. He'd asked around and apparently, Henry Lockhart did not ride at all. He could understand why Henry kept the racehorses but why the others? What was the point?

He ran a hand over the mare's wiry mane then down over her long nose. "There you are, girl. How did that feel?" He leaned forward and kissed her, inhaling her sweet hay fragrance.

"You are a charmer, Alex! Felicity is making eyes at you now."

He turned to find Mina leaning over the stall door, grinning.

"You have no idea," he replied, returning her smile.

"I have news!" she announced.

Alex grinned. Mina was such a whirlwind, so chatty and excitable, constantly full of energy and enthusiasm for everything. She loved her job, loved the horses and loved the stables. She was warm, bubbly and funny, and Alex was thrilled to now count her as a friend.

"You do, Mina? Did you spot a ladybird on a primrose? Or a dragonfly on the pond? Or did you hear that *Horses and Hounds* is holding a flash sale with fifty percent off all equine products?"

Mina stuck out her tongue. "None of the above. Now... How do you fancy attending a party this evening up at the big house?"

Alex frowned. His heart fluttered.

"It's not that unusual, you know," Mina said, opening the door and entering the shadowy stall. "Mr. Lockhart hosts a lot of parties and sometimes he does invite us employees. I've been to a few of them just to check out the celebs as much as anything. Even got me a few autographs." She paused as if waiting for Alex's approval. "And there will be champagne, of course!"

"I'm not sure, Mina." He wanted to keep a low profile. That was the point of moving to a new location. He wanted to work with horses but avoid human company as much as possible. His room over the stables was cozy and comfortable. With cable TV and an Xbox, plus an e-reader full of books, he didn't need much else. At least he tried to tell himself that he didn't. He could survive without human contact, without sweet words and hot kisses and the promise of future plans that would never be realized.

"Oh come on!" Mina mock punched his arm. "It'll be fun. Besides, if you don't go, I can't go."

"Why not?"

"The other grooms will be taking dates and I'll just look like an idiot turning up alone." She pouted and swayed from side to side, reminding Alex of a little girl trying to manipulate her parents into taking her to the fair.

"Mina… You do know…that I don't…"

"Alex, you have nothing to fear from me. I do not fancy men. *At all*. I like the fairer and less hairy gender." She waggled her eyebrows. "So please come with me."

"Why don't you have a date to take?" Alex asked, taking in her pretty face and shiny brown hair.

"I'm sworn off relationships at the moment. My last lover went back to her husband and…" She rubbed a hand over her chest.

Alex nodded. He knew how that felt. Married men — and women it seemed — had a way of hurting and humiliating their extra-curricular lovers, especially when said lovers had no idea that the person they were dating was married.

"Okay, Mina. I'll come."

"Yippee!" She jumped up and threw her arms around his neck then proceeded to blow wet sloppy raspberries there like an overly energetic puppy. Alex wriggled out of her embrace. He was very ticklish and Mina had zoned in on his weak spot.

"I hope I'm not going to regret this," Alex said when he'd ensured that Mina was a safe distance away.

"I promise you won't," Mina said then danced out of the stables like a jodhpur-clad Cinderella on her way to the ball.

Felicity nudged Alex with her warm nose, gently reminding him that she was still waiting for his attention. He turned back to her and rubbed behind her ears.

Horses he could manage. Women, as platonic friends, he could deal with. But rich handsome men who wielded their attraction like a sharpened sword… Alex had no room for them in his life at all. Henry Lockhart might be intriguing and downright attractive but he was everything that Alex had sworn to avoid.

He just hoped that he had the willpower to stick to his guns. It wouldn't be that hard now...would it?

Chapter Three

Alex allowed Mina to tuck her hand into the crook of his arm as they made their way up the gravel path toward the Grange. It was a large and impressive country house built from local cream and brown quarry stone with well-preserved Victorian bay windows and even a tower, which Mina told him housed an impressive library.

As they neared the house, Alex could hear the soothing lilt of a Celtic ballad being played on a harp. He recognized the tune and it brought a wave of sadness as it mingled with the sounds of voices and laughter. Images of his childhood flickered through his mind and he had a sudden yearning to speak to his mother. But he couldn't. He wouldn't be able to speak to her ever again.

"Hey. Are you okay?" Mina asked.

"Yes. Why?" He coughed, embarrassed that he had just let his guard slip in front of a new friend. He didn't want to carry his grief here, to this new place. It was best left behind in the town where he had grown up.

"You just squeezed my arm tighter." Mina stopped and turned to him. Her hair was stylishly pinned up on her head and she'd lined her brown eyes with dark shadow. Her lips were bright red and her skin glowed in the twilight.

"I'm a bit nervous I guess. I don't usually attend social gatherings like this."

"Well time to get used to it," Mina replied before planting a kiss on his cheek. "The life of a groom can be a social whirl—especially when you work for Henry Lockhart. He likes everyone to be involved at all levels. It's all about the networking."

Alex knew that it could be that way. It was something he'd dreamed of as a teenager when he'd helped his uncle out at his small farm in South Wales. But even then he'd not thought much about the actual socializing and how difficult that might be. Alex had just assumed that he'd grow into a confident, articulate man. That was what growing up was about, right? Unfortunately, he still felt like the same shy, awkward boy inside and any confidence he displayed was more of a front than he'd care to admit.

Moving away from Wales had been partly to do with his disastrous love affair, partly because he'd lost his mother and partly because he longed to reinvent himself—to become the man he'd always hoped he'd be.

Alex lifted his chin. Tonight he *would* be the man he wanted to be. Confident, self-assured, in control of his own destiny. He would push all hurt, doubts and negativity aside and enjoy the evening as he carved out his new life. He just hoped that his handsome boss stayed out of his way, because a whiff of that mouthwatering scent and a glimpse of those piercing blue eyes would turn his newly established — and rather fragile — veneer to rubble.

* * * *

Henry circulated amongst his guests. He was an enthusiastic host. He ensured that glasses were full, people were entertained and talking to those they desired to network with, and that the food in the drawing room was replenished regularly. He sipped his own champagne slowly, determined to keep his wits about him this evening. He had no intention of getting pissed and taking another cheesy celeb to his bed. It wouldn't be one of *those* parties.

Although spring had not yet turned into summer, it was warm out, so he'd opened the French windows that led onto the stone veranda. The harpist's soothing melody washed over him and he felt a sense of peace. Music had always calmed him and lifted him, just like riding. His stomach tightened at the thought of being on a horse, of feeling the beast between his legs as it became a part of him while they galloped across the land. Henry had never ridden professionally, but he had always ridden for pleasure. Felicity's big brown eyes came into his mind and he swallowed hard. It had been two years since he'd taken her out. Two whole years since he had allowed himself to feel the freedom he had once believed he couldn't live without.

But then he didn't deserve to feel it, did he?

In fact, he hadn't even been able bring himself to visit Felicity because of the pain it caused him. Callum… The name circled the perimeter of his mind but he pushed it away and focused instead on the harp.

He threw back the rest of his drink, forgetting his vow to stay sober as grief teased at the edges of his control, then grabbed another from a passing waiter and made his way outside. The breeze had picked up and the plants in the large beds danced to the harp's refrain — elegant, mournful, beautiful. Henry gazed at the extensive and perfectly groomed gardens. He was lucky to own such a property at his age — he reminded himself of the fact every day. Not many thirty-five year olds had what he did. And yes, he had been born privileged, but he had worked hard since leaving Cambridge to ensure that the wealth he possessed was of his own making. Henry Lockhart was no lazy scrounger. He had been employed in one way or another since he'd been sixteen and had joined the army at twenty-three after leaving Cambridge, where he'd studied law. He'd served several tours of duty in Iraq before returning to England and making his fortune through security consultancy for the wealthy. He'd soon been able to employ a very efficient team to run the company for him. When Callum had been alive, Henry had really enjoyed being able to focus on the horseracing circuit instead of day-to-day business matters, but since his passing, Henry had struggled to maintain his former enthusiasm.

He turned to go back into the house when something caught his eye. In the window of the tower room, he could see a dark figure. Staring right at him. Even though he couldn't see the person's eyes from the lawn, he knew that they were watching him.

* * * *

Alex stepped away from the window, his cheeks flaming. *Shit!* Henry Lockhart had stared straight at him, no doubt wondering what his groom was doing nosing around in his library. He placed the book he'd been perusing back on the shelf then turned to leave. But it was hard to do so. The room was beautiful with its cozy, circular space, deep-set fireplace and floor-to-ceiling bookshelves. The carpenter had set the shelves at angles so that they followed the shape of the walls and the books had been arranged so that they fitted the spaces perfectly. Someone had spent hours categorizing the books into genres and authors and editions. Someone who clearly loved books as much as Alex did.

Reading and horses. They were the only things that had mattered to Alex growing up. He'd spent his days helping out at his uncle's farm and his nights escaping the claustrophobia of the small Welsh valley by reading. He had been a regular at the local library, often waiting weeks for books to come in, and admittedly it had not helped with how others had treated him. They — the small-minded boys of his school year — had labelled him the *gay bookworm*. Even before he had really known himself that he felt no attraction to women, the other boys had honed in on him and singled him out. Anyone who didn't excel at rugby or shag the local girls on a Friday in the shadows of the dilapidated leisure center was automatically labelled gay, weird or a loser.

Yes, Alex had been glad to escape.

He gave the room one more lingering glance then reached for the door handle but the door swung wide, causing him to take a step back. His heart leaped as he laid eyes on the one man he really didn't want to bump into this evening. Ridiculous, really, when that man was his boss and hosting the party. But hey, he could always hope, couldn't he?

"Alex Castillo."

Alex stared at Henry Lockhart, stunned at how his own name rolled off Henry's tongue and affected him like an erotic caress. He felt it deep in his stomach and it tightened his balls.

"The new groom…browsing my private library? See anything you like?" Henry stared straight at Alex, his blue eyes as penetrating as an X-ray.

Alex nodded. His tongue was suddenly thick and dry and he didn't trust himself to reply.

Henry held out a glass of champagne, and Alex took it gratefully, gulping the cold, bubbly liquid. "Thank you."

"You're welcome. There's plenty more downstairs. Unless you'd like to spend the evening up here, of course." Henry licked his lips. "You like my library, Alex?"

"It's very impressive, sir. You have some rare books here."

"You know much about rare volumes then?" Henry asked, taking a step closer to Alex.

"Yes… I…uh read a lot."

"We'll have to compare notes, Alex. I like a man who reads."

"I'd like that, sir."

"Don't call me *sir*, Alex. I might be your boss… I might have some power over you in that respect…but I'm not your Dom. Call me Henry. Please." He grinned, and Alex smiled back, relaxing a little, though the idea of being ordered around by the gorgeous man who now stood within touching distance made his heart rate increase. If Henry Lockhart was to tell him to strip right now…to kneel before him and surrender to his will…well, he'd have no choice at all, would he?

He shook his head. What was he thinking? Where had his vows to stay away from men like Lockhart gone? Up in a puff of smoke, like his decision to remain single.

"I should like to get to know you better, Alex. Would you like that too?" Henry moved his eyes over Alex, from his head to his toes then back up again, and Alex felt as if he'd been physically caressed. Goosebumps rose all over his body, his nipples tightened into hard points and blood rushed to his groin. *Not now!* He moved his jacket over his stomach and adjusted it to cover his burgeoning erection.

"I…I would, Mr.…I mean, Henry."

"Good. But right now I have guests to entertain. So, shall we?"

They left the library and as Henry closed the library door behind them, he leaned closer to Alex and whispered into his ear, "You intrigue me with your soft brown eyes and your air of innocence. It's not what I'm used to, Alex." Then he placed a large hand in the small of Alex's back and gently guided him toward the staircase, all the while circling the base of Alex's spine with his thumb, causing Alex's heart to beat wildly and his cock to strain painfully against the front of his trousers.

Chapter Four

The guests had thinned out and glasses and plates had been cleared away. A few stragglers were gathered around a card table in the drawing room, and Alex watched them from the huge leather armchair he'd slumped into as the champagne carried him from a gentle buzz toward sleepy relaxation. The fireplace to his left was clean and cool, a pile of decorative logs and fresh herbs filling the space that a fire would occupy during colder months. Alex rubbed his shoes over the purple fireside rug, watching the deep pile as it rippled with his movements. He could clearly envisage lying in front of the hearth on a winter's evening, basking in the glow from a roaring fire as Henry lay in his arms, sated by passionate lovemaking.

Foolish, drunken thoughts. But ones that made him smile, nonetheless.

The group of card players finally rose and laughed as they staggered out of the room. Alex was left alone in the hollow calm that permeates a house once the revelers have gone. It was not unpleasant and he wished he could remain there all night, settled in Henry's big leather chair.

Mina appeared through the French doors and Alex smiled. He'd forgotten all about her since he'd come down to the party with Henry's hand planted firmly on the small of his back. He'd been enchanted by the handsome and wealthy businessman and his thoughts had been clouded all evening.

"Hey, Alex!" Mina stumbled toward him, her dark hair tumbling from its clips and curling around her chin. She grinned as she swayed—she'd enjoyed the free champagne too.

"You okay, Mina?"

"Yesshhh." She squinted as she approached him. She was trying to negotiate her way across the carpet without any mishaps.

"Is it time to call it a night?" he asked.

"Oh no." She shook her head. "The night is young, dear Alexsh. I'm heading into town with some of the othersh…and a celeb or two. Wanna come with?"

Alex frowned, the alcohol haze slipping away suddenly as concern for his friend washed over him. "Are you sure that's a good idea?"

She nodded. "Yesh, be fine. Tim's coming too." She waved a hand dismissively.

Tim was a senior groom at the stables and Alex knew that he kept a watchful eye over the younger grooms, kind of like an older brother, so Mina would be safe as long as he was there. "Well just stay with him, all right? No wandering off."

Mina saluted. "Yesshh, Alex! I promishe I will be shafe and shenshible."

With that, she blew him a kiss and disappeared into the inky blackness of the night.

Alex sighed and placed his champagne flute on the stone hearth. He'd volunteered to take the early shift tomorrow to spare some of the other partygoers, so he should try to get some sleep. He rose and smoothed out his trousers then retrieved his jacket from the back of the chair.

"Leaving so soon?" The voice he already knew so well captured his attention. Henry stood in the archway that led to the grand entrance hall. He had removed his tie and jacket and now stood there in his pure white shirt, unbuttoned at the throat to reveal a triangle of smooth, tanned chest, and with the sleeves rolled up to his elbows. Alex eyed the blond hairs that covered Henry's thick forearms and had a sudden yearning to run his fingers over them. He would be safe if held in those arms. He knew it.

But it would never happen.

"Seems I'm the last one, Henry. Everyone else has gone." Alex approached his boss, his heart thudding, his stomach tight.

"I was hoping you'd hang around," Henry said.

He ran a big hand through his floppy blond hair and brushed it back from his forehead. The tiny hairs at Henry's hairline were white blond and Alex wondered if the hair on Henry's body was the same color or darker.

"You're blushing, Alex."

When they'd descended from the library earlier, Henry had directed Alex toward a group of grooms from other stables and Alex had listened to the men as they'd discussed the coming races, breeding stock and social calendar. He had listened and tried not to appear awestruck, though inside he'd been open-mouthed and wide-eyed. These people lived a life he had only ever imagined in his wildest dreams and now — he had to pinch himself—he was becoming a part of it. He just hoped that he could blend in and not be too obviously different, not be the outsider he had always been growing up. All he had ever wanted was to belong, to fit in with other people, to not stand out like an ugly duckling. The free flowing champagne had helped eased his nerves, as had Henry Lockhart—rather unexpectedly. It was as if Henry saw Alex's apprehension, as if he recognized something within him. Whenever Alex looked up, Henry was watching him, smiling and nodding, and it excited him. Alex had spent his youth longing for approval, support and acknowledgement and within the space of an evening, the extremely handsome, rich and elegant Henry had given him all these things. Alex had been filled with warmth as the evening had progressed, it had emanated from his belly and spread out to his limbs, easing his stiffness and relaxing him so much that after a few hours of polite chat, he'd been happy just to sit by the fireplace and observe everyone else. But he didn't feel like an outsider, he just felt that he was home.

No doubt it was the champagne. It was the good stuff, not the five quid bottles that his mother used to buy for celebrations.

"I noticed that you have photographs of some of your winning horses along the hallway," Alex said, keen to diffuse the tension and to remove the focus from himself for a moment.

"All winners," Henry replied. He gestured at the first photograph, which showed a racehorse and jockey crossing a finishing line.

"The Grand National?" Alex asked.

"A few years ago. Beautiful stallion, that one. Strong, powerful and feisty." He raised his eyebrows slightly and Alex's stomach flipped. Was Henry telling him that he liked his rides feisty? "Of course, for racing purposes, a horse needs to have a certain edge to it. That special something. Don't you agree, Alex?"

"I do."

"But for everyday purposes…well…I think something more reliable, perhaps not predictable yet…I don't know quite how to explain this." Henry chewed his full bottom lip.

"I think I understand."

"I'm a man who likes to be in charge, Alex. I like control. Yet…I also like to be surprised."

Henry was his opposite. Alex had always wanted someone to take charge, to guide and nurture him. To celebrate his willingness to submit. On a horse, Alex was always in control. But in bed, in relationships, he needed to be cherished.

He returned his gaze to the photographs. "And this one?" he asked, pointing at an image of Henry and another man. They were grinning at the camera, their faces relaxed and happy. Henry's arm was wrapped around the man's shoulders, and Alex felt a pang of jealousy to see Henry so happy with someone else.

Henry stood before the photograph and myriad emotions crossed his handsome face before he carefully composed himself.

"Oh, that's nothing. Just me and an old friend. A long time ago." He shrugged and turned his back on the picture.

Alex gazed at it for a moment, taking in the men's windswept hair and sun-kissed skin. There was something in their eyes that Alex recognized. He'd felt something similar at one point. It was the look of men in love, that self-satisfied contentment that came with believing that someone had your back. He had believed that he'd found that for a while, until his lover had admitted to being married with a family, that was. So just because he'd thought he'd found it, didn't mean that he had. But where had Henry's lover gone? Was it par for the course that all love ended in heartbreak and disappointment?

Better to stay single and safe.

"Thank you for this evening." Alex held out a hand. He had a moment of doubt as Henry stared at him. Had he upset Henry by asking about the photograph? He really didn't want to lose his job at the stables. But then doubt melted away as Henry enveloped Alex's hand in both of his. Henry's hands were large, smooth and warm. Alex's stomach flipped. Just moments ago, he'd been reminding himself that love ended badly. That sex was the route to heartbreak. But Henry was so big, so powerful, so masculine, and he made Alex acutely aware of how easily Henry could take him. With or without his consent.

But I would consent to make love to this man.

Henry pulled him closer until their joined hands were squashed between their bodies. Alex gazed into Henry's face and his heart fluttered at the dark desire he saw there.

"Alex...I know that I shouldn't be doing this. Allowing myself to be near you goes against everything I promised myself I would avoid. But I can't help myself. You're warm and inviting. Intriguing. Vulnerable yet brave and strong."

Alex grazed his lips across Henry's broad jaw, breathing deeply of his delicious, fresh and heady scent. He paused for a moment and watched Henry, wondering when the rebuke would come.

"Henry, I could fight this. I know I should. But I have the feeling that this is just the tip of the iceberg."

Henry suddenly pushed Alex's hand lower and pressed it against the hard bulge in his trousers. "Talking of tips... I have one I'd like you to start with right now."

Alex smiled and caressed the generous erection. "It would be my pleasure."

As he rubbed up and down, he mused at his own confession. He had been so honest with Henry, so unguarded. Was this just a physical attraction, a raw, primal need that could be fixed with a quick, hard fuck? It was possible, he knew that. And a fuck would be so good right now.

But he hoped, deep down, that it would turn out to be much more.

Henry took hold of Alex's face and stared into his big, brown eyes. They were gentle, inviting, needy. He lowered his head and pressed a soft kiss on Alex's lips. He tasted of champagne. He delved into Alex's mouth with his tongue, tasting and savoring. Alex responded and they drifted into desire, their kisses deepening in intensity.

Henry released Alex's face and ran his hands over his young, lithe body. He was overwhelmed by the urge to tear away Alex's clothing and kiss every inch of him before claiming him with his cock. The image of fucking Alex hard made his balls ache and he groaned.

"What is it?" Alex pulled away, his lips puffy from kissing, his eyes dark with need, yet also bearing his confusion and anxiety. This was not a man confident in his appearance, his personality or his demeanor. Alex was a man who evidently had scars beneath his handsome veneer.

There was an air of vulnerability about him that reached out to Henry's heart and made him want to fuck him hard yet also hold him close and protect him. Was that wrong? Could he be attracted to a man who would need him, want him and love him. Just as… He shook himself. He should not do this. Henry could not allow himself to take another man, a man whom he could fall in love with. It would not end well for either of them.

He took hold of Alex's arms and pushed him away, hard enough to let Alex know that he wanted this to stop.

"Did I do something wrong?" Alex asked, his brown eyes wide, a tiny frown marring his olive skin.

Henry shook his head. "No. It's not…" He was about to use that old cliché, *It's not you it's me.* And that was not fair, not fair at all. "I just don't think I'm ready for this, Alex. It would be unfair on you."

Alex shook his head. "No. No, Henry. It's okay. I want this." He stepped forward and pressed his body along the length of Henry's, ran his hands over Henry's front, dangerously low until he caressed Henry's thighs.

The sensation of Alex's fingers sliding over his clothing was so erotic and Henry sighed as he grabbed Alex's hands and stilled their movement.

"I just can't." Henry stepped back and placed a hand on Alex's chest, feeling the rapid thudding of his heart. "Not now. I'm sorry."

His own heart thudded with longing, as Alex's eyes clouded and his expression changed. The innocence and lust was replaced with something else, something colder and wounded, and it was as if Henry now looked at a different man.

"Thank you for your hospitality," Alex said. He straightened his clothing and rubbed his face. "I'll be off then."

"That would be best," Henry said, grinding his teeth together as Alex turned to leave. He wanted to follow Alex and turn him around, to pull him to his chest and hold him tight. But that would be madness. He barely knew the handsome groom. They had shared a moment of passion, nothing more, nothing less. This was why he only indulged himself with those he knew he couldn't hurt, men who wanted sex and nothing more. Henry had made a decision—after losing Callum—never to get involved again.

It was a decision he intended to stick by.

* * * *

Alex was confused, fucking hurt and confused by the rejection, as he made his way down the driveway and took the path that led to the stables. The evening breeze had picked up strength and he shivered as it ruffled his jacket.

He had made a big mistake this evening. It would be preferable to blame his cock rather than admitting that he had given in to the urges of his need to be cared for. Henry Lockhart was not the type of man to really care for someone, especially not for a needy groom who worked for him. He had been a total fool and his cheeks burned as he realized how needy he must have seemed as he'd tried to persuade Henry to let him stay.

What the fuck…?

He passed the dark stable block and walked around the back to the staircase that would take him up to his room. His single man's room. Room for one. Just like his heart. No room for love. Just enough room for Alex to survive. Yet as he unlocked his door and entered his private space, he couldn't help wondering why, if Henry was the seductive charmer that his reputation suggested, had he let Alex go? Why hadn't he used him for a quick fuck as he did all the others who came his way? Didn't that suggest that Henry actually had some integrity, something redeeming about him?

Alex flicked on his television and browsed through the channels, unable to focus on anything. Everything seemed so trivial, so petty, so insignificant. Life was still happening out in the world, people were still getting married, killing each other and making promises that they would break. But Alex couldn't care about them. Not at all. His inner turmoil was surfacing slowly like bubbles drifting to the top of a fizzy drink.

One of the bubbles held the least favorable of possibilities regarding Henry's rejection of him, yet it was also the most likely one— Perhaps Henry simply didn't find Alex attractive. That, Alex could understand, though it wounded him deeply and ripped new holes in his already shaky confidence.

Chapter Five

Henry perched on the stone steps of the veranda and ran his hands through his hair. His eyes stung in the morning light. He hadn't slept a wink after the party. Instead, he'd played the scene with Alex over and over in his head, each time trying out a different ending to the one that had left him feeling like shit.

He was such a dick. He'd abused his position as Alex's boss and that was unforgiveable. He'd witnessed the hurt in Alex's eyes, seen the pain and self-doubt that clearly haunted him.

Henry had floated along for the past few years— numb, full of self-loathing, oblivious to everyone and everything else. Including Felicity. A lump formed in his throat as he thought of the horse, of what she had meant to him and of how he had abandoned her as depression and grief consumed him. What must she have thought?

Henry jumped up and ran down the steps, across the lawns and through the trees. He emerged through the greenery to see Alex saddling up Felicity and he skidded to a halt. The dark-haired groom was so careful with her, talking to her all the time as he secured the saddle under her belly then flipped the reins over her neck. Mina approached Alex, leading another of the older mares. Alex sprang into the saddle and guided Felicity across the yard and out to the open paddocks. Mina followed on her horse and Henry followed on foot.

His heart thundered as he observed Alex warming up, walking Felicity before encouraging her into a trot. He rose with her rhythm, effortlessly, professionally and as fluidly as if he were a part of her.

And Henry knew right there and then what he had suspected since he had first laid eyes on the groom — Alex was special. Henry had only known him for a brief time but he recognized something in him. Henry's heart had been broken. He had begun to heal but his scar tissue was tough and twisted. Could he ever open his heart to another man, allow himself the joy of a true loving union?

He leaned against the fence and let the tears that stung his eyes fall slowly down his hot cheeks. It had been two years since he'd lost Callum and he knew that he had pushed his grief away, punishing his body instead of allowing the suffering to really emerge. But he also knew that the pain wasn't as sharp as it had been and that time was easing his loss. He doubted that it would ever fully leave him, and that Callum would always be a part of who he was, but he could finally admit that the prospect of seizing life by the reins actually held some appeal at last.

He just really didn't know if he could move on enough to love again.

* * * *

Alex settled Felicity in her stable. He caressed her nose and smiled as she nuzzled him, her soft lips tickling the palm of his hand. Horses had always been more straightforward to him than people. The light shining through the stable door was suddenly cut off as a figure blocked it. Alex turned, expecting to find Mina, but instead he met the curious blue gaze of his boss.

"Henry." His heart flipped and his mouth dried up. How would things be between them after their moment of 'almost' intimacy? Had Henry come to fire him?

"Alex." Henry entered the stable but stayed back. The straw covered floor might as well have been a football pitch with how far away he seemed to be. "How are you today?"

"Good thank you."

"Alex…about last night. I'm sorry. It's just…my life is complicated."

"I understand." Alex ground his teeth together. Henry had no idea what he'd been through himself. He wasn't accustomed to throwing himself at other men. Did Henry see him as another frivolous wannabe?

Henry's brow furrowed. "Look, Alex. I'm your boss. I have a responsibility towards you. I can't just screw my employees."

"I know that. It's just…" Alex kicked at the straw. What was the point? He'd only sound as if he was trying to justify his own horny behavior.

"Just what? Tell me, Alex. I need to understand."

"It's stupid." Alex's cheeks flamed.

"No. I want to know."

"I mistakenly felt that there was something between us. I know it's ridiculous but I just did. I don't go around sleeping with every man who'll have me, you know. But I stupidly felt some connection to you.

There. I've said it. Now you can go away and laugh at me."

The silence hung in the air between them as Henry shifted from one foot to another. "I don't think that's stupid, Alex. It's just that I'm not in the habit of trusting my instincts anymore. I take what I want from men then I send them on their way. I'm not proud of it but it's who I've become. And I like you. Already. I don't want to fuck that up."

Alex swallowed his surprise. That wasn't what he had expected to hear.

"Look. I'm free this afternoon. Do you want to come for a ride?"

"I've just been on one. Felicity might be a bit tired right now."

"Not on a horse."

"Don't you ride, Henry? I thought that Felicity might be your mare."

Henry's face darkened, and Alex immediately regretted asking the question.

"I haven't ridden a horse in two years. And yes…Felicity is mine. I just can't."

The horse nudged Alex and he smoothed her neck. He considered asking Henry why he hadn't ridden her but sensed that now wasn't the right time.

"So what did you want to ride?"

"Why don't you get showered and changed and I'll show you?" Henry smiled and his eyes sparkled.

"Sure." Alex nodded. He was trying to stay cool and calm but it was difficult. Just then, Felicity brushed past him and approached Henry. Henry's smile dropped. He quickly opened the door and left the stable.

"Come up to the house when you're ready!" he called as he disappeared from sight.

Alex stood next to Felicity at the stable door and leaned his head on her muscular shoulder. "What is it, girl?"

The horse shook her head as if in reply and stamped a foot.

"It's something we need to figure out. I'll try to get some answers for you." Alex hoped that he would have the opportunity to speak to Henry about it. He couldn't imagine not being able to ride anymore. The freedom of being on horseback was exhilarating. It could heal and offer a freedom that not many activities could match. Perhaps it would help Henry to deal with whatever demons he was battling.

Perhaps.

* * * *

Alex approached the house. Henry was keen to share his love of riding with Alex. Not horse riding but something that he had found as a thrilling alternative.

"Here I am." Alex smiled.

"I hope you're hungry," Henry said as he gestured for Alex to follow him.

"Famished."

Henry led Alex around the side of the house and toward the extensive garages that were built out of the same stone as the house.

"Wow! I didn't realize these were here."

Henry grinned at Alex's surprise. "Wait until you see inside." It was good to see someone else impressed by the house and surroundings. He'd owned it for four years and had been wowed when he'd first bought it but now, with all that had happened, he sometimes worried that he didn't appreciate it all. Henry pressed the fob to raise the first garage door and waited. "How about you close your eyes, Alex?"

"Seriously?" Alex raised his eyebrows.

"Or not. Up to you." Henry shrugged.

"Okay then." Alex shut his eyes, and Henry gazed at the dark lashes as they fluttered on Alex's cheeks. Yes, this was a beautiful young man. He suppressed the urge to kiss Alex, worried that if he started, he wouldn't be able to stop.

Henry took Alex's arm and guided him toward the garage. "Just a few steps forward. And...there. Now open your eyes."

Alex blinked and stared around him before fixing on the shiny Harley. "That's your ride? It's a handsome motorbike."

"This isn't just a *motorbike*, it's a 2003 Harley Davidson Dyna Super Glide Sport with custom T-bars." Henry winked at Alex. "It has a V-twin, four stroke, engine with 1449 displacement and is powder coated black."

"I don't know what that means but it sounds impressive." Alex's cheeks colored, and Henry immediately regretted boasting. He'd only wanted to show Alex that he knew about bikes, not to dent Alex's already shaky confidence.

"So you fancy a ride?"

"I...I've never ridden a motor...a *Harley* before."

"Now's your chance. As long as you're happy to ride pillion." Henry bit his cheek. The thought of riding his Harley with Alex behind him, holding onto him, sent shivers of pleasure throughout his body.

"I'd love to. But I'll be honest. It does make me a bit nervous. I mean...what if I fall off?"

Henry shook his head. "That won't happen, Alex. I won't let it. Just hold on tight." He picked up the two leather jackets that were lying over the saddle and offered the smaller one to Alex. "It should fit. I guessed at your size."

Alex slipped his arms into the sleeves and reached for the zipper but Henry stopped him. "Let me." He slowly slid the zip up to Alex's throat then laid his hands on Alex's shoulders. It suits you." He leaned forward and pressed his lips against Alex's.

Henry pulled away and met Alex's brown eyes. He knew that whatever he did, he didn't want to hurt this man. He wanted to nurture whatever it was that existed between them, even if it was just lust. For the first time in a long time, he didn't want a quick fuck followed by a lonely night. He grabbed his helmet from a shelf and a spare, which he offered to Alex.

He cocked his leg over the bike and kicked the footrest up then put his helmet on. "You coming?"

Alex nodded then slipped on the helmet, climbed on behind Henry and wrapped his arms around his waist.

"Don't let go," Henry called over his shoulder. Alex's grip around him tightened and Henry's heart lifted.

He had a feeling that he was going to enjoy the afternoon.

* * * *

They flew through country lanes and fields and trees whizzed past them in a blur of luscious springtime green. The excuse to hold tightly on to Henry was welcome and he enjoyed the sensation of the Harley roaring beneath them. The softness of Henry's leather jacket over his hard, toned body was arousing and Alex's balls ached with need.

Finally, Henry drove into the carpark of a pretty little country inn. It was set within its own grounds but was surrounded by an emerald patchwork of fields and dry stone walls. The beauty of the scenery took Alex's breath away.

Henry waited for Alex to dismount then he flicked the stand into place with his foot and slid his leg over the saddle. "So? How did you find it?"

"Exhilarating," Alex replied. And it had been, though his legs were shaky and he yearned for a cold drink.

"It is isn't it? I tried a few different rides before I settled on this one but she sure is smooth. And fast!" He grinned, and Alex's heart fluttered. When Henry smiled like that, the small lines around his eyes relaxed and his face positively glowed with youth and vitality.

"Shall we get something to eat?"

Alex pushed open the wooden door of the inn and breathed in the familiar smells of beer, food and an open fire. They went straight to the bar and were greeted by a small, gray-haired woman who offered them a friendly grin. "Hello, gentlemen. What can I get you?"

"I'll have a Coke as I'm driving but, Alex, what about you? They serve some fine ales here." Henry gestured at the bar.

Alex considered just asking for a Coke but realized that a proper drink might help him to relax. "I'll try the Dragonhead, please." Alex pointed at the nearest pump.

"Good choice," the woman said.

They took their drinks to a table in front of the large hearth and Henry handed Alex a menu. "The food here is amazing. Good hearty country meals."

Alex sipped his ale. It was smooth and creamy. The cold soothed his dry mouth and throat. "This is good."

"Cheers!" Henry raised his glass. "To new friendships."

"And more," Alex said, then bit his lip. His stomach growled and he realized how empty it was. "The alcohol has gone straight to my head."

"So do you think you could get a taste for riding a Harley?" Henry asked as they perused the menus.

"I could get used to it." *If it meant that I got to ride behind you every time.*

"How does it compare to horse riding?"

"Nothing will ever outshine that," Alex replied. "Ever since I can remember, I've loved being on a horse. Back in Wales…" He bit his lip.

Henry raised his eyebrows. "In Wales?"

"Yes. Where I grew up, I used to ride my uncle's horses. He had a small farm. And, on the mountains there were wild ponies. During the summer I'd even ride a few of the tamer ones."

"Really? You weren't afraid of being thrown or trampled?" Henry asked.

Alex paused for a moment. Was Henry mocking him? "No. It wasn't them I feared."

A young woman appeared at the table to take their orders and Alex took the opportunity to brace himself. He had never divulged the secret pain of his youth and he couldn't believe that he was going to do it now. But it felt natural with Henry, like he wouldn't be judged.

"Who did you fear, Alex?"

"I was different to the boys in my area."

"Because you're gay?" Henry's direct question made Alex start then he realized that it didn't matter because Henry was too.

"Yes. They just wanted to screw the local girls but I had no interest in that. I tried to stay out of their way but they just sought me out. Every day. They were relentless."

"Physical?"

"Sometimes. Mostly verbal jibes, though. That can wear a person down over time. Being with horses was my escape. They didn't torture me or attack me or abuse me. They accepted me. That's why I mostly prefer horses to people."

"Mostly?" Henry's mouth turned up at the corners.

"There are some people I have liked almost as much as horses."

"So did the bullying stop when you left school?"

"Yeah. I worked with my uncle for a few years then took whatever jobs came up at local stables and farms. I couldn't afford to go to university and I had no qualifications because I'd missed so much school, so my only experience is of the equine variety."

Alex raised his pint glass and noted that it was two thirds gone. *Better slow down.*

"I hate that they bullied you. But it happens everywhere. I went through something similar."

"You?" Alex stared at Henry. "But you're...so... You're..."

"Say it, Alex." Henry laughed.

"You're so big and attractive, Henry. I mean...I'm a mouse. But you."

"A mouse? There is nothing mousey about you, Alex. You are gorgeous. Do you know how fuckable you are? How hard it was to resist you?"

Alex forced his mouth shut. He was fuckable?

"Those shitheads probably picked on you because you made them want you. And I bet all the girls wanted to fuck you too and that pissed them off." Henry finished his Coke. "And as for me, I'm so big because I built myself up. I spent my youth at boarding school. My busy parents never wanted to be parents. They don't mind me so much now I'm all grown up but when I was a kid they wanted me off their hands.

Boarding school was all right most of the time and I liked some of the teachers, but what boys get up to in dorms…well…at least you got to escape at night."

"I thought that was all movie stereotyping."

Henry shook his head. "Sadly not. I always knew that I felt no attraction to women, but let's just say that I had a thorough knowledge of how to pleasure a man by the time I turned eighteen."

They were interrupted by the waitress as she served their meals.

"Tuck in!" Henry said as he did the same.

"So what happened after boarding school?" Alex pushed a slice of steak around his plate with his fork before stabbing it.

"I went to Cambridge and studied law then I joined the army. I did a few tours of Iraq then realized I could utilize my knowledge and experience. I set up a security company and made my fortune."

"It's not your parents' money?"

"No. I'd hate to be dependent on them. Though I know that I was lucky to have contacts I made at university."

"Everything helps, eh?" Alex said. "But you've stayed single?"

Henry lowered the forkful of food from his mouth. He hung his head and Alex's stomach clenched.

"No. There was someone. A few years ago. It didn't end well."

"The man in the photograph?"

"He died."

"I'm so sorry. What happened?"

"A car accident. We'd had an argument and he stormed off. It was raining heavily and a lorry swerved across the motorway and… Look, Alex. Do you mind if we don't talk about this right now?"

"How was your meal, gentlemen?" The old lady from behind the bar looked at their plates. Alex's was empty but Henry still had half of his pie left and a few potatoes. "Would you like me to come back in a bit?"

"No, thank you. It was good. I'm just not that hungry." Henry leaned back in his chair. "More drinks would be good, though."

"Of course." She took their plates and cutlery then returned to the bar.

"Sorry, Henry." Alex reached out and covered Henry's hand with his own. He expected Henry to pull away but he didn't. Instead, he turned his over and curled his fingers around Alex's.

"It's okay. Really. Just hard to speak about it."

"I had someone too." Alex wanted to show Henry that he too had been hurt.

"You did?"

"I met him at the town library. He was a university lecturer. Older. Charming. We hit it off over the romantic poets. He was…my first."

"Really?" Henry's eyebrows disappeared beneath his blond hair.

"And only." Alex squeezed Henry's hand as his cheeks burned.

"That's sweet, Alex. Did you love him?"

"I think so. At least, I believed so at the time. But he was married and he deceived me. He had no intention of leaving his wife and children, and when I found out I wouldn't have wanted him to. I was just so hurt at how he'd lied to me. He led me to believe that he was someone he wasn't. I just couldn't trust anyone after that. Not that there was much opportunity to meet someone else where I grew up."

"So you're obviously wary now." Henry leaned toward Alex. "I don't blame you. Stay away from the closet gays, young man." He smiled. "Find someone who will love you like you deserve to be loved."

As Alex stared into Henry's eyes, his heart thundered and his cock stirred in his jeans. Henry was so much more than just a hunk. He was everything that Alex could want. Gorgeous outside and in.

* * * *

Henry swirled the remains of his Coke around in the glass. He'd found out quite a lot about Alex in the past two hours. He had a hunger to get to know Alex better and it surprised him. He wasn't used to caring about other people at all. When Callum had died, Henry had thought that a part of him had died. But now, it was as if that part of him had been resurrected.

Yet why couldn't it be possible? If losing someone could have such a devastating effect upon the human heart then why couldn't a new person create the adverse effect?

"So, Alex, do you have any family?" He placed his glass on the circular wooden table.

"No."

"Are they all gone?" He tried once more. If Alex didn't expand on his answer, Henry would leave it and find another topic to discuss.

"It was only ever my mother and my uncle. Well, he wasn't even really my uncle. Just some second cousin to my father I think. However that works. I never knew my father. He wasn't interested, so I don't actually know if he's dead or alive. Sad, eh?" Alex swigged his ale then swallowed and licked his lips.

"Alex, I don't think many people have the traditional family unit. If it ever really existed. I think that people used to stay together for financial reasons more than anything but now things are different. In some ways it's sad but then why should humans stay together if they're not happy. Everyone is entitled to happiness, right?"

Alex's face darkened, and Henry realized that he'd hit a nerve. "As long as they don't hurt others along the way, yeah. My father…he hurt my mother."

"In what way?"

"He worked in Spain for a while. That was where he met my Spanish mother. She fell in love with him and when he returned to the UK, she foolishly followed. But by then she was pregnant and she didn't know what else to do. My father didn't want to know."

"So how did she manage?"

"She was too ashamed to return home to Grenada so she found a job and worked until I was born. Then she went back to work. She placed me with whatever cheap childminders she could find until my 'uncle' contacted her and informed her of the family link. He told her he was ashamed of my father's behavior and that he wanted to help if he could. So I spent a lot of time at the farm as I was growing up. Sadly, he lost the farm a few years back because of debts." Alex's mouth became a thin line. "He just lost the will to keep going after his home was repossessed and he died of pneumonia after having a particularly bad bout of flu. I mean…who dies from flu these days?" Alex raised watery eyes to Henry's face, and Henry's heart flipped.

He moved his chair closer to Alex's and took his hand.

"I guess it's not necessarily the flu that's the problem, but the complications it can cause."

"He just didn't want to fight it. So he gave up. Broke my mother's heart. He'd been her only friend."

"Were they ever...close?" Henry asked and felt Alex tense beneath his touch.

"Not that I know of. He was much older than my mother and I never saw any clues that suggested that they might have been. She just... She never stopped loving my father. The bastard that he was."

"That's so sad," Henry replied, and Alex squeezed his hand. "I'm sorry, Alex."

"My mother followed him six months ago. A sudden heart attack. I think that she was exhausted. All those years of working eighteen hour days just burnt her out. I contributed what I could from my bit part jobs but it was still a struggle. And she was just so stubborn...she wouldn't move away in case my father ever wanted to see her or me. But he never did."

"You've had it rough."

"No rougher than many others." Henry saw the boy that Alex must have been with his large innocent eyes and olive skin, his dark hair and earnest, intelligent expression. No wonder he'd been bullied. He was an Adonis. And many human beings could not cope with real beauty. It scared them to the point that they felt that they had to retaliate against it, as if they needed to repay the universe for making such perfect beings when they were so very flawed themselves.

"Alex, I..."

"Shhh." Alex placed a finger over Henry's lips then leaned forward. "We've done enough talking for now."

Henry held his breath. Then Alex removed his finger and replaced it with his lips.

And time stood still.

Chapter Six

The ride home passed in a dream for Alex. He clung to Henry as they passed the fields and hedgerows, the dry stonewalls and isolated farms. The landscape reminded him a lot of Wales with its vast, wild and open expanses. Was it possible to make your home somewhere else? After all, he had no real ties now, did he? His family was gone. His lover had abandoned him and made it quite clear that there was no future for them, and Alex didn't want the man after how he had deceived him. He had proved to be false. Many people were the same — his own father, for instance. But there were good people too. Alex was sure of it. He had to be, because without that hope, then what was there? His mother had been the person she'd portrayed herself to be. She had not concealed anything from Alex or the world. And that, sadly, had been her downfall. She had exposed herself to rejection and had never healed. Thinking of her brought the familiar pain back to Alex's heart and he instinctively pressed closer to Henry. Henry responded by squeezing his hand and Alex was comforted. Henry now knew so much about him that Alex felt he had nothing to lose by trusting him.

Henry pulled into the driveway of the Grange then parked up in the open garage. When he cut the engine, Alex stayed where he was, holding tightly onto Henry. He didn't want the afternoon to end.

Henry removed his helmet and peered over his shoulder. "You okay?"

Alex nodded then took off his own helmet.

"I've been thinking about getting another Harley. I could arrange lessons for you. Then we could go out together. Might be fun."

"I'd like that. I think." Alex smiled. He'd be downright terrified but as long as Henry was there, he'd find the courage. "And what about you? You think you'll ever ride a horse again?"

Alex got off the bike, and Henry followed. "I'd like to think I might do. I miss riding. It's been a while but I really care about Felicity."

"I'm sure she misses you."

Henry placed both of the helmets on a shelf in the garage then removed his leather jacket, and Alex handed him the one he'd borrowed.

"So what now?" Alex asked. He really didn't want to go back to his room alone.

"I have a few calls to make. Business. I'd rather not, but even with managers, I still have to oversee things." Henry smiled but Alex's heart sank. He had hoped that their afternoon would lead into the evening and that they would talk more.

"Okay. Well, I'll head on down to the stables then."

"Alex." Henry held out a hand, and Alex took it then allowed Henry to pull him close. He rested his head on Henry's shoulder and wrapped his arms around Henry's waist. "You smell so good."

"So do you."

Alex pressed himself closer and moaned softly as Henry slipped his hands down the back of his jeans. He raised his face and met Henry's lips and they kissed, gently at first but soon their kisses were hard and needy. As they devoured each other, Alex let all cares slip away. It had been so long since he'd just given in to desire. So long since he'd been physical with someone. He needed to surrender to Henry here and now.

"Fuck me, Henry."

Henry paused to meet Alex's eyes. "No. I promised myself that I wouldn't. I don't want to hurt you."

"It will hurt me if you turn me away right now, Henry. I need this. I need to feel you inside me."

He watched Henry pause for a moment, evaluating the situation.

Would it really be so wrong just to give in to their bodies, to submit to desire and to enjoy each other?

Henry suddenly slipped to his knees in front of Alex and reached for his zipper.

"No, Henry. There's no need."

"Shhh! Allow me to pleasure you. I want to."

"But…"

"Enough."

Henry was in control, and Alex knew that he had to allow Henry to do as he wished. He wouldn't fight him. Henry would look after him and it would all be okay. He sighed as Henry released his cock and caressed it from root to tip.

"Impressive," Henry whispered before licking the shiny end.

Alex leaned against the Harley, reassured by the heavy weight behind him. He was nothing but sensation as Henry took him deep into his throat and sucked him hard. He bucked into Henry's warmth, as

Henry worked him. His pleasure rose and his cock twitched with each flicker of Henry's tongue. "I'm going to...fucking...come, Henry. Stop."

"Never." Henry cupped Alex's balls then pulled his mouth right to the tip of Alex's cock before swallowing him again. Alex was unable to hold back and he cried out as he exploded deep into Henry's throat.

They stayed that way for a while as Alex's erection waned then Henry got to his feet and pulled Alex in for a tender kiss. "You taste like fucking heaven, Alex. Do you know that?"

Alex stared into Henry's eyes. He blinked to clear the tears that threatened to fall. He couldn't believe the pleasure he had just experienced and how he had been able to give in to it so easily, so naturally.

"Now I really do need to get some business done."

"But don't you need..." Alex's voice squeaked out.

"I'm good...for now."

"I want to please you too," Alex said as he tucked his cock into his boxers.

"Shhh. You have." Henry stroked Alex's cheek then led him out of the garage.

They walked around the house together then Henry paused at the French doors. "See you later," he whispered and winked.

Alex didn't know what to do but he knew that he couldn't just walk away from Henry feeling like he did. "I'm coming inside, Henry."

"What?" Henry smiled but his eyes were wide with surprise.

"After that...in the garage. I can't just walk away."

"You don't want to do this, Alex. I'm trying to protect you."

"I know what I want, Henry. Take me inside."

Henry stared at him for a moment then took his hand and led him into the house. They started kissing at the bottom of the stairs and Alex stripped off his shirt and jeans. Henry covered his chest with kisses then pulled off his own clothes.

They kissed as they climbed the steps and by the time they'd reached Henry's bedroom, they were both naked. Alex eyed Henry's body. He was everything he had expected him to be. A perfect, sculpted male. Every muscle was well defined, his chest was smooth and hairless, his cock thick and smooth as it jutted out from a mass of golden curls. He allowed Henry to guide him to the bed and push him back onto the soft covers.

The linen on the king-sized bed was white and crisp and he stretched out as Henry climbed over him and kissed him, slowly and sensually. Their erections bumped against each other and Alex gasped as Henry ground his hips into him, showing him what he could expect very soon.

Alex's stomach clenched. He had only ever been with one other man, and though the sex had been good, it hadn't been great.

"Roll over," Henry instructed as he opened a bedside drawer.

Alex did then he pulled a pillow beneath his chin and dug his fingers into it. Henry took hold of his hips and lifted them slightly then ran his hands over Alex's bottom, cupping the cheeks and smoothing them. Alex's stomach flipped with desire. He had never yearned for anyone this much before.

"Relax, Alex. I won't hurt you. Are you sure that this is what you want?"

"More than anything."

Henry slipped a hand between his cheeks, and Alex gasped as Henry spread coldness there. *Lube.* "Sorry. This stuff never seems to warm up."

"It's okay. It feels good." And it did as Henry slid his fingers up and down from Alex's balls to the base of his spine. Then Henry circled his tight entrance before slipping a finger in and gently probing him. As Alex relaxed into the sensation, Henry added another finger, and Alex moaned with need. "I want you so much, Henry."

"All in good time."

Henry took hold of Alex's cock then he spread the lube over him. Alex bit his lip as Henry eased two fingers back inside him then rubbed one large hand up and down Alex's erection as he fucked him with the other. Just as Alex was at the brink of climaxing, Henry removed his fingers and slowed his movements.

There was a tearing of foil. "Are you ready to take me now, Alex?" Henry asked.

"Yes. Please."

Then Henry was pushing at Alex's body, easing himself into him inch by inch until Alex was full.

"God help me, Alex. You're so tight." Henry pulled out of Alex then plunged back in and they moved in unison. Alex became one with sensation and with desire. He moaned into the pillow. It was so good, it was all too much, and suddenly he was shaking as Henry pumped him hard and he came.

Then Henry slipped out of him and pushed him onto his back. He slipped a pillow under Alex's hips and pulled his legs over his shoulders. "I want to see you when I come, Alex."

Henry pushed inside him again and Alex panted as Henry fucked him hard. Alex stared into Henry's eyes, overwhelmed by the emotions sweeping through him.

Henry groaned as he came and heat erupted deep within Alex's body.

Henry pulled out and collapsed on top of Alex, wrapping his arms around him and pressing his face into Alex's neck.

* * * *

Alex opened his eyes and Henry was perched on the edge of the bed. He turned as if sensing that Alex was awake.

"You okay?" Henry asked, his face etched with concern.

"Never better," Alex replied, though he was already wondering what would happen now. He realized that he'd be missed at the stables if he didn't get back soon.

"It's quite late, Alex, and I still have to make those calls."

"Of course." Alex's heart sank as he looked around for his clothes before realizing that he'd left them downstairs. Henry pulled on a pair of sweatpants then passed him a dressing gown and smiled.

"I'll see you out."

Alex pulled on the robe then followed Henry down the stairs and quickly dressed.

"Henry..."

"It's all right, Alex. I promise. I just really have to make some calls. I'll see you later." He pecked Alex on the lips then opened the door for him.

Alex walked down through the grounds and toward the trees, following the short cut to the stables. He didn't know what to feel. Had he expected to stay for dinner? To be spooned for a while longer? He didn't know.

He fought the urge to turn around to see if Henry was watching him. If he was, Alex knew that he'd run straight back into his arms. If he wasn't, Alex knew that his heart would break.

* * * *

Henry tossed and turned in bed, drifting in and out of sleep. He heard screams and moans as he ran through the halls of the Grange, his body glistening with sweat, his vision blurred.

He realized that he was dreaming.

Then there was an explosion, and everything went white.

Henry sat up in bed. His heart thundered and he rubbed his temples, trying to free himself from the dream. It was dark in his room yet the blackness was occasionally pierced by flashes of light from behind the thick curtains.

There was a storm.

And more.

He jumped out of bed and ran to the window. He pushed the curtains aside and stared into the gloom. Thunder boomed above then within seconds lightning flashed again. But beyond the trees, down at the stables, was a bright orange light.

"What the hell?" He dragged on his sweat pants then slipped his feet into trainers. As he pulled a T-shirt over his head, panic rose in his gut.

Something was wrong.

Very, very wrong.

* * * *

Alex slipped a harness over Felicity's head and tried to encourage her toward the stable door. Panic rose in his gut. He *had* to get her out. A bolt of lightning had set an old tree on fire and sent it crashing into the far end of the stables. Even though it was raining, it wasn't heavy enough to douse the fire that was spreading rapidly. The fire brigade might not make it in time and they had to get the horses out immediately.

The pleasant afternoon had become a muggy evening and a storm had followed. The horses had been restless and he'd been unable to sleep. He was glad of his insomnia now.

"Come on, girl," Alex spoke softly, attempting to hide his own fears from the horse, but she refused to budge.

Felicity was obviously terrified.

"Alex, come on!" Mina poked her head around the stable door. "Hurry up. The fire's taking over."

"She won't come!" Alex cried.

"Then you'll have to leave her." Mina's face was tear-stained and her eyes were wide with terror. "We've got to get the rest of the racehorses out. They're too valuable to risk. Come on!"

Alex paused and looked at Felicity. Her big brown eyes rolled and she reared as lightning flashed again. "Come on, Felicity. I won't leave you here. I just can't." He knew as well as any groom how valuable the racehorses were but Felicity was important to Henry. Alex couldn't stand the thought of her coming to harm, or the idea of how losing her would affect Henry — he would never recover. Alex wrapped his arms around Felicity's neck and stroked her flicking ears. He'd never be able to forgive himself if he walked out on her.

Thunder cracked and Felicity jumped. Alex cradled her large head, whispering to her, telling her it would all be okay, when really he knew that it wouldn't. He would have to try riding her. It might be the only way to save her.

"Alex."

Alex's stomach flipped at the familiar voice, the voice that had stopped him in his cleaning of the stables just weeks ago, the voice that he loved to hear caressing his name.

"Henry." He turned from Felicity and met Henry's eyes.

"What are you doing, Alex? Get out of here!" Henry said.

"She won't come with me, Henry. And I won't leave her here."

Henry approached him and wrapped an arm around his shoulder. "So you'd prefer to stay here with her and risk your own life?"

"I can't bear to abandon her, Henry."

"I've never met anyone like you, Alex."

Screams from outside alerted them to the increasing danger. Henry released Alex then took hold of Felicity's bridle. "Come on, girl. Come with me." He took a step backward, beckoning to Felicity with his free hand. "Come on, girl." Felicity held firm, rooted to the spot with fear. "You have to come, Felicity."

"Henry, you'll have to ride her."

Henry turned his shocked gaze to Alex. "I...I can't."

"You can. Callum would have wanted you to. You need to get back in the saddle, Henry. Right now. Face your fears and help Felicity to face hers."

Henry paused, his eyes as full of terror as Felicity's, then he grabbed Alex's head and pulled him close. He kissed him so fiercely that when he released him, Alex was gasping for breath.

"Let's get out of here!" Henry ordered then sprang lightly onto Felicity's back. She stamped for a moment then Henry tapped her with his heels and she moved forward, through the doorway and out into the night. Alex followed, blinking hard against the tears and smoke that filled his eyes.

* * * *

The next day, Alex and Henry sat on the steps of the Grange, watching the sunrise. Gray clouds drifted across the horizon but the rain had passed and left the air clear and calm. They sat close together, wrapped in a patchwork quilt and nursing mugs of tea. The fire had raged most of the night, destroying the stables and the grooms' accommodation. The horses were all safe and Henry had arranged for them to be stabled in a large old barn in one of the paddocks. Some of the grooms, Mina included, had chosen to sleep there with the horses, the others were lodged at the Grange.

Henry had dealt with everything calmly and efficiently, and Alex wondered if anything ever phased the man. His heart swelled with admiration and awe.

"Thank you for last night, Alex. What you did...saving Felicity. I'll never be able to make it up to you."

"*You* saved her, Henry."

Henry slipped his arm around Alex's waist and pulled him closer. "But you told me how."

Alex leaned closer, and Henry kissed him. He opened his mouth and Henry delved between his lips with his tongue, exploring and tasting him. When Henry pulled back, Alex sighed, but Henry took hold of his chin in both hands and smiled. "There's something here, Alex, I know it. But we're just at the starting line."

"Like with a horse race?"

"Exactly. But unlike a horse race, we don't have to hurry. We can take our time, reach each hurdle when we're ready. We don't need to rush the jumps. I don't want us to fall, Alex. I want this to work."

"Me too. But right now, I'd like to learn a bit more about you." He got to his feet and held out a hand. "How about we start upstairs?"

Henry grinned, pushing his blond hair out of his eyes. "So life's not just about horses and Harleys?"

"Not anymore," Alex replied, "and I'm looking forward to coming along for the ride."

About the Authors

Bailey Bradford

A native Texan, Bailey spends her days spinning stories around in her head, which has contributed to more than one incident of tripping over her own feet. Evenings are reserved for pounding away at the keyboard, as are early morning hours. Sleep? Doesn't happen much. Writing is too much fun, and there are too many characters bouncing about, tapping on Bailey's brain demanding to be let out.

Caffeine and chocolate are permanent fixtures in Bailey's office and are never far from hand at any given time. Removing either of those necessities from Bailey's presence can result in what is known as A Very, Very Scary Bailey and is not advised under any circumstances.

Morticia Knight

M/M Erotic Romance author, Morticia Knight, enjoys hot stories of men loving men forever after. They can be men in uniform, Doms and subs, rock stars or bikers—but they're all searching for the one (or two!) who was meant only for them.

When not indulging in her passion for books, she loves the outdoors, film and music. Once upon a time she was the singer in an indie rock band that toured the West Coast and charted on U.S. college radio. She is currently working on more instalments of Sin City Uniforms, The Hampton Road Club, as well as the follow-up to Bryan and Aubrey's story from Rockin' the Alternative and Dylan and Zero from Biking Bad.

Helena Maeve

Helena Maeve has always been globe trotter with a fondness for adventure, but only recently has she started putting to paper the many stories she's collected in her excursions. When she isn't writing erotic romance novels, she can usually be found in an airport or on a plane, furiously penning in her trusty little notebook.

L.M. Somerton

Lucinda lives in a small village in the English countryside, surrounded by rolling hills, cows and sheep. She started writing to fill time between jobs and is now firmly and unashamedly addicted.

She loves the English weather, especially the rain, and adores a thunderstorm. She loves good food, warm company and a crackling fire. She's fascinated by the psychology of relationships, especially between men, and her stories contain some subtle (and not so subtle) leanings towards BDSM.

Ethan Stone

Ethan Stone has recently returned to Oregon and is working on re-growing his web feet. He has been obsessed with two things in his life: books and all things gay. After spending years trying to ignore the voices in his head, he finally decided to sit down and listen to them.

What he discovered was a perfect union of his two obsessions. Ethan used to have a day job that paid the bills. He wore a uniform to work and he looked damn sexy in it. Now he gets to wear sweatpants and watch movies all day.

Molly Ann Wishlade

Molly Ann Wishlade has always been an avid reader and writer of stories. Her lifetime of reading has taken her from the magical worlds of The Faraway Tree and The Borrowers, to the Greek myths and legends, to Sweet Valley High and Judy Blume's Forever, to Asimov's science fiction, Jane Eyre's torment and Stephen King's masterpieces. More recently she has wandered through the vivid historicals of Philippa Gregory; the bubbly, gritty delights of Adele Parks and the fast paced thrillers of James Patterson. She loves getting lost in a novel and often regrets finishing one as the characters are usually missed like old friends. She regularly indulges her insatiable hunger for romance and passion in the delicious worlds created by romantic novelists and is working on several of her own!

What precious spare time she has is spent with her family (one gorgeous husband and two bright and beautiful children), taking long walks around the beautiful Welsh countryside (although she's still waiting for the rescue greyhound she wants to accompany her), cooking her own secret recipe curries, drinking Earl Grey (in copious amounts) and discovering delicious wines. Oh, and she also loves to ski and can't wait to go again! And buying shoes!

She wants to take readers on the rollercoaster that is life through the creation of her own characters, relationships and worlds.

She appreciates feedback, recipes and wine recommendations.

All of the above authors love to hear from readers. You can find their contact information, website details and author profile pages at http://www.pride-publishing.com.